# ISLAND TWILIGHT

*Other B&W titles by Nigel Tranter*

THE STONE
THE QUEEN'S GRACE
BALEFIRE
BRIDAL PATH
THE GILDED FLEECE
FOOTBRIDGE TO ENCHANTMENT
NESTOR THE MONSTER

# ISLAND TWILIGHT

## NIGEL TRANTER

EDINBURGH
B&W PUBLISHING
1993

Copyright © Nigel Tranter
First published 1947
This edition published 1993
by B&W Publishing
Edinburgh
ISBN 1 873631 22 7

British Library Cataloguing in Publication Data:
A catalogue record for this book is available from
the British Library

Cover illustration: *Auchenhew Arran* by James Nairn
Collection Andrew McIntosh Patrick,
courtesy The Fine Art Society

Cover design by Harry Palmer

Printed by Werner Söderström

FOR perhaps the thousandth time, on that racking interminable journey, the wagon lurched and jolted to a stop, and the creaking and groaning of its sore-tried frame subsided. And in its place that other groaning, that had been its accompaniment and undertone throughout the weary day, rose and persisted. From their huddled misery amongst the blood and filth and rags of the floor-boards, the sick and the wounded and the dying moaned and cried, and cursed anew their agony, their fate, and their Maker.

The man sitting, crouching, in cramped discomfort on an empty ammunition-box near the tail-board, shook his head dumbly. He had done what he could—little enough, heaven knew. With his instruments, his few medicaments, even his hoarded stock of brandy, gone, he could do nothing. These poor devils were past the words of comfort, the quips and pious hopes and bawdy songs with which he had started their ghastly journey—except perhaps poor Finlay, here, to whom words could mean more than to the common soldiery. The water itself was done, the last bottle empty, finished these two hours. Twisting head and shoulders gingerly, he peered out into the shadowy glades of the forest, this seemingly endless grim-peopled Forest of Soignies, through which they had trundled and jarred and crept their painful way all afternoon and evening. Plenty there were to call on for help—but how many would answer, could answer? There would be few full water-bottles amongst those staggering bleary-eyed battle-grimed men, and fewer still who would part with one. He did not blame them; not many of these men had eaten or slept since yesterday's battle. Aeneas Graham had been campaigning long enough to know the value of a man's water-bottle, especially in this dusty Belgian summer. Still, he could try again.

He called out to the trudging straggling files, pleading in the name of Christ's own wounds, offering a crown, two crowns, for a bottle, for half-a-bottle of water. He got no response. Possibly the men did not comprehend, did not even hear him. In the main they were English, exhausted raw levies of Lord Hill's Fourth Division, with few veterans amongst them—and yet they had given a good account of themselves yesterday on the field of Quatre Bras, when they had stood their ground against all Ney's bludgeoning; their retiral today, enforced only by Blücher's collapse at Ligny, was all the more bitter therefore.

The plodding columns were succeeded by a troop of rattling, clanking artillery, Brunswickers, the drivers making great play with their whips amongst their wild-eyed horses and stragglers of the infantry. Their Duke had fallen in the battle, it was said. No use appealing to them.

Behind streamed more marching men. The forest was full of them. These were Germans mainly—Hessians, Hanoverians, and Nassauers, with some Swedes and Belgians amongst them, of Alten's polyglot force, the scrapings of war-torn Europe with little, now, of discipline or order in their ragged columns. Graham tried his halting German on them, but with no success, and cursed them, but without conviction.

"It's no use, Aeneas," a voice said, a voice weak but never weakly. "Never heed. They need their water as much as we do, poor souls. More perhaps—they've still . . . to live."

Graham looked down at the head resting on his knees, the face gaunt and worn and lined beneath the stubble of beard, the deep-set eyes glittering feverishly below the wide crag of brow, all under an incongruous shock of fair curly hair, boy's hair it might have been. He ran his hand over that hair, lightly. "And so have you," he declared. "So have you, Finlay MacBride—more to live for than most of these others."

The other shook his head, though only briefly and with pain. "No, my friend," he said. "That dream is dreamed. I will not see Erismore again. My race is run. I have been foolish, I fear. My place was there—it may be I should never have left it, at all. There was—there *is* so much to be done." He sighed, a sigh that ended in a choking cough, violent, frame-racking.

Drawing him up higher, seeking to ease him—and he was painfully easy to lift, big-boned as he was—Graham waited for the paroxysm to pass, grim-faced. But when he spoke, his voice was gentle. "Tell me about Erismore," he said.

The sick man, flushed and panting, achieved the ghost of a smile. "My patient Aeneas, and you weary of the sound of that sad isle, by this, for sure." Nevertheless, his eyes lighted up with a gleam distinct and so much warmer than the strange glitter that had come to them of late, a gleam that the thought of Erismore never failed to light in these the eyes of her wandering pastor and son. It was the only medicine that Doctor Aeneas Graham could give to his friend, in that nightmarish forest.

"Was I wrong to leave it, Aeneas?" the priest demanded, with none the less urgency for having demanded it an hundred times before. "They would not heed me, they were not ready for me . . . or, perhaps, God forgive me, I was not ready for them. But they needed me, they need me now, desperately. And it is too late." He overbore the other's automatic protest with a thin gesturing hand. "Will they get another shepherd, in their need, I wonder? Will another be appointed in my place?" His tone of voice and the shake of his fair head answered his own question. "Then have I failed in my duty? Which was my duty—to stay where I was not wanted, or to go with the men that I was sending to their deaths?"

He had half-risen in his excitement, and the surgeon's hand pressed him back, gently. "Hush, Finlay—these are crazy words," he said. "You are sick, your mind is tired, confused. Think of Erismore itself, your green island, with its cliffs and sandy bays, and its little fields and heather hills. You've told me so often. If you want to return to it, don't torture yourself with these imaginings. . . ."

"But it's true, I tell you," the Highlandman cried. "It was to their death I was sending them—and I knew it, God, I knew it! I thought that was my duty, too. So many duties! I felt that I owed it to Dunalastair, who had put me in Erismore, rebuilt me my church—even, I thought that I owed it to the English king! So I recruited men, calling it a duty, and more men and more men, till I no longer could stay there my own self and face the women's eyes. As Dunalastair's chaplain I would be with the men, and doing my duty again—and not seeing the reproach of all Erismore! And now Dunalastair is dead like the others, and I am dying, and the new lord will put no minister in Erismore. I have failed them, and they are shepherdless." He struggled up again, fiercely. "And that means that they are lost. Lost to the Devil. They are damned, all of them—and myself with them!"

Forcibly Graham pushed him down, and exhausted he sank back, gasping for breath. From the dark back of the wagon, above the undertone of groaning, a hoarse voice rose, urgently. "Guv'nor—this cove 'ere next to me's bad, I reckon. Feels like 'e's twitchin'—a-gurglin' in 'is throat. . . ."

Thankful even for this interruption, Graham carefully disengaged himself, resting MacBride's head and shoulders heedfully on his stained greatcoat, and half-stepped, half-crawled, stiffly over the huddled bodies on the floor-boards, cautiously, on all accounts; his own left shoulder and arm was bound and slung in bandages, where a musket-ball had done its work. The casualty in the corner, a mere lad, of their own 92nd, had merited his neighbour's apprehension. Even as the surgeon reached him, his head rolled sideways, jaw sagging down, and the gurgling ceased. Sighing, Graham pulled the boy's coat up over his face, and turning, retraced his difficult way to his stance by the tail-board.

"Young MacIan's troubles are over," he said. "Poor lad."

And after a tearing cough, weak at first but strengthening as it went on, the priest's voice rose, vibrant, passionate. "God Almighty, into Thy hands we commend the soul of this our brother. Depart in peace, thou blessed soul. . . ."

Alten's Germans were now past, and in their place a rabble of stragglers, walking-wounded, broken men, the hangers-on of an army, a disorderly array. But still the wagon remained stationary, and behind it a long column of similar vehicles had formed, baggage-carts, limbers, commissariat-wagons; presumably it was the same ahead. Presently, through the press, a single horseman appeared, pushing his way with difficulty and unconcealed irritation, a handsome young man conspicuous in the spectacular uniform of the Staff, made even more noteworthy by the addition of a flamboyant plaid of yellowish tartan. Graham recognised him at once—young Campbell of Ardtoran, formerly a captain in one of their own companies of the 92nd, now an aide of General Abercrombie's.

"Ardtoran!" he cried. "Here, man—over here."

The officer stared, slewed his charger's head round, and plunged towards them, swearing comprehensively in Gaelic-English-German at the thronging crowd. "Lord, is that yourself, Mr. Graham!" he shouted. "Months it is since I've seen you. What are you doing in that?"

"All I could get," he was told, tersely enough. "Have you got any water, Ardtoran? I must have water. I've got this damned cart full of wounded, and not a drop of water for hours."

"Water, is it?" The newcomer slapped the flat pannier-bottle strapped to his saddle. "Surely. This ought to be full, I think." Unbuckling it, he came up with them. "Here you are. But man, you've caught something yourself, Aeneas? Shoulder, is it? A bad business for a doctor! And, Mary Mother—who've you got there? It's not Mr. MacBride? *Dia*, but I'm sorry. I heard that he'd been poorly, but . . . This is bad, bad. Mr. MacBride, I am distressed indeed. This is the devil of a war, for sure." He peered within. "And you've got a full load in there, too. Poor lads. This would be yesterday's doing—you caught it from Ney? It was good work, if bloody, I hear. I can't say as much for old Blücher. I've been over with the Prussians for three days, with Sir Ronald. Yesterday Boney attacked near a place called Ligny, and Blücher got a real drubbing—had his horse shot under him, too, and got rolled on. He's lost thousands. . . ."

"We heard," Graham interrupted grimly. "Isn't that why we've been retiring all day through this utterly damnable forest! How much further we've got to go I don't know—but I'm going to get these poor devils out of this wagon before much longer, whatever the rest of the army does. It's sheer murder. . . ."

"You won't have to go far now, I think. I'm told that I'll find the Duke at a village at the edge of this forest—Waterloo, it is called. No more than two miles now, at the most. I have dispatches from Blücher—he's at Wavre, and will stand there. If the Duke decides to stay at this place, it looks like another battle, and a big one, for Boney's in a hurry. . . . And so am I, for that matter. I'd better be off. See, Aeneas"—and diving into the skirts of his coat, he produced a chased silver flask—"this is better than water. Give some of this to Mr. MacBride—it's from our own mountains. And take some your own self—you're looking none too spry."

"My thanks. I lost all my own things last night—stolen during the battle, I imagine. And, Ardtoran—on your way forward, will you see if you cannot get this confounded baggage-column started again? Heaven knows what's holding it up—but there's hundreds, maybe thousands, of wounded in it, and they'll be dying like flies. Probably the drivers are drunk or asleep. . . . Use the flat of your sword, if necessary, but get them to move."

"I will, yes, for sure. There's a good three miles of it behind you, too. A disgrace it is, b'Gad. I'll be off, then. Good luck to you, Aeneas—and Mr. MacBride. The war is no place for a priest, at all. *Beannachd leat!*"

"Goodbye, and thank you. And my respects to your General and tell him that, at this stage of the war, it is cheaper to heal men than to get new ones!"

Night had brought a thunderstorm and driving rain to the heavy torpor of the day. In a corner of the dark barn, lit only by the smoky light of a couple of flickering lamps and intermittent lightning flashes, with the scents of cattle and hay mixing strangely with the heavy reek of sweat blood and death, Aeneas Graham sat by his friend. It would not be long now; Finlay MacBride would not see the dawn. His cruel wasting disease had run its course, assisted potently by a chest wound and the rigours of war. For some time he had been delirious, but now he was quiet, gazing up into the murky rafters with great unseeing eyes. Getting softly to his feet, the surgeon left him, to make another round of that place of shadows.

More than one hundred men lay in the barn, and more were without in the sheds and cattle-court of the little farm-stead, laid in tight rows on the ground, as though mown down by the Great Reaper's scythe, with only the surgeon-major to attend to them, and those of their fellows whose incapacities still permitted them to crawl about to their assistance. The army was economical in its medical services. Graham prayed only for two able-bodied men, that they might remove the dead as they expired and so permit more of those left outside to be brought in.

Taking one of the lanterns, he moved about amongst the recumbent ranks with a pail of water and a pannikin, adjusting a dressing here, easing a sufferer's position there, speaking a brief word of comfort or hope, giving a drink where it was sought, and covering the faces of those who no longer required his ministrations. Nine of the latter he found, on that round. It was the killing hour of the night.

The little that he could do, done, he made his way back to Finlay MacBride. He seemed not to have moved, in the half-hour's interval. He might not be fully conscious. Stooping over him, to peer more closely, Graham found the deep lustrous eyes full on him, and as fully aware.

"Aeneas," he whispered, "thank God you're here. My time is short, now, and I have something, much, to tell you— a service to beg of you. I was afraid that you might not come in time. . . ."

Graham took the groping hand in his own, and sat down at the other's side. "Never fear, Finlay," he said, tight-voiced, and could think of nothing else to say.

"I do not fear death," the priest took him up, quickly, "I, that have been death's doorkeeper so long—only of leaving so much undone." His thin fingers were gripping tightly, tensely. "There is so much I have left undone, so much that I have no time now even to tell to you . . ." With an obvious effort he sought to calm himself. "Aeneas," he went on, urgently, "there are two favours I would ask of you, in friendship's name. Frances, my sister— will you go to her, when you get home? She lives in Edinburgh now, with our aunt, widow of a writer named Munro, in Queen Street. Mrs. Munro of Balvithie—you will find her easily. Tell her, tell Frances my sister, that I came to see that she was right, in the end. She was against my leaving Erismore . . . she loves that place, too. Tell he that I meant to go back. Ask her not to be judging me too harshly. She sees very clearly, does Frances . . . I wish that I could see as clearly. Always, I see two or three or four sides to a problem, one as telling as another. . . ." He sighed, a long quivering sigh. "Dear Frances, my little *piuthar*. *Tha thu coart. Tha mi duilich. Feumaidh mi t'fhagail.* . . ." He relapsed into a long stream of his native Gaelic. The surgeon let him talk on, and soon, incomprehensible as the speech was to a Lowlander, he recognized it to be wandering, a muttered delirium. Leaning back against the stone walling, Graham watched and waited, grey-faced, leaden-eyed, in his heart a great pity, something of bewilderment and the stirring of a blind indignation. This then was the outcome, the miserable end of a selfless life, a fine, a noble life, dedicated to the service of others. This was his friend, his eager, generous, vital, friend, who loved his fellow-men to a fault and his God without limit or question, the unique flower of their ancient Scots Kirk, and the closest follower of his Master of any of His ministers that he, Graham, had ever known or heard of, struck down in his youth, discarded. It was so wrong, so utterly wrong. He had seen many young men die, so much youth snuffed-out, suddenly, inexorably, with the satanic prodigality of war, and grieved over them, friends, even his own brother amongst them. But this was different; they all, the best and the worst of them, had been soldiers and sinners, heroes perhaps, but quarrelsome, lecherous, boasting, impatient, ordinary men, pressed unwilling warriors frequently, but fighting and living as fighters, and gaining some satisfaction, some lustful fulfilment from it all. But not this man, Finlay MacBride. He was a man dedicated, apart. Hating war, with all its evil and degradation and brutality, he had forced himself to embrace it, to be part of it, forsaking cherished life's-work, to serve those whom he held to be in direst need, voluntarily, indeed against all opposition and the stric-

8

tures of his kind. One of the few priests in Wellington's army, nominally he was there as chaplain to Dunalastair his Chief, Colonel of their Regiment, but actually his mission was to all who needed him, minister to a profane army, catholic, indiscriminate, and beloved. And there he lay, broken, with all. . . .

A desperate spasm of coughing, violent, frustrative, aroused him, and bending over, he lifted MacBride up into a sitting position. This could be the end; already he had had two hæmorrhages; the third would be the last. But presently the fit died away, and its victim, shivering though bathed in sweat, sank back limply, spent. Gradually the cruel heaving subsided, and he lay silent, eyes closed.

And presently, too, the heavy eyelids of the watcher drooped and closed likewise; he had not slept for more than uneasy minutes in thirty-six hours. Above, the tattoo of the rain was incessant.

It might have been a minute or an hour, when he was aroused. Finlay MacBride was speaking again, his voice husky, unsteady. ". . . and they would not listen to me. They smiled, but there was evil behind their smiles. I know it. They confessed Christ, but served the Devil. Lachlan Macgillivray . . . Rudha nan Altair . . . If only I could find out . . . *Tha e fuathail.* Frances, *a graidh, tha mo chridhe goirt . . .*" Suddenly the rambling voice gained strength, direction. "Aeneas—someone must go to Erismore before it is too late. They must be saved, or I shall never lie in peace! It is my sin that I left them, and them needing me, desperately." He shook his head. "They would not admit it, and almost I believed them. Almost I believed that it was such as you that they needed—a doctor not a priest! That is what I told myself—a doctor before a priest, fool that I was. I told myself that they were not ready for me, in my arrogance. And them slipping, slipping into nameless evil. I tried, before God I tried . . . but they shut me out of their hearts. But I would have found out, in time . . . I would have fought, and in time, with the Lord's help, I would have saved them . . . And then the war, the recruiting . . . I thought perhaps, if some of the men were to get away from the island, out into the world, it might help. So it began . . . and here it ends! *Ochan, mise'n diugh . . .*"

A vivid flash of lightning and a fierce clap of thunder from directly overhead, brought a cry or two from the other sufferers in that place. With a word to his friend, Graham got up stiffly, to walk amongst them and reassure them, telling them that it was only a storm, and that their battles indeed were over. He went outside too, splashing through the streaming steading, to speak a word or two with the unhappy occupants of the sheds and byres, to bewail with them the leaking roofs and the lack of any sort of equipment and to curse the war, the Government, and Bonaparte impartially. Reeling a little, slightly light-headed himself from lack of sleep, pain, and loss of blood, he made his way back to his corner.

Finlay MacBride was waiting for him, burning-eyed. "Aeneas—did I ask you to go and see my sister? She lives in Edinburgh. . . . Yes, then. And will you see the new Dunalastair, too—the Colonel's brother? Ask him, plead with him, to send another minister to Erismore. He is a hard man, and violent . . . but perhaps he will heed you, perhaps God will soften his heart. Say it was my last, my only wish, my charge, in the name of Christ. . . . Tell him that the Devil has his claws on Erismore— Erismore, where Christ's message first was spoken in all Scotland, cradle of the Faith. *Dh' fhairtlich orm.* Tell him . . . *tha mi guidhe ort . . .*" He began to cough, great harsh reaching coughs, deep, horribly regular, convulsing his whole wasted body. Graham held him, biting his own lips. Three times the priest strove to speak, desperately, through that torture. At last he got the one word out, "Erismore . . . !" and then, choking, the red flood overwhelmed him. Finlay MacBride had peace.

## 2

ENEAS GRAHAM sat on the edge of his chair and drummed fingers on knee, with what served him for patience. Having seen enough of the darkened room, he stared out of the window. The house stood at the corner of Portman Square and King Street, and from his seat he could look both up, to the fashionable parade of the Square, and down, along the busier thoroughfare towards the barracks, where, if there was less elegance there was more stir to catch the eye. And, at nearly noon, it was time that there was some stir, too—more especially in No. 14 Portman Square. Glancing at the great timepiece on the elaborately carved white mantelpiece, he shifted on his chair again, and puffed heavily. Aeneas Graham was not notably a patient man.

In ten minutes more he was pacing the floor, with the short quick steps that would have suited his late uniform better than this new civilian outfit. He paced between his window and the inner wall, where a large and ornate mirror, cracked unfortunately, confronted him on each approach with the image of a dark-browed youngish man whose naturally rather sombre features were presently marred by a frown, and whose passably modish and well-cut coat was distressingly halved diagonally by the broken reflection. And, mid-route, as it were, he methodically made circuit of a large and apparently recent stain on the thick carpet, which he charitably assumed to be wine, and rounded, near the mirror, a single shoe, a woman's shoe, gilt, tawdry, and much worn. As well, perhaps, that the curtains of the windows other than this were still drawn, and the great room consequently discreetly darkened. The stale frousty smell was eloquent enough—sufficient for the visitor to be sorely tempted to open his window. Aeneas Graham did not like the room, any more than he liked being kept waiting. And he did not like his mission, either.

11

He was searching about for a bell, to summon the insolent and unkempt manservant who had admitted him, to demand his hat, when the door was flung violently open and a man stumbled into the room, to stand swaying a little, one hand shading his eyes, one holding on to the wall.

"Well . . . ?" he demanded, thick-voiced. "If my interfering mother sent you speiring after my health, you can go back and tell her that I'm perfectly well, better than she is, the auld bitch. And you can tell her, too, that if I ever need a doctor, I'll find my own, sir, I'll find my own!"

Aeneas stared—but not so much because of the words as at the man himself. He would hardly have believed it; this was no more than a caricature. As like the Colonel as a man conceivably could be—and yet as different in all that mattered as to be practically an opposite. Almost identical in build and feature and colour, the difference in carriage and bearing and expression was grotesque. Where the Colonel had been tall and handsome and hawk-like, this man was tall and handsome and vulturine. Where the one had been broad-shouldered, lean, and upright, the other was broad-shouldered and weedy and sagging. One had been fine-drawn, open-featured, frank, the other was fine-drawn, suspicious, cunning. Both looked what they were, sons of a proud line of autocrats—but what different sons.

"Lord Dunalastair . . . ?" Graham wondered. It seemed impossible that this man, lined-faced, blotchy, trembling, with temples greying beneath the night-cap that still sat askew on his head, could be younger brother to the Colonel.

"Naturally, sir." He drew up his long dressing-gowned figure with some dignity.

"M'mmm. Then, I'm afraid that you are under some misapprehension as to my identity, my lord. I have not the, er, felicity of your mother's acquaintance, and am not in the least concerned with your lordship's health . . ."

The other frowned at the tone of voice. "Indeed. But you style yourself some sort of a doctor, I'm informed . . . ?"

"Yes, I am a doctor," Aeneas agreed. "Graham, by name, lately Surgeon-major, the 92nd Highlanders."

"So!" Lord Dunalastair's rheumy eyes narrowed. "One begins to see light—one of my foolhardy brother's, h'm, adventurers . . . perhaps one of the new army of place-seekers? I hope, sir, that you have not encouraged yourself, that, for my brother's sake, I can exert my influence to find you occupation? Though, so help me, I imagine that there must be a great demand for prison doctors, with most of the hulks and gaols full of your Wellesley's rabble!"

The younger man opened his lips, shut them again, and took a deep breath. "You are pleased to jest, my lord," he said, with hard-won if grim civility. "My mission is quite otherwise—and not on my own accord."

"Indeed. But you do want something? It is my experience that everybody would like something, Mr., Dr., er Graham."

"*I* would like," Aeneas stopped himself abruptly, and swallowed. "For myself, I would like many things," he said; then, evenly, "but none, I think, from you, sir. My mission concerns the late Reverend Finlay MacBride, and the island of Erismore."

"The late . . . ? Then the fellow's dead too, is he?"

"Yes. Finlay MacBride died on the night before Waterloo—the day after your brother."

"So." The other, who neither had sat down himself, despite his unsteady stance, nor offered his guest a seat, moved a few paces into the darkened room, and back. "So the ranting warrior's dead too, is he! Poetic, sir, and not unsuitable. Is there not something in the Scriptures about he that taketh the sword perishing by the sword?" And, at his caller's expression: "I can't imagine that you expect me to shed salt tears at your news, Doctor?"

"No," Aeneas agreed briefly. "And I had not expected it to be news to you."

"But yes—and not unpalatable news either, my friend, despite the barbarous hour of the day you chose to deliver it. It saves me considerable trouble and weariness, and something like seventy pounds a year! The latter I might have attained anyway, of course—but not without the former."

"I take it that you mean Mr. MacBride's charge, his stipend?"

"Exactly, sir."

"And his successor in Erismore . . . ?"

"Erismore will get along very well without a parson—as it did before."

Aeneas considered the carpet for a moment or two, tight-lipped. "Lord Dunalastair," he said, "it was on this subject that I called. Finlay MacBride, whom I am proud to have called my friend, died in my arms. He asked me to tell you that it was his last and only wish that Erismore should not be left without a minister—apparently he judged your attitude with some accuracy! I imagine that you are scarcely a religious man, but you are Chief of Clan Tormaid as well as laird to these people, and surely you owe their moral welfare some consideration . . . ?"

"I owe them nothing," Dunalastair interrupted hoarsely. He was part-leaning, part-sitting, on the edge of the large central table now, his shaking hands gripping its support tensely. "The boot's on the other foot, b'Gad—most of them owe *me* plenty; my brother was inefficient at collecting rents, as at much else. Erismore, sir, is a very small and damned unprofitable portion of my lands, and if I was to saddle myself with what you call the moral welfare of these people, I'd be fit for the madhouse or the pauper's gaol—and deserve it, too."

"And the Kirk? Will the Kirk of Scotland just let you deliberately close down one of its churches?"

"The Kirk will do nothing—like it did for more than a hundred years before our fanatic cajoled my feckless brother into rebuilding the church, and putting him into it as minister. The church is mine, not the Kirk's—and I'm the only heritor. Erismore did fine without it for a century; it'll do so again."

Aeneas stared at the other blankly. What was to be said? Obviously the man was fully armoured against all appeals, whether to reason or sentiment or charity. There would be no reaction to pleading save insult and abuse—not that pleading was in Graham's line, anyway. The only approach there was that could have any effect on this scion of nobility, was self-interest. It went against the grain, but . . .

"Lord Dunalastair," he said, "am I to take it that your

objection to replacing Mr. MacBride is purely financial? If that is so, some arrangement might be made. I have a little money—not much, but enough to help . . . and others, perhaps—the Kirk itself . . . ?"

"Man, you're mighty keen, so help me!" Dunalastair blinked his suspicion. "What sort of a doctor are ye? A devilish holy one, b'Gad, and a deuced unlikely soldier . . . ?"

"That is a matter of opinion—and there are moments when I feel far from holy, I assure you!" he was answered, significantly. "But Finlay MacBride was the finest man it has been my good fortune to know, and I value highly both his friendship and his dying wishes."

"Aye." Dunalastair sniffed his unbelief. "Are you sure you're not wanting the place for a friend of your own . . . or thinking of turning parson yourself? A nice easy place, with little work, remote, do what you please and no questions asked, eh? For if you are, my friend, you can do your preaching in a cave and baptize your converts in the sea—for as long as I'm Dunalastair you'll not have the church, you nor any man. You've come to the wrong man, Graham—I've no cause to love the Kirk, damn it, with its black corbie-crows, b'Gad I've not! Do I make myself clear?"

"More than clear—transparent!" Aeneas gave back, tersely. "I will not trespass further on your lordship's obviously valuable time. And I can take back to Scotland with me a quite memorable picture of the Chief of Clan Tormaid!"

"Aye, you can, my mannie!" Dunalastair lurched off the table, and crouched his long body towards his caller, venomously. "Go you and tell them that Dunalastair, now, is a man that kens his own mind, that damns the Kirk that rules Scotland, and all its ranting hypocrites—not a weak fool that thought a red coat and a drawn sword, leading a wheen of bare-kneed savages, was glory, and that the King's Shilling was better than his own rents. Tell them that. And if you go to Erismore and try missionarizing those heathens, tell them from me that I'll have every penny they ever owed me, before I'm done, so help me! Now, get out!"

15

"With pleasure." Aeneas turned in the doorway. "But before I go, I have an admission to make. I lied when I said that I had no concern for your lordship's health. On the contrary, I am much concerned, gravely concerned. All the symptoms are most evident. I cannot imagine that Clan Tormaid will long be favoured with its present chief. Good day to you, my lord."

## 3

LICKING the salt spray from his lips, Aeneas Graham steadied his shoulder against the shrouds, to counter the sway of the ship, gripped the ratlines, and knew that it was good to be alive. That it was the first time that he could have said as much, for many a long month, did not occur to him. He seemed somehow to have got out of the way of appreciating life, of late—since he returned to his native land, indeed. Nothing appeared to be so good as it had seemed from the battle-torn fields of wasted Europe—nothing even so good as he remembered leaving it. London had not commended itself to him—but then, he never had loved the place; Edinburgh, despite the briskness of its clean wind-swept streets and spreading views, had appeared to him an alien place, peopled with a hurrying but tired and complaining folk, a folk weary with more than a decade of war and all its attendant restrictions and scarcities—and with returning soldiers; even St. Andrews, his own town, had seemed to fail him, its streets meaner and dingier and dirtier than he had thought them, his one-time friends and acquaintances changed into strangers or gone altogether; and in the tall ancient stone laird's-house within its ring of leaning beech-trees on the breeze-blown shores of the Ness of Fife, that was his home and cradle, he had found a sombre brother bent on prosperity, who had eyed him a little askance, a tight-mouthed sister-in-law who wondered how long he would be staying, and a small unknown nephew who apparently had been well-warned as to the demerits of the soldiery. His widowed mother dead, his sister married and gone, he had not remained long in the green Kingdom of Fife, that for so long had been his promised land. He would go back, of course, one day.... How many others, he had wondered, had come home, thus? How much more of Europe's manhood, swallowed suddenly into the cruel maw of war, and as suddenly disgorged, found itself thus at a loss, out of touch with its stay-at-home fellows, eyed askance, almost unwanted? Was this ever the lot of the returned wanderer?

But it was geography that Aeneas Graham was considering at the moment, not psychology. He turned to the man at his side. "If that's Mull, then, Mr. MacNab—which is Erismore?"

"Och, you'll not can see Erismore from this, Dr. Graham," the mate told him. "Wait you till we round the Ross o' Mull, and Iona, and you'll maybe can see the tops of its hills beyond Tiree and Coll. It's not that easy to come by, Erismore."

"Of course—it's at Coll that I've to get off, isn't it?"

"Aye, Arinagour of Coll. It's as far as we can take you, and us due in Tobermory by night. But you'll be getting a fishing-boat to take you the rest of the way, sir, easy enough—to Eorsa, anyway, if not just to Erismore itself."

"Eorsa—that's nearby, isn't it?"

"Och, yes—five or six miles, no more. The next island, it is, and a better sort of place whatever, as I'm told. Not so remote, if you understand me, Doctor. . . ."

"But if there's only the five miles between them . . . ?"

"Aye, but Eorsa's got an anchorage and a bit harbour, and there's good land on it, for the crofts. But Erismore's no more than hill and rock and sand, they say, with a bad coast and no landing-place. Myself, I was never there, at all—it is not often that they have any visitors, I reckon. It'll just be a sort of holiday you'll be on, Doctor, I expect?" That was only a polite inquiry.

"Something of the sort, Mr. MacNab." And that was only polite, likewise.

The *Cormorant* was two days out of Glasgow, two grey soaking, heaving days, wherein chill wind and rain had been as drearily constant as the driving white-laced seas, and land no more than an occasional infrequent blur, uncertain, unlikely. But, abruptly, an hour ago, all had changed; a shaft of sunlight had pierced the serried clouds, dispersed, vanquished, and banished them, the sea, still white-laced, was blue now, shot with amethyst and deepest violet, and glittering to hurt the eyes, and land was sharp-etched and full of colour the distant purple of the mainland mountains, half-a-hundred islands, low and green, cliff-bound and rocky, hill-girt and heather-stained, and all the legion of the tortured skerries, naked and black and spray-drenched. The mate had pointed out and named for him certain of the isles and landmarks—over to starboard green Colonsay, backed by the twin Paps of Jura and the Islay headlands, landwards, above little Scarba and the Isles of the Sea, the jagged teeth of Cruachan and all the mountains of Lorne, northwards the long promontory of the Ross of Mull with the tip of Iona beyond, and to the west only the glistening plain of the limitless ocean. Aeneas stared at it all, and saw that it was very good.

It had been no easy task getting himself even thus far, and frequently in the last two weeks he had cursed himself for a fool, an aimless fool, and a stubborn fool. Which, had he considered it, might have made his present satisfaction the more noteworthy. There was a time, in Glasgow, when he despaired altogether of getting a passage into the North-West at all; there was little traffic to this remote seaboard, little to tempt the Glasgow merchants to send their ships up into these dangerous narrow waters, especially since the so-called improvements of the last few years had emptied so many of the glens. During the war, it seemed, there had been occasional transports sailing into the North to collect recruits, and men-of-war scouring the more accessible islands with their press-gangs, but this commerce was now practically at a standstill, with both the demand slackening and the supply failing, and few vessels indeed found occasion to voyage farther north than the comparatively civilized ducal area of Inverary, except for an odd immigrant ship. And indeed, it was in just such that Aeneas had been fortunate enough to purchase a passage, prevailing on the captain to go the few miles off his route and drop him at Coll, on his way to Tobermory of Mull, where the *Cormorant* was to pick up a ship-load of unhappy colonists for the Canadas, ferried over from some cleared and improved estate in Morvern. How Frances MacBride had managed to transport herself, and alone, to these fastnesses, Heaven alone knew; her aunt's failure to insist on accompanying her, strange as the word of it had appeared to the man, was the more understandable.

For it was on Frances MacBride's trail that he was bound. Frances MacBride was leading him, all unwittingly, this merry dance—though he probably would have preferred to say that it was his sense of duty, his promise to a dying man, his conscience, or even his justifiable urge to run counter to the new Dunalastair's ill-graced wishes and designs; any or all of these, rather than admit that he was chasing a young woman to the ends of the earth, that he might thereby delay making up his disgruntled and disillusioned mind as to his own immediate future. Men have made use of thinner excuses, ere this, on the same account . . . and wasn't a promise a promise? He had followed Finlay's directions and repaired to the house of Mrs. Munro of Balvithie, in Queen Street of Edinburgh, on his way home to Fife, there to discover that his bird was flown. Frances MacBride had departed for that heathenish and horrible island, as her aunt had named it, a month before, on receipt of the sad letter Aeneas had sent anent her brother's death. Mrs. Munro, cheerful Lowland soul, had agreed that it was a fair scandal for a bit lassie to be travelling all that long road—and to such a place—all on her lee-lane. But what could she do with the girl? She would pay no heed to her old auntie—never had done—and would gang her ain gait, like her poor brother, poor Finlay, who never knew what was good for him, either. She had things to settle up, so she said, the lassie—she had kept house for Finlay in the Manse of Erismore, before, as Dr. Graham would ken, and it was her home in a manner of speaking—and she made out that there was a great lot to be done. There was no stopping her, and she wouldn't have her aunt's company, either—though she had offered to go—for which Mrs. Munro shed only a brief tear, for she was no traveller, especially on the sea, and that place Erismore garred her grue. That had been the burden of much of the widow's complaint—the barbarous and baleful influence of that nasty island; what they could see in it, beat her. But always those bairns had loved it, Guid kens why; they hadn't been brought up on it, but on Eorsa, the next island, where their poor

20

father had been the minister—but there it was like a magnet drawing them both. Poor Finlay had wasted and broken himself on it, and the lassie was in a fair way to doing the same; it was no place for a young lady at all, at all—even Frances MacBride, the independent hizzy. If she—her old auntie—had carried on the way that bairn did, she'd have been skelped and shut up in her room till she learned better, she would so! Though she could look after herself, could Frances, she'd say that. As to when she might return, Dr. Graham's guess was as good as her own—she'd come back when she wanted to, and not a minute sooner; but having gone all that road, and taking maybe two weeks to the journey, she'd likely stay a matter of months anyway. As well her poor father couldn't see her from his grave—though he was a wild-like creature too, in his fashion . . . these Hie'lant folk! Aeneas, with a fairly vivid mind-picture of the said Frances MacBride, had smiled grimly, and taken his leave. And when he had so quickly savoured enough of his home-coming, and even found old Doctor Burnet of St. Andrews, whom he had hoped to partner in his practice and eventually succeed, dead and buried and supplanted by an insolent puppy newly graduated from University, he had shaken the dust of the East Neuk of Fife from his feet, and come travelling. Had he been a fool, then— weak, drifting . . . ? Well, couldn't he afford a holiday—wasn't he entitled to it? For seven, eight years he had soldiered and campaigned, with precious little of holiday-making about it. He had lived moderately, modestly, not spending all that came to him. Need he hold the reins so short, now? He need not, confound it . . . but why was he here, just the same? The man shrugged. Let that fly stick to the wall, meantime . . .

The red granite cliffs of the Ross of Mull were behind them now, along with the rock-torn western strands of Iona and all the twisted, racked, and moulded contours of the Treshnish Isles. Far far ahead were the blue mountains of Rhum, and nearer, beyond the red towering precipices of lonely Staffa, were the long low outlines of Tiree and Coll, hull-down, as it were, against the wide Atlantic.

"And that's the place for you, sir," the mate pointed out to

21

him. "We'll have you there in a couple of hours, and that will be you."

"M'mmm. I suppose it will," his passenger agreed, doubtfully.

It was a dazzling morning of sun and breeze and shadow, when Aeneas, glad enough of the exercise, for the wind across the sea was chill, helped to push the heavy coble down across the rounded pebbles of the far, western beach of the island of Coll, and into the jabbly waves. There were four fishermen, whom the innkeeper had bargained with to row him as far as Eorsa—but no farther—and all of one family by their looks, fierce of aspect but inoffensive of expression, and they had not one word of their passenger's language between them. But a smile is the same in any tongue, and they smiled politely whenever they happened to look at him, which, of necessity, was frequently, for they sat facing him in his seat in the stern, two to a thwart, each pulling deeply, strongly, on a long-bladed oar, with the new-risen sun in their faces and the west wind at their backs. And they sang or crooned or hummed as they rowed, a slow, simple, elemental melody of no more than half-a-dozen notes, in time to the rhythmic sweep of the oars, a curious haunting air, only a fragment of a tune, without beginning or end. And the squat boat lifted and sank, lifted and sank, to the heave of the waves, and the oars creaked steadily and in unison, and the waves slapped and gurgled under the counter, providing their own suitable accompaniment, and Aeneas found no fault with any of it.

As the sun rose higher and the level glitter lifted off the water, Aeneas could see that an island lay ahead—how far, he found it hard to guess, the difference in the prospect and perspective from a small boat thus low in the water, and the deck of a tall ship, was astonishing. It seemed a big place, low-lying on this near side and rising gradually north-west-ward, till, far off, it culminated in high rugged hills, even now just emerging from their night-caps of heavy mist. "Eorsa . . . ?" he asked, pointing.

As one man the four smiled, nodding vigorously.

But hadn't MacNab yesterday indicated that Eorsa was a flattish place with good land for crofts, not hilly like its neighbour? Those then must be the mountains of Erismore beyond. He stared at them, stern, aloof, stained with sable shadow, uncertain against the clear sun-bathed shores and slopes of Eorsa, wreaths of white mist climbing out of their valleys and corries to join the sombre clouds that clung to their brows. This, surely, was more like Mrs. Munro's horrible and queer place, than Finlay MacBride's green and pleasant isle!

Presently the boatmen raised a small dark-brown crotal-dyed sail of some heavy hand-woven fabric, to reinforce their efforts with the oars, and they made better time, tacking north-west and south-west into the wind. On the former tacks, their passenger recurrently obtained an increasingly better view of the more northerly end of Erismore, as it crept out from behind Eorsa. The fierce and soaring cliffs, even at this distance, frowned darkly, threatening, and the inhospitable nature of its coast became ever more evident. Along most of its visible south-east side, the hills sloped steeply to great precipices dropping sheer into the sea, over the rims of which tumbled innumerable foaming streams, half their substance blowing away like steam, on their dizzy fall. And where the cliffs lowered and broke, westward, jagged rocks and stacks and thrusting skerries took their place, round whose grim bases the angry seas boiled whitely.

With the bulk of Eorsa beginning to shelter them from the breeze, the fishermen turned their boat due southward to skirt the coast of weedy strands and shingly bays and stretches of silver sand. It seemed strange that two islands so close together and so remote from others, could be so differently fashioned. There were crofts to be seen here, scattered small irregular fields, and many cattle grazing amongst the turning bracken of the slopes and hummocks—a kindly place. In time, round the long green peninsula that formed the southern tip of Eorsa, they turned, and there, in a sheltered bay, was a cluster of houses, one larger than the others, a little whitewashed church, and a stone pier. Into this bay the coble's bows swung.

And as they pulled in towards the pier, another boat pulled out from it. A similar craft to their own, it appeared, but with more people in it, six at least, it drew away at right angles to their own approach, heading out toward the westernmost reach of the bay as they came in from the south. With their backs to it, the Coll rowers did not see it for some time, till, with a half-glance to his right, one of them spied it. Quickly he spoke to the others, and they all looked round. Then the first turned to Aeneas, urgently. "Erismore . . . !" he said, pointing. "*Bàta . . . nan Erismore!*"

Vigorously his passenger nodded, and the fisherman, cupping hand to mouth, shouted lustily, his companions assisting.

That they were heard in the other boat, no more than three hundred yards off, was apparent. Its oars were rested, and all faces were turned towards them. There seemed to be four rowers in this also, a man in the bows and two in the stern.

Leaning over his oar, the Coll fisherman shouted, in the Gaelic, and gestured towards Aeneas, most obviously requesting a passage for him to Erismore. To reinforce his plea, Aeneas stood up, and raised a hand.

There seemed to be a hurried consultation in the other boat. One of the rowers leaned forward to the older man in the stern, pointing. His companion there, Graham could see now, was a woman, her hair blowing loose in the breeze. A hail, and a few sing-song words came to them across the water.

The Coll spokesman shook his head, said a few words to his colleagues, and turned to Aeneas doubtfully. "*Tha mi gle dhuilich . . .*" He shook his head again, eloquently, apologetically. "Erismore . . . *nach bochd sin!*" and he shrugged.

The position was only too evident. Graham frowned, and lifted his own voice. "I want to get to Erismore," he shouted. "I've come a long way . . . I'll pay you well. . . ."

He saw the other people talking together, the woman—a young woman, it was—amongst them. Then, a brief word or two was flung to them, curt, conclusive, and the oars dipped once more and the boat moved forward. And it kept on its previous course.

Tight-lipped, Aeneas Graham sat down on his seat again, and the fishermen, avoiding his glance, pulled strongly for the little pier.

The Reverend Mr. Keith shook a grey and sympathetic head. "It is very unfortunate, Mr . . . Graham, is it? . . . very unfortunate indeed. But no doubt they'd be mistaking you for Dunalastair's new factor, as I did myself. I got the word that he was coming, a whilie back, at a Presbytery meeting at Tobermory. You'll understand that the puir folk here are no' exactly looking forward to his visit, having heard tell of the new laird's notions about rents and the like . . ."

"But surely, sir, they might have given me a chance to explain . . . ?"

"Aye, they might . . . but they're a wee bit difficult, the folk over at Erismore, and no' that fond of strangers. It's no' often we get a gentleman like yourself coming to the islands, sir, especially to Erismore. Myself, I canna just mind of such a thing happening before, at all. You'll be connected with the Government, likely . . . ?"

"No, I'm a private individual, on a private visit, sir."

"Oh, aye. Iph'm'mm." The minister's watery old eyes transferred to the red stones of the pier. "It is a very fine day for the time of the year, is it no'? I was just down to the pier here, to see off a friend in yon boat. Will you just come away back to the Manse with me, Mr. Graham, and have a bite of dinner? There's a bit sort o' inn downby, there, but I think you'll do better with Mrs. Keith."

"You are very kind, sir . . . but I think I'd better see about getting another boat, across to Erismore."

The other smiled faintly. "Och, you'll have plenty time for that, Mr. Graham. You'll no' get across today, nor yet, maybe, tomorrow—Erismore's no' a place you can just flit across, like the Ulva ferry."

"But it's only five miles . . . ?"

"Five miles across the Sound, aye—but from here to the only place you'll land a boat on Erismore, it's liker fifteen. And no' to be done in rough weather, either. It's an ill place to reach, is Erismore. And a'body that could take you is out at the fishing just now, forby, and will no' be back till night . . . so you might as well come and have your dinner, Mr. Graham."

Aeneas summoned such wisdom as he had, and swallowed his temper. "Thank you, Mr. Keith," he smiled, if grimly. "Perhaps you're right."

The Manse was a square, substantial house, unlike the church, slate-roofed, and standing in a pleasant garden, even with some small trees in it. The minister pointed these out with some pride—the only ones on the island, apparently. "A wonderful place, a garden, Mr. Graham," he said. "A man can be as near to God in a garden, as anywhere bar the Kirk itself."

Aeneas was interested to see this house, where Finlay MacBride had been born and raised. He had heard about it, and its garden, that his father had won out of the bracken and the rocks and the machar. "Do you still have the water-garden and the fish-pond?" he wondered.

"Aye, but the fish are dead this long whilie . . ." Mr. Keith stopped, and turned to stare at his companion. "But how did *you* ken about that, Mr. Graham?"

"Finlay MacBride told me."

"Finlay MacBride . . . ?"

"Yes. He was my friend. That is why I am on my way to Erismore."

"So that's it. Man, I'm glad to know you, if you were a friend of Finlay's. A fine laddie, Finlay, and a strong servant o' the Lord . . . if a wee thing impatient. His death was a sair blow. But the pity you hadna' been here an hour earlier; yon was his sister Frances, in the boat, there. She'll be right sorry to have missed you."

His companion looked doubtful. "Missed me . . . ? Well, I suppose you could call it that. So that was Frances MacBride . . . !"

"You havena' met her, then? She's a fine lassie, and bonny, too." He blinked. "And with a mind o' her ain—like her brother . . ."

"So I noticed," the younger man said, perhaps too promptly.

"Och, but you must no' be too hard on her, Mr. Graham— how was she to ken? Forby, it was Duncan Og Macgillivray's boat, not her's . . . no' that she's that keen on factors herself, like the rest of Erismore!"

"You'll have to tell me all about her . . . *and* the rest of Erismore," Aeneas said, thoughtfully.

"Time enough for that," the minister answered. "Come away in, and meet Mrs. Keith."

Time there was, too, and enough. For three long days a gale of wind and rain blew steadily out of the west, violent, unfaltering, buffeting and drenching and shrouding the islands in its chill venom, deaving them with the incessant roar of breakers and surf, and drawing a grey curtain of spray and mist and driving rain between Eorsa and Erismore and the rest of the world besides. And in Eorsa, perforce, Aeneas Graham remained.

He stayed at the Manse, on the insistence of Robert Keith, strongly supported by his bustling buxom wife, who, a Lowlander like her husband, but who had never mastered the alien Gaelic, was unfeignedly thankful for some civilized company to talk to. It was by her, rather than by her more cautious spouse, that Aeneas was informed. He learned that Frances MacBride was a warm-hearted, cool-headed partisan, clearer-minded if rather less saintly than her brother, but as headstrong. That she had a hatred of governments, factors, and authorities generally—all in fact who would oppress her poor islanders. That rather unaccountably she loved Erismore passionately, but was worried about the place, without any manner of doubt. As to Erismore, he heard much of dangerous coasts and frowning cliffs and fearsome mountains, of worthless land and barren crofts, of superstition and sickness and death, of a proud and backward people. But he *learned* only that it was a place that kept itself to itself, and could continue to do so, as far as Mrs. Keith was concerned.

The minister he found reluctant to talk about it. Pressed, he admitted that in a way, he supposed it might be looked on as a part of his parish now, especially if, as he informed him, the new Lord Dunalastair was not going to fill the charge again—for certainly the Synod of Argyll would not, could not, attempt to put a new man in against the proprietor's wishes and without his support; they were short enough of priests as it was, for their established parishes, and still more so of funds, to seek to perpetuate what had been little more than a whim of the late laird, urged on him by his friend Finlay MacBride. It was a pity, of course, for Finlay's sake—but the laddie would insist on that crazy caper of going away to the wars, and leaving his parish . . . ! For himself, his services were always available—if they were asked for, wanted. But it was difficult . . . and he was getting an old man, and the folk didn't seem to want him. They had their Elder and Catechist, Lachlan Macgillivray. . . . If the Presbytery officially joined Erismore to his parish, of course, he'd have to try and do something, hold a service there occasionally, but . . . the place was inaccessible. . . ."

In that, at least, Aeneas Graham agreed with him. And the storm persisted.

## 4

A ENEAS could see no break in the ominous foam-crested line of the skerries that circled the place like a girdle. Bearing down on it thus, and with a following westerly wind, appeared to be crazy. But presumably the boatmen knew what they were doing; they had refused to bring him yesterday, because the seas were still too high after the gale, so evidently they were not merely foolhardy. Anyway, there was nothing that he could do—not even speak their language.

Erismore, glistening wetly in the pale sunshine, lay before them like an open horseshoe, with low ground in front, centrally, near to the succession of rock-ribbed sandy bays of the shore, rising quickly, behind and on either side, in ridges and sweeps and folds, to the stern cliffs and great hills and soaring peaks that made the body and soul of the place, cradling around the shore a scattering of small houses. And westwards, a barrier guarding these unlooked-for pleasant sandy bays, about half a mile from the beach, the jagged teeth of the skerries gnashed the long Atlantic swell.

The boat, a black wide coble similar to that which had brought him from Coll, and which appeared to be standard in the district, bore down on the line of boiling waters at an alarming pace. The oars were out, but for steering rather than propulsion, for the boat was rudderless. Aeneas, in the bows this time, under the scrap of sail, looking aft, noted that the grey-bearded man in the stern who guided them by brief words to this rower or that, had his eyes fixed, not on the threatening cauldron ahead but on some distant point, or points, on the island far behind. Landmarks to be kept in line, no doubt. Might they be accurate!

The regular rise and fall that the boat had maintained on the great rollers ever since they had turned in towards the island, began to alter. A shorter erratic pitching motion took its place, punctuated by sudden violent lurches forward, hovering pauses, or sideways rolls, as the backwash from some submerged ledge struck them. Then suddenly they seemed to reach, and tremble on, the lip of a long smooth slope of water. Down it they plunged, sickeningly, down, with the evil knowledge of dark rocks below, gliding down into the very maw of the sea, to check abruptly, giddily, under a high overhanging cornice of wave, and to climb steeply, slowly, ever more slowly, so that it seemed that they must drop back into the trough and be overwhelmed, to climb and falter, and then to find the toppling crest and sink and dissolve under them, and to lunge onward. Now the steersman was shouting, the oars threshed and dug deep, the rowers galvanized into sudden furious action. Spray was in their faces, all around was broken water, roaring breakers, and flying spume, with, disturbingly near on either hand, the black heads of the skerries, trailing streaming weed, like the yellow hair of the drowned. Like a mad thing the coble jerked, swirled, and stalled. Grunting, the rowers pulled and strained, the boat heeled, steadied, and leapt forward. With a sort of gasping cheer, the oarsmen relaxed, the grey-beard sat back, grinning, and they slid out into quiet water. Aeneas Graham's breath exhaled in a long quivering sigh. Now he knew why they called Erismore inaccessible, inhospitable.

The three or four men, working at the nets near the little pier, took the Eorsa boat's arrival with noteworthy calm. A brief wave, a hailed word or two, and they went on with their net-mending—but that they watched his disembarking with some interest, Aeneas had no doubt.

Picking his way over the rough boulders that constituted the pier, followed by two of the boatmen with his baggage, he nodded good-day to the group at the nets, and had it only formally returned. There was no need to ask the way; the track led up, keeping company with a shouting boisterous stream, past drying nets and an upturned boat or two and a dilapidated shed, to the houses. There was no village, no street, no sort of order to their placing, each cot-house just set down where the rocky hummocky ground permitted a levelish stance and a little greensward, primitive stone and turf cabins, thatched with sprouting reeds, and each surrounded by its patchwork of tiny fields, massively if ineffectually enclosed by a network of tumble-down dry-stone walls. And some distance up, on a prominent knoll, stood the church, low and squat and severe, distinguished by its glazed small windows and a modest belfry. Indicating to his companions that they leave his baggage near the pier meantime, Aeneas walked on alone. From within dark doorways and around the corners of walls, his progress was contemplated by great-eyed ragged children and watchful silent women.

He had not gone far when he noticed a man leave a somewhat larger house ahead, with something like a steading round it, and walk down the track towards him, slowly but deliberately, and with a sort of dignity. He was an old man, and tall, and though his great frame was lean now, he bore himself erect, with none of the stoop and shuffle of age. His hair was long and gleaming white, as was his beard, and the breeze ruffled it as he walked, bare-headed.

A few paces from Aeneas the old man halted, and raised a veined hand, and inclined his head, in a single courtly gesture of greeting. "I give you welcome to Erismore, indeed, sir," he said slowly, in the soft careful English of the West. "It is a very fine day, but the sea is rough yet, whatever. It would not be a comfortable voyage you would be having. Myself, I am Lachlan Macgillivray." The old man's voice was deep and strong and vibrant.

"Good day to you—and thank you, Mr. Macgillivray," Aeneas said, surprised. "You are kind. My name is Graham— Aeneas Graham. It was a rough passage, as you say. Coming through the reef, there, was quite an experience."

"Yes, then. It was not the day to be coming that way, at all. We name that Maclean's Gate, and it is the best way through the skerries in the good weather, but after a storm from the west, it is bad. Myself, I wondered to see your boat take it—better it would have been farther on, at the other channel. You will be the new laird's factor, likely, Mr. Graham . . . ?"

"No, I'm not," he was told, rather shortly. "I have nothing to do with Lord Dunalastair, the Government, or anyone else. I am on a private visit, a holiday, if you like. . . ."

The old man's rather strange eyes, brilliant somehow despite their faded blue, widened a little, but he spoke with the same unhurried calm. "Surely. May your visit be a pleasant one, whatever—with the time of the year that's in it!"

Aeneas Graham's quick glance could discover no visible trace of mockery. The other's face was half-turned from him to gaze out over shelving land and limitless sea, and in the fine aquiline features only a quiet gravity was apparent. "I hope so," he said.

"Yes, then. Can I be directing you to any place, Mr. Graham— if you will be stopping for a space?"

"Well . . . yes. Is there an inn here, or anywhere that I could put up?"

"Och, the pity it is. There is no inn, at all." The old man smiled gently. "Myself, I would not like to be innkeeper on Erismore. But I think I could be finding you a house where you could stop, maybe. . . ."

They moved on together up the track by the chuckling burn, past the house from which the patriarch had emerged, and their going did not pass unobserved. They agreed on the weather, the state of the crops, and God's goodness in bringing the creature Bonaparte to book at last.

Up near the church, Aeneas descried a larger house with two storeys beneath its thatch and a wooden porch to its front door. "That will be the Manse—where Miss MacBride lives?" he suggested.

"That is so, yes." His companion's glance was keen. "You know Miss MacBride, then?"

"No, I have not met her yet. But her brother, Finlay MacBride, was my friend."

"So." The old man nodded slowly. "I see. Mr. MacBride was your friend. It was bad that he had to die, bad, and him so young. But God's will be done. May he rest in peace."

"M'mm. Yes, of course. It was a tragedy. He loved this place,

32

Erismore. He told me all about it . . ."

"And what would he be telling you . . . about Erismore, Mr. Graham?"

Something in the way that was said, made Aeneas turn quickly. He found the other's eyes fixed on him, intently, with an expression that matched but ill their washed-out colour. But his grave smile followed, easily.

"A small barren island, it is, and us quiet, humble folk, you see. . . ."

The younger man nodded, briefly. "Quite. It was the beauty of the place he talked about, it's remoteness, his work here . . ."

"And why not, and him strong in the Lord's work! A great worker, Mr. MacBride. It is good that he loved Erismore. . . . But this is my grand-daughter Mairi's house. She will be able to look after you, I think. It is a good house—the biggest on the island besides my own, and the Manse, of course—also she has the English, and me teaching her my own self. If you will sit on the seat there, by the door, Mr. Graham, I will speak with her."

It was another two-storeyed house they had come to, by a sandy side-track from the main climbing road of the place, white-washed and tidy and clean-seeming within its enclosure of yellowing berry-bushes, and having the appearance of a small farm rather than of just the usual croft. For once, the farm-buildings were set back a little, behind the house, nor did the midden rise predominant at the front door, as his doctor's eye had noted was the convenient normal in these parts. Aeneas waited, by the rough-hewn bench at the door, and watched the last untimely bees crawl in and out of the three hives beside the Michaelmas daisies, and a cynical-eyed goat extend its ears over the garden-wall to crop the remaining leaves of a suitably-placed currant-bush.

Preceded by the murmur of voices, the old man emerged with a comely young woman, dark-haired, high-complexioned, deep-bosomed, dressed in green homespun, short-skirted and bare-footed. She smiled at Aeneas, shyly, and he thought that her brown eyes were gentle as a calf's. "This is Mairi Macgillivray," her grandfather announced. "Ewan Beg, her man, is out at the

33

fishing, but she will take you in. It is no grand house, for a gentleman like yourself, but I think that she will make you comfortable. Will you not, then, Mairi?"

"Och, yes—I will be trying, anyway," she answered, and her voice was soft and pleasant, like the rest of her. "If the gentleman will just come away inside . . . ?"

Aeneas Graham decided that Erismore was a better place than he had been led to believe, which was a pleasant experience, for so far, since he had doffed his uniform, he had been consistently disappointed, disillusioned perhaps, with what he had returned to, so consistent that sometimes he had begun to wonder, away at the back of his mind, if it might not be himself that was at fault. But this was different. He had met with courtesy and hospitality. His room, up a steep white-scrubbed stair, was clean and bright, with a neat comfortable bed, and a view to dream into. He had had an excellent meal of soup and fish and curds and heather-honeyed scones, in the big low-ceiled kitchen below, and just tasted an admirable whisky which Lachlan Macgillivray apparently had sent up for him specially, from his own still. And he liked this Mairi Macgillivray, as would any man, indeed.

"I have to go and see Miss MacBride," he told her, now. "She stays alone at the Manse?"

"She does, yes. And it is not right, at all."

"Why not? She'll come to no harm, surely?"

"Och, it is not good to be living alone. She should have a man, a husband. She is beautiful and strong and kind. A woman needs a husband—myself, I know it. This Erismore is no place for her, whatever."

"Ah," said Aeneas. "Um'mm. Well, I'd better go across to the Manse, anyway. . . ."

The girl shook her head. "She is not there, at all. I saw her go, a small time past. Up the road, there, to the hills. She had her basket—she will be for Camusnacreagh. There is a woman there that she visits, sick, and her man dead at the wars. . . . Och, not very far at all—half an hour, it could be. Peig Macleod, the first house, it is past the forest—you will be finding it, easy. . . ."

He walked up the sandy gravelled road towards the hills, thoughtfully. It was a pleasant road, lifting and coiling its way by strips of cultivation amongst outcropping rock, across the green and black of a peat-bog with stacks of drying peats like smaller versions of the cot-houses themselves, around grassy knolls and braes of whin where small shaggy black cattle grazed, and over bare moorland where black-faced sheep and scattered stone were one and indistinguishable, but always mounting, by small hills or great, up out of the yellowing bracken to the fading heather, to the rock-strewn bases of the ultimate mountains. All this, within perhaps a mile and a half, so steady was the climbing. Nor did his track end at the hill-foots; right ahead the wall of mountains divided to the cleft of a deep glen, and into its green defile the track wound, to disappear amongst the cloak of its woods. For, unlike Eorsa and what he had seen of Coll, there were trees on this island, alder and hazel, oak and pine and rowan, and, more abundant than the others, the slender graceful birches that now made a golden glory of all the lower brae-sides with the delicate tracery of their turning leaves. Probably it was the tall hills that did it, giving some protection and shelter from the searching sea-winds; Aeneas did not know. But Erismore was the richer therefore.

He had passed perhaps half a dozen crofts, near the road-side, by the time that he reached the glen, squat, low-browed places, with rounded backs like crouching beasts nosing back into the earth out of which they had risen, and seen others scattered about the surrounding slopes, but of these a good proportion seemed to be deserted. And though he glimpsed some women and a few children working about them, he saw no man, all that road.

The hills now dominated everything, tall and steep and rock-bound above their skirts of birch and hazel, their dark heather flanks scored by innumerable foaming streams and the long grey scars of screes. There were many peaks, bare, stern, remote, and one that soared austere and terrible in its stark detachment above them all, and into the daunting press of them the glen

35

pushed its way.

Within the valley, it was pleasant open woodland, thick as it had seemed from a distance, with the slim silver boles of the birches, and their bronze and ochre canopy of tiny heart-shaped leaves, screening the frowning ridges and summits above, as the kindly grey-green lichen covered the nakedness of the fallen rock below. The stream, that the track had followed faithfully all the way from the shore, here sang a softer song to the trees, its boisterous shouting stilled to a mild murmur as it slipped smoothly, swiftly, over basalt shelves, or chuckled quietly where it spilt over polished ledges or swirled round tumbled boulders. And from the tree-tops a wood-pigeon cooed softly, persistent, and amongst the roots and ferns and mosses small sounds stirred and were still, and now and then, as the birch boughs swayed gently and as gently sighed, a yellow leaf fluttered down lightly to join its sleeping fellows. And on the rustling carpet of gold and copper that they laid down for him, Aeneas walked, and, knowingly or not, trod softly.

He heard the singing before he saw the singer, a warm contralto voice that came to him from round a bend in the track, lilting a simple tuneful song, natural, unaffected, melodious, that did no violence to the wood's tranquillity. He knew that song, "Bonnie Mary o' Argyll," and liked it well. And it occurred to him that it was being sung in English. He waited.

# 5

SHE came, presently, round the clump of rust-red junipers, walking easily, unhurriedly, as one would to that song, her empty basket over her bare arm, her eyes adream and her head in the air, as adequate a picture, in her fitting half-sleeved knitted jersey of saffron, and knee-short skirt of crotal-brown—Highland length, but none the worse for that—as the autumn woodland itself. So she did not notice, at first, the man who stood beside the dark Scots fir, and her singing went on, unfaltering. Aeneas had a few moments to consider her, and did not waste his opportunity. That she would be good-looking he was prepared for, well-built and character-full—but it was some quality of vitality, of vividness almost, about her, even in her present air of abstraction, that struck him most strongly. Not that he need have been surprised, of course; her brother had been vital enough, in all conscience—and she was very like her brother, even though her hair was dark where his had been fair; the wide brow, high cheek-bones, finely cut nose and chin, were the same, and the mouth, if less large, was generous still. But her colour was different, warmer than Finlay's pale intensity. Also, her tall lissomeness had not the incipient stoop of her brother's lanky big-boned frame. That much Aeneas perceived, before, not wishing to introduce himself by alarming her, he stepped out of the pine's shadow and up the track towards her.

"Bonnie Mary" stopped short with distressing finality. Her walk, after a brief initial hesitation, quickened rather than faltered. The basket dropped from the crook of her arm to her hand, where it began to swing as to some purpose. Her head, that had been in the air, did not sink noticeably, even if the eyes no longer dreamed.

At half a dozen yards, Aeneas smiled, to the best of his ability, and doffed his hat. "Good afternoon," he bowed, "Miss MacBride, I believe?"

It took her a few steps to answer that, even with a stiff incline of her head, and he noted that she had hazel-brown eyes, where Finlay's had been blue-grey. Also he noted that, whatever their potential warmth, they held little of it now, and that she headed rather apparently to the far side of the track, and beyond it, as she came up with him.

Hurriedly, abruptly, he went on, and though he did not realize it, his black brows frowned their blackest. "I was told that I'd find you hereabouts—some cottage past the wood. I heard you singing—in English . . . so I knew . . ."

She had not stopped, only slowed her walking, and that slightly. "Indeed, sir."

He positively glared. It would be so easy to say who he was, to stop this foolishness—but something prevented him, some deep-seated, only part-acknowledged urge to confound, to humble her. "I have come a long way to see you," he said, even-voiced. "Our last encounter, off Eorsa, was hardly satisfactory, either!" Did he only imagine the pale beginnings of a flush at that? "I'd be obliged if you would spare me a moment."

She stopped then, but without fully facing him. "As you will, sir. But I cannot imagine what business you can have with me . . . unless it is the Manse? I can move out of there whenever I must . . ."

"It is not the Manse. I am no factor, Miss MacBride. And my business has brought me all the way from the Low Countries." He frowned again, but at himself this time. That was cheap, hollow, and unnecessary, and he knew it. Therefore he spoke the more harshly. "My name is Aeneas Graham!"

"Oh!" Her hand lifting to her mouth in dismay, she turned to him, then it dropped lower as though to still the sudden and noticeable heaving of her bosom, and her eyes widened, shot with a variety of emotion . . . He should have been satisfied with his achievement.

Instead, he felt a fool sudden and complete, and something of a knave and a boor into the bargain. His hand went out in an urgent gesture. "I'm sorry . . ."

"I'm sorry . . ."

In unison they said it, so inevitable, so inadequate, and stopped. Then, as their eyes met, wary, confused, ashamed, he blinked, smiled, grinned, laughed outright, an uneven and rather fearsome laugh, harsh with disuse, and his out-thrust hand reached for hers. "I am an abject idiot," he announced, as with conviction. "Please forgive me, Miss MacBride."

"It is myself that should be asking that," she claimed, and there was no denying her flush now, a rosy warm flood that did her almost chiselled good-looks no harm at all. "I am really terribly sorry—you must think me horrid, rude. I thought . . . I had no idea, of course . . ." and her glance quite promptly shed some of its unaccustomed meekness. "I couldn't possibly be expected to know. . . ."

The man nodded gravely. "And you disapprove of factors on principle, I believe?"

"Well, it's not so much that, perhaps. . . . It is because—well, you see, I've been worried about the Manse. I suppose I've no real right to be there, now. When the new minister comes, of course, I'll have to leave . . . unless he wants a housekeeper. When I heard that the new factor was coming, I was sure that he would want to turn me out . . . and it is my home, you see, and, well . . . I've been dreading it. . . ."

"You are very fond of Erismore?"

"Yes, I suppose so. I feel that I belong here, in some way." She looked away from him, and smiled, fleetingly. "And if I have to leave the Manse, I'll not really have any excuse for staying here—I'll have to go back to Edinburgh. . . . So, you see . . . ! And we get so few visitors here—we don't get any, in fact. It never struck me that it could be anyone else but the factor. But I was very rude—I was not too happy about the boat at Eorsa, too . . . and I was not singing very well . . .!"

"You were a lark, a nightingale," he assured her, soberly. "And 'Bonnie Mary' is a favourite of mine. I understand the position perfectly. Anyway, I am glad I've found you at last—despite my childishness a minute ago."

"But is it possible that you really came all this way just to see me, Dr. Graham?" she wondered. "I can hardly believe that.

Surely you had some other reason, as well . . . ? You were so very kind, about Finlay—and your letter, but . . . ?"

The man looked a little uncertain himself. "Well . . . yes, it was to see you that I came to Erismore—at least, if you had not been here I would not have come, that is certain. But I suppose there *is* more to it than that. Finlay told me so much about this island; it was quite a passion with him. It made me curious, anxious to see it. And I felt that I deserved a holiday, after all these years of campaigning. I have felt rather out of sympathy with things, too, since I returned to this country—conditions have changed, people too. . . . And when I got home, I found a situation that quite altered my half-formed plans for settling down there." He shrugged. "I think, perhaps, I was quite glad of this excuse for putting off having to plan my future, for a bit. You see, I promised your brother, just before he died, that I would come to you, and give you his message. I am only fulfilling my promise."

"And a fine dance I've led you!" the girl said, ruefully. "You must have regretted your promise, Dr. Graham. But, Finlay . . . ?" She looked down. "Was he . . . was it very bad, at the end? Did he suffer a great deal . . . ?"

Aeneas spoke carefully. "I think that he suffered more in his mind than in his body. He was very anxious, about Erismore, mainly—his charge here. I think, once he realized that he was not going to be able to return, that he regretted ever having left. Not selfishly, of course, but for the sake of the people here. He was worried about the place, desperately. He wanted me to tell you that he came to see that you were right, in the end, and that he always intended to come back."

"Yes," she said, and suddenly started to walk. "Yes. Dear Finlay. Oh, why did he ever leave Erismore? This was his place. . . . Oh, God, why did he have to die! He was . . ." Abruptly, chokingly, she was silent, and the man, opening his mouth to speak, closed it again and strode on beside her, wordless. And presently, he laid his hand on the handle of her basket. "Let me carry this," he suggested.

She shook her head, keeping her eyes to the front. "No—it is

40

nothing. No weight in it. It was just some things I was taking to a woman up the glen. She is very sick."

And since her words came unsteadily, struggling through tears, he took her up quickly. "Sick? What is wrong with her?"

"I don't know. Something internal, I think. She has a lot of pain, poor soul. It is very sad, and her with two children. I do what I can, but it is not much . . ." Then she stopped in her hurrying, and turned to him. "But you are a doctor! You could help her, perhaps?"

"We-e-ell." He nodded, but slowly, to her new eagerness. "I could have a look, anyway."

"Would you? I would be very grateful. Poor Peig, she has had a bad time. Her husband, Torquil Macleod, was one of Finlay's recruits, and was killed at, at . . . I think it was Estramadura."

"Torquil Macleod! Of course—I knew him. He was a piper—in Fraser's company. Poor fellow, I had to amputate, I remember. . . ."

"Then would you come and see her, now, since we are so near? It is no distance. It would be a great comfort to her." Already she had swung about, and was starting back the way that she had come.

Aeneas followed perforce, but doubtingly. He had effected his introduction certainly, and had banished the tears which he had dreaded—but what had he let himself in for, now!

She led him, hurrying, through the wood; obviously, this one was not apt to be lukewarm about her projects. He said no more anent Finlay and his anxieties, meantime, but told her of his own call on her aunt, and of his journey north.

Presently the trees began to thin, and the glen to open out, and they came out into a deep basin of the hills, green amongst the brown of enclosing heather, with a small reed-fringed loch at its centre, grey now, denied the afternoon sunlight by the jealous hills. And, below a knoll near the head of the lochan, was the croft of Camusnacreagh, built slantwise up the slope, with its hunched back, indeed, burrowing into the rising ground behind.

"So that is where Torquil learned his piping," Aeneas said. "The home he played to!"

41

"The home that he should never have left!" the girl amended shortly.

Through the skinny scurrying poultry, barked and growled at by a yellow-eyed lean black-and-white collie, they came to the dark gap of the doorway. Frances MacBride went in first, and man and dog remained outside glaring at each other with mutual antipathy, where, in a little while, they were joined by two half-naked children, wide-eyed, unwashed, and as gaunt as the rest of the establishment. The visitor's smile achieved no response, and open-mouthed they contributed to the silent inspection.

Stooping in the doorway, when Frances called him within, Aeneas at first could see little or nothing. The place was black as the pit; there appeared to be only the one window, and it was small and unglazed and hung-over with what appeared to be an ancient sheep-skin; there was a hole in the roof, above the peat-fire which glowed dully in the centre of the floor, but little light filtered through from there, with the smoke to contend with, while his own bulk blocked the doorway; and all within, floor and walls and the few simple furnishings, were so darkened by soot as to be practically an even black. Black-houses he had heard these cabins named, seemingly with justice. But if the eyes failed him, his nose did not; peat-reek, humanity, and dog, the stuffy smell of poultry, the oily tang of fleeces, and the warm heavy scent of cattle, struck him with almost physical force. Coughing, he pressed in against it, stumbling over the unseen clay of the floor, and from somewhere amongst his feet, a hen fled in squawking uproar.

He perceived Frances MacBride standing near the fire, and beside her a slight woman, sitting on a bench, who rose as he approached and dropped him a curtsey, before the girl's hand on her shoulder pressed her down to her seat again. She was small and old-seeming, in her dark shawl of tartan, to be the wife of Torquil Macleod, who had been but thirty, but more than years can make a woman old. Aeneas, peering close, at eyes and skin, felt her pulse, and nodded to himself. He asked her questions, Frances interpreting, some of them embarrassing, where he was

42

gruff, Mrs. Macleod hesitant, and the girl resolute. He asked for a light, and was found a cruisie-lamp of fish-oil, which burned but smokily. Also for a wash, and was directed to a bucket of water beside the door. Then he directed that the silent woman get on to her bed. "She will need to remove some of her clothes," he said shortly. "I dare say I can manage, myself."

Frances indicated the dark box-bed built into the wall of the cabin. "I will hold the light for you," she said calmly.

He nodded, unspeaking, and thus he made his examination in silence, save for, once or twice, Peig Macleod's hastily-suppressed gasp of pain, and the recurrent gusty sighing of the milch-cow stalled beyond the partition. Frances held the lamp closer, at his sign, and closer still, and once he shivered involuntarily at the tickle of her hair against his cheek.

At length the man straightened up. "No wonder she has been suffering, and complaining of a discharge," he said. "She has a great abscess, there...."

"An abscess...? That is serious, isn't it? Can anything be done?"

"It should be opened, cleaned out. It is draining away her strength."

"And you could do it?"

He nodded. "I think so. I have some things in my baggage . With assistance!"

"Of course. I will tell her. When?"

"The sooner the better. Tomorrow—the next day? But it will not be pleasant, for her . . . or the assistant!"

She shook her dark head quickly. "That must not matter. I will speak to her, now."

"Tell her that it will be painful, but not dangerous." He washed his hands again at the door, and issued thankfully into the fresh air.

Outside, she joined him, presently. "Tomorrow, she says," Frances told him. "You will tell me what you need?"

"Yes." He frowned up at the frowning hills. "You are rather like your brother," he said.

43

## 6

THEY walked back, into the wood and out of it again, speaking little. The years of his soldiering had atrophied any faculty that Aeneas had ever possessed for polite conversation with the opposite sex—or with anyone else, for that matter—and he was overmuch aware of it. Which did not help. And here and now he was careful of what he had to say—which was of no assistance, either. He made his judicious statements, on innocuous subjects, and that was that. The girl considered him out of the corners of her brown eyes, and wondered.

The sea was spreading before them, illimitable and still burnished with the late afternoon sun, that their side of the island had lost, when he spoke up. "What is wrong with Erismore?" he asked abruptly.

His companion, after a swift glance, and a few paces, replied without answering. "What *is* wrong with Erismore then, Dr. Graham?"

"I don't know. I thought that you might be able to tell me. There seems to be an idea that there is something wrong with it. All that know the place hint, infer, as much—not that they are many, I agree. Nothing certain, specific. It is not liked. Why?"

She kept her eyes on the ground, and said nothing.

He went on: "I've heard it called horrible, queer, and unchancy—your aunt, that was. The Coll folk looked at me strangely when they heard that I was coming here. And the Keiths at Eorsa have no love for it, were definitely reluctant to discuss the place. Difficult, Mr. Keith called it. But it was Finlay's own attitude that impressed me most. He was fond of the island, almost to an obsession, as you know—but he was worried, anxious, about it. And his worry became desperate latterly, when he recognized that he was not going to be able to return to it. At the end, of course, it was difficult to know how much of what he said was real and how much delirium. He talked about it being lost, damned even, unless he could get back to it, confessing Christ but serving the Devil. That sort of thing. I remember, one time, he said that the folk here were slipping into a nameless evil. The phrase stuck in my mind. . . . What did he mean . . . ?"

The girl was frowning, now. "I don't know," she said. "I wish I did. I would tell you if I could. I know that there is something wrong, of course—something more than just the obvious things that you would expect in such an out-of-the-way place— backwardness, superstition, and that sort of thing. There is something hidden, deep-hidden . . . but I've only the vaguest ideas as to what it is. We've known it for a long time—years before ever Finlay went away we were trying to find out. He felt it interfering with his work, and I know how it worried him. I have been trying to discover what it is, ever since. . . ."

"But surely you must have some idea?" the man cried. "If you can feel so strongly that there is something wrong, surely you must have some sort of notion as to the kind of trouble? I mean, is it the people, their attitude or the way they live—morals, and so on—or do you think it has something to do with the place itself?"

"Oh, it is the people—though possibly the place has something to do with it, too. It is all so terribly difficult to put into words, Dr. Graham. There is so little to grasp hold of, as it were. It is more feelings and suggestions, than anything else, impressions that one gets suddenly, undeniably, of something hostile and evil. You will probably think that I am just a foolish hysterical girl, over-imaginative . . . though Finlay felt it even more than I do. And other people have felt it, too. We had a minister here from Tiree, once, who told us he would not stay here, for any inducement. . . ."

"Yet you don't want to go away—you say that you love the place!"

Frances nodded. "Yes, that's true. I love Erismore, and the people, or most of them. I feel somehow that the evil, or whatever it is, is from without, as though the people are more sinned against than sinning. It is so difficult to explain. . . ."

45

"But you do believe that there's some sort of wickedness going on?" Aeneas insisted, bluntly.

"Yes."

"Something that's been going on for a long time—possibly before you or Finlay ever came to the island?"

"Yes." She glanced at his dark set face, and then away again. "But it's getting worse!"

"M'mmmm," the man said.

They walked on in silence for a space.

Frances MacBride turned to him, hesitated, and then spoke in a different tone. "Dr. Graham—tell me about my brother. Tell me his message."

"The heart of it, I have already told you." Aeneas answered her. "About how in the end he came to see that you were right, and that he should never have left the island, and how he always had intended to return. But, mainly, I think, he wanted me to try and explain to you why he had acted as he did. I gather that he felt that you never fully understood . . . ? There had been a disagreement . . . ?"

She nodded, tight-lipped.

"I remember, he said that you always saw so very clearly, so much more clearly than he did, who always saw two and three sides to a question. That could be his weakness, perhaps, as well as his strength."

"Or mine!" she interjected quickly.

The man used no words to answer that. "Finlay saw far," he said. "Too far, for any peace of mind, perhaps. He loved his fellow-men too much, and, unlike most of us, was not content just to say so. He had to *do* something, always. That is one reason why he left here, I imagine; the life here, for all his striving, was too passive, too easy. He felt that the men who had gone needed him more than those who were left. And perhaps they did—if you could have seen the conditions he worked in, the help and comfort and peace he brought to hundreds, thousands even. . . . You will say, but that was not his sphere; his place was here, where he was ordained priest. He knew that, too—but he meant to return, you see. He said, once, that Erismore was not quite ready for him—while these men that had gone to fight, needed him urgently."

"I know—I know all that," she cried, but not unkindly. "We discussed, argued it all. But it seemed so clearly a parish priest's duty to stay with his charge, especially such a parish as this, that had been neglected for centuries. His first duty, surely . . ."

"His first duty! That was Finlay's trouble. He saw so many duties, and was apt to put the most urgent first. A calmer, more prudent man might have taken the long view, the wiser view—a view that he could see, mind you, as he saw the others, only too clearly. But he was not calm or prudent or wise—he was warm and strong and generous and fine. Finlay MacBride was the finest man I ever knew."

The girl's voice quivered. "Dr. Graham, you must not think, because I question what he did . . . you must not think that I am cold, unnatural. . . . I loved my brother, deeply I loved him—more deeply, I think, than is usual between sister and brother. Always, we did everything together. We were inseparable. We came here, to Erismore, together. We had planned it, even as children. We were going to be missionaries, to bring Christianity to Erismore, together. It sounds presumptuous, I know—but it was our lifelong ambition. And there was much that a woman could do. You will know that this was one of the earliest outposts of Christianity in the Highlands, if not *the* earliest—St. Ninian is said to have founded a colony here a hundred years before Columba came to Iona. It was terrible that it should have sunk back almost to heathendom. And it had, you know; even now, I sometimes think, its Christianity is only skin-deep. My father did what he could, from Eorsa, but he had no authority, and he was a sick man, and the sea made him ill. Besides, he was a pastor, and no evangelist, I'm afraid. . . . When Finlay managed to convince Lord Dunalastair to rebuild the church here, and revive the charge, we were overjoyed. It seemed something fine, splendid . . . but you see how it has turned out! That is why I was so upset when he decided to go off to the war. It seemed like throwing away all that we had worked for. I knew

Finlay—his enthusiasm, how he would throw himself into the thick of everything, never spare himself. I knew, too, that like Father, he had no great reserves of strength to squander . . . I knew that he might well never come back, whatever he said. And I was right. So we quarrelled, for the first time, and . . . and I never saw him again."

He nodded, unspeaking. Clear-sightedness might have its drawbacks too, it seemed.

She resumed again, after a moment. "That is one reason why I had to come back when I heard that he . . . when I got your letter. I wanted to carry on with his work here, our work, in such small measure as I could. Not that there was much that I could do alone, a woman. . . . But I thought that I could keep his name before the people, his memory, a reminder of the work he had begun. . . . But now, I am not so sure. I cannot feel that I have been very successful. And when he was replaced, I could tell his successor about him and about his plans, and about Erismore. In that way I could perhaps help a little to complete his work . . ."

Aeneas cleared his throat, glancing at her under down-drawn brows. "I'm afraid, Miss Frances, that you're not going to be very successful in that, either," he said. "Finlay is not going to be replaced. I saw Dunalastair, the new man, myself. He is very definite. There will be no minister to follow Finlay."

Her eyes lifted, from the road, over the shadow-filled moors and the stark hill-slopes, to the lambent sea, into which all the light of the land had drained. "So . . . !" she said, in a long sigh. "You brought that word, after all! It was that that I was afraid the factor had come to tell me, more than any other fear . . . I had expected that, too, you see. Poor Erismore!"

They had come to the edge of the peat-bog and the last slope above the scattered crofts that fringed the shore. Already, with the early dusk upon them, the houses, with their turf and reed roofs, were fading into the land, but each was marked by the blue plume of peat-smoke lifting gently on the evening air. The girl paused beside a great outcrop of stone.

"I often come here, about this time, to watch the boats come in with the darkening," she told him. "Sometimes the sunsets are almost beyond believing. Tonight it is very quiet."

Aeneas considered. Below them the land met the sea in a wide sickle, a long arc of bay, containing innumerable smaller bays, facing west by south between two massive headlands, dark towering cliffs that reared themselves sheer for hundreds of feet, before shelving back in great bold steps and ledges, still fiercely steep, to flat bare summits, level as table-tops, with, stretched between them like a string to the bow of the bay, the black line of the skerries. Within the sickle the sea, like the land, gloomed dark in shadow, deepest violet edged, as were the skerries, with the dead white of breakers. But beyond, was no gloom at all, no shadow, no hue, nor feature, nor any certainty; just the vast empty shimmering plain of the sea, translucent, softly refulgent, seeming not to reflect the stark vacancy of the sky but rather to glimmer gently with its own luminosity, unrelated to brightness or light, even, or any colour. And there was no end to it, no horizon, no meeting of sea and sky, just void, nothingness, to all infinity, ultimate, terrible. The eyes beheld it, and shrank from it, and did not consider it. "Yes, I suppose that it is quiet," the man agreed, heavily. "It is no sunset, anyway."

Frances scraped a pattern on the gravel of the path with the toe of her brogue. Twice she glanced at the man before she spoke. "Dr. Graham . . . the Manse . . . Finlay would have expected you to stay in his house. It is at your service. There is a room for you, Finlay's room. . . ."

"No," he said quickly. "Thank you, but it is not necessary. I have found a place. There is no need . . ."

"It would be no trouble . . . if you would prefer it." She lifted her head, her chin. "No need to care what people say! It is the least I can do."

"No. You are kind—but I will be all right where I am. The old man Macgillivray found me a good place. . . ."

"Lachlan Mor!" She turned swiftly. Perhaps she was glad to change the subject. "So he has taken you up! He has been quick."

"Yes. He met me almost as soon as I landed. He had been watching the boat, he said—surprised that we came in the way we did. He was very civil, courteous. I was quite impressed."

"Yes."

"He is rather a remarkable man, is he not?"

"Yes."

"He was different from anything I'd expected. The men at the pier looked at me a bit askance—but he was quite hospitable, helpful. I gather that he is some sort of patriarch in the place?"

"Oh, yes. He's that, and more—Elder and Catechist, tacksman, school-master, quite the uncrowned king of the island."

"I see. He seemed to be interested that I was a friend of Finlay's."

"He would be, yes." Suddenly she leaned forward, pointing. "There are the boats, now—just rounding the headland, there. Can you see them?"

At first he could not pick them out, against the pale sheen of the water, but on her directing, he discovered them, half a dozen tiny-seeming craft, like water-beetles creeping over the transparent skin of the sea, beyond the lesser, southern-most, cape. On they came, so very slowly, as his own boat had done that forenoon, moving parallel with the skerries, but well to seaward.

"They look very small, frail." Aeneas mentioned.

"Small, yes—but they are very important to Erismore those few boats. Without the fishing, the folk here could not manage. The crofts are not enough, the ground too barren, to provide a family with a living. Without the fish they would go hungry. But they take their toll. Erismore is no haven for boats."

"I believe you, there," the man agreed. "There are accidents, then, sinkings?"

"Continually. It is a constant dread. There is not a croft on the island that hasn't lost a man to that sea. It has always been like that on Erismore. The women have no rest from the fear of it. And there are so few men now, anyway. . . ."

They walked downhill towards the township. The boats had not yet turned in towards the island, heading for the farther, more northerly, gap in the skerries. Small lights were beginning to gleam from one or two of the houses, but most of the people, as Frances pointed out, would be down at the pier to watch the boats come in. They had not been out for five days, the recent storm prohibiting, and with the seas that still were running, their landfall was yet a matter for concern. Also, the fishing had not been so good, of late, and a new fishing-ground was being tried today; the luck might have turned.

With the dusk, and the shadows of the bay, they could not see as far as the skerries now. But presently, something like a cheer floating up from the shore seemed to indicate that the boats were through. At the Manse gate, they paused.

"Will you come in, and have a bite of supper?" the girl invited.

"No—no, thank you. Another time, maybe. I told Mrs. Macgillivray I'd be back ..."

"Mrs. Macgillivray ... ?"

"Yes—that is her name, isn't it? Mairi, the old man's granddaughter. Or is that only her maiden name?"

"No—that is her husband's name, too. There are many Macgillivrays on the island. So that is where Lachlan Mor put you!"

"Yes. Is it unsuitable, in any way? It seems very comfortable. The young woman seems very pleasant ..."

"Oh, yes—you will be comfortable with Mairi. She is a good girl, kind, and clean too. Ewan Beg is nice, as well, if a little weak, maybe. But ..." She shook her head, suddenly, decidedly. "Well, time I was making my supper. Thank you so very much, Dr. Graham, for all your kindness. I do appreciate your coming here like this, all this way, and your loyalty to Finlay, and your interest and patience. It has been, will be, a great help to be able to discuss matters with you—I'm afraid that I've rather got things here on my mind, out of proportion, perhaps. Having had no one to talk them over with, I've rather bottled them up, I suppose, and brooded. I was probably beginning to see things, to imagine things that weren't there. . . . Your coming is just what I needed, I think. Sometimes I have been a little bit

51

frightened . . . I am grateful." A couple of steps she moved, and then: "And thank you, too, for being so kind about Peig Macleod. Will you come over in the morning, and tell me what is needed? Let me give you dinner, and we will go up to Peig in the afternoon?"

"Thank you. You are kind." He coughed. "And do not be frightened any more. There is nothing to be frightened for, I am sure."

"No. Goodnight, then." She was some yards up the path, when her voice came back to him. "Have you told Lachlan Mor about . . . that there is no new minister coming?"

"No," he answered. "Why?"

"I think, perhaps, it might be as well not to mention it, meantime . . . if you don't mind." And, uncertainly: "Maybe it would be wise to be careful what you say, over there—just at first. . . . Good night."

Frowning, the man turned, to walk slowly back towards the farm-house. It was time that he had come, it seemed. Finlay's sister was needing him. Perhaps Mairi Macgillivray was right; it was not good for a young woman to live alone . . . a MacBride, especially.

## 7

EWAN BEG MACGILLIVRAY was an inoffensive young man, open-faced, freckled, cheerful and uncritical—almost as pleasant as his wife, if without the same depth of character. They had come up from the shore together arm-in-arm, he with a string of gleaming fish across his blue jerseyed shoulder, and Mairi had introduced him to their guest. Whether or not he had been glad to hear that they had a lodger to share their comparatively newly-married bliss, he greeted Aeneas with a boyish cordiality. His English was barely as good as Mairi's, but he used it without embarrassment, substituting his own Gaelic naturally when he did not know a word, with generally understandable results. He was very proud of his wife, obviously, and of his house and farm, which was, after his great-uncle Lachlan Mor's, the best on the island, and of his boat, the *Eala*, of which he was the owner and skipper. He was proud, also, of today's catch of fish, the best for weeks, and that it was himself that had led the way to the new fishing-ground. And Mairi was proud of her husband, if in a different fashion that shook her dark head over him at times, and they laughed together a great deal. The newcomer, whom they accepted with neither uncomfortable awe nor undue freedom, found his own little-used smile receiving unwonted exercise at and with their young blitheness. And he was all of thirty-four.

So, after a sufficient supper of porridge and new-caught creamy mackerel and thick floury oatcakes, Aeneas was in no hurry to retire to the fire which Mairi had kindled in his own room, content to stretch in front of the glowing peats in the kitchen, and listen to Ewan Beg extolling modestly the fertility of Ruaigmore's dozen acres of tilth, the quality and spirit of its score of black stirks and half a hundred shaggy sheep, the size and speed and sea-worthiness of his eighteen-foot *Eala*—and inferentially, perhaps, the seamanship of her skipper—and the few merits and curious notions and terrible temper of the woman that was married on him, God forgive her—with just a hint, maybe, of the strong and masterful sort of man one had to be to husband her. And to watch, discreetly, the play of light and shadow on the girl's warm comeliness, the swift kindling of eye and cheek and throat, the eager parting of lips, the ready laughter, and the rapier-quick flame of retort and remonstrance. To listen and watch, and to feel pleasantly how remote and contradictory all this was from the gloomy hostile mystery that Frances MacBride's lonely brooding had conjured out of Erismore—except very occasionally and only transiently, vaguely, when Ewan's talk of the sea drew a sudden stillness across the young woman's mobile features and a fleeting curtain over the sparkling eyes.

Not once, either, was the stranger asked to give any account of himself.

It was, perhaps, an hour after supper when Lachlan Mor arrived. The young people were quiet in his presence, and the laughter stopped. But he was very affable and urbane, and blessed all within that house with quiet dignity, before seating himself on Ewan's high-backed chair before the fire. He had come to see that the gentleman was comfortable, he announced, and whether there was anything else, at all, that he might be needing? They were poor and humble folk, but anything they had, whatever, was at the service of a friend of Mr. MacBride.

Aeneas acknowledged this kindness gratefully, assuring him that he was more comfortable than he had any right to expect, disclaiming any further needs for the present, and thanking him for the most excellent whisky.

The old man said it was a pleasure; the whisky was poor stuff, no doubt, compared with what the gentleman would be used to, though it was the oldest matured that he had, and the Erismore water was good for it. Yes, he distilled it his own self. He would be running some more one of these days, and would be glad to show Mr. Graham the way of it . . . if he was thinking of staying any time at all, that was?

Aeneas did not know yet how long he was likely to stay, but

it would not be for very long, he thought. He would be very glad to see the distilling process, should the opportunity occur.

Yes, it would be a pleasure. Anything at all. The winter seas were not the best for getting away from the island, and later in the year there were the fewer ships to get passage to the South, from Coll or Tobermory or even the Oban itself. But Mr. Graham's work here might not take him that long . . . ?

That was agreed, without elaboration.

Yes, the gentleman would do as he thought best, whatever. And Miss MacBride herself might be going South with him? It was a long road for a lassie like herself to travel, alone, especially with the year wearing on. The winter on a place like Erismore was coarse, coarse.

Mr. Graham was sure it was, but had no knowledge of Miss MacBride's plans.

Of course. A very fine young lady she was, too, with the grand spirit in her. They were proud to have her amongst them. She must be greatly fond of the island to be staying all this time, alone? Nothing but love of it would keep her on their poor barren rock of a place, for sure.

Aeneas thought that perhaps she felt she could be helpful.

Lachlan Mor agreed that there might be that in it, the kind young heart of her. Not that that sort of work was the thing for a gentle bred young lady the like of herself, maybe. Their own stronger women were the more suited to it, perhaps. But Miss Frances would never consider her own self, at all—it would be others that would have to be doing that for her. And he had heard that Mr. Graham and herself had been away up to see Peig Macleod, Camusnacreagh, that afternoon? The poor creature would be better, perhaps?

Hardly, yet, he was told. She had rather a bad abscess, that would have to be opened and drained.

Was that so, indeed! And fancy them finding out a thing like that! And who would be able to do the likes of that, for the poor woman?

Coughing, Aeneas admitted that he was a doctor.

The old man, stroking his white beard, turned from the fire

to consider the younger man thoughtfully, his colourless eyes searching, unwinking, unswerving. Meeting the stare of them, the impact, almost with a shock, the other was put in mind of the cold remote glitter of the evening sea that he had beheld and shrunk from not so long since. Strange eyes indeed, and no more to be fathomed than that other chill vacancy.

After an appreciable pause, Lachlan Mor nodded. A doctor! Was that not a surprise! An honour, indeed. Never had they had a doctor on Erismore, before. Himself, he was interested in a very humble way in the art of healing—only as a child might be, before the knowledge of a real doctor, of course. Any doctoring that the folk of the island had had, himself it was that did it. But this was interesting, indeed.

For a while there was silence in that lamp-lit room. Since the old man's coming, the young people had barely spoken half a dozen words between them. Ewan Beg crouched on a low three-legged stool, drawn back some distance from the fire, and Mairi stood at his back, her hands on his shoulders. Both stared into the glow of the peats, but without any appearance of disinterest or inattention. They merely waited. Aeneas waited, too—for it was the old man who dominated the room, who by some power of personality controlled the tempo of their intercourse as he did the substance. And now he sat quietly, and stroked his beard.

So Mr. Graham was a doctor—and a friend of Mr MacBride! And he had come all the way to their island, the busy important man as he must be! That was a very wonderful thing—nothing like that ever had happened before. It would not be for nothing that the likes of himself would come that long road—Mr. Finlay must have spoken well of the place, to be sure?

He spoke much of it, anyway, Aeneas temporized.

Just that. Dr. Graham had seen a lot of Mr. MacBride, then? He would be soldiering with him, no doubt? A necessary thing it was to have a doctor with the soldiers—the Government would see to that, no doubt. And here was them having a Government doctor coming to Erismore! No, no—of course he understood that Dr. Graham was just on a sort of holiday, whatever. He would have to see that he did not let any little sicknesses that they might have on the island interfere with his holiday, then. That would not do, at all.

The younger man sounded non-committal.

And if Dr. Graham had been in the Army with Mr. MacBride he would know the laird, the old laird, MacTormaid himself, the Lord Dunalastair, as they called him? A fine man, indeed, and a great fighter—too great a fighter for the like of Erismore, perhaps! Maybe he had told him about the island, too?

It had been mentioned, Aeneas conceded.

Of course. And it might be, that the Doctor had met the new laird, also? A great gentleman, living in London, they said, but not forgetting his tenants in the North, at all! He might be a friend of Dr. Graham's, too?

No. This time his informant was very definite. The new Lord Dunalastair was no friend of his, and his visit had nothing to do with him.

Lachlan Mor did not suggest it, at all—and him on a sort of holiday. If the laird wanted information about the island, he'd be sending his new factor, for sure. There was word that the rents were to be increased, which would be difficult, and many of them hard put to it enough as it was, and the crofts with little worth to them. They were expecting the new factor, indeed, and he would see for himself—and maybe he would tell them if they were getting a new minister?

In the pause, Aeneas cleared his throat. That would be a matter for the laird and the Kirk, he supposed, carefully.

It would, no doubt. Not that they were not managing along well enough, of course, on their own. As Catechist and Elder, he held a sort of service, now and then, and saw that the young folk were instructed—not the same as Mr. MacBride at all, of course, but the work went on. And Mr. Keith was not that far away, and them needing a minister for anything. If need be, they could manage along, as they did before—though they were grateful for all Mr. MacBride's work, to be sure. And he had worked hard, in the Lord's work. Had he told Dr. Graham of his work . . . ?

Aeneas was becoming restive, when a knock at the door

heralded the arrival of two more men, both middle-aged, who stood uncertainly within the doorway, turning their bonnets in their hands. Lachlan Mor, after a grave stare at them, introduced them as Callum Ruadh Macgillivray, his nephew, and Nial Maclean, Ardaig, and Mairi, discovering her voice, invited them into the circle of the fire, drawing up a form for them to sit on. But though they came forward, smiling, they did not sit down. Ewan Beg said a few words to them, in Gaelic, which they answered in monosyllables. Each time Aeneas glanced at them, they smiled. It seemed evident that they had come to see the stranger and since they did not speak his language, they were not going to be so rude as to chatter in any other in his presence. Lachlan Mor had fallen silent now too, but Mairi took up the talk, if with some constraint, bringing her husband in with her. Ewan, at a nod from his great-uncle, produced the whisky-bottle and a number of horn cups. Filling them liberally, the old man lifted his own to just below the level of his eyes, those curious palely brilliant eyes that looked at Aeneas fixedly.

"God's wisdom guide us all," he said gravely, "—especially the Doctor!"

More visitors arrived, singly and in pairs, till the kitchen was full, of men and the smells they brought with them—sheep and fish and pitch and the tang of sweat-permeated homespun clothing—for no woman came amongst them. In the main, they were elderly quiet bearded men, though there were a few who were younger, but, for the present, equally quiet. Of the former, Aeneas recognized the man who had sat in the stern of the boat that had refused him passage at Eorsa, a big man, massively built and sombre-visaged, who was introduced to him as Duncan Og Macgillivray, Lachlan Mor's son. He was confused already with all these Macgillivrays, but he would remember this man.

Aeneas had intended to retire to his own room before this, and would have been glad to do so now, but it seemed obvious that all these people had come here on his account, either to pay their respects or to inspect him, and to withdraw himself too promptly might appear churlish. Not that they made any attempt at conversation with him—few of them knew any English, probably—but their attitude was civil, and their interest natural without being impolite. But an unease prevailed that was undeniable; even Lachlan Mor seemed to have withdrawn himself into silent meditation and Mairi, suitably, had disappeared. Aeneas contemplated his room upstairs with some longing. He would give them ten minutes more.

Then one of the younger men spoke to Ewan Beg, making a proposal, obviously, and others supported him. Glancing at his great-uncle, who, after a moment, nodded wordlessly, Ewan stared into the fire with some concentration, and, with a gulp, broke into song.

He had a rich and tuneful voice, and, after a hesitant start, sang with an easy confidence, a rousing air, simple and strong, with the company joining in the refrain. A boat-song, most evidently, with the roll of the sea, the creak of the oars, and the sigh of the waves in it, and the singer kept the rolling rhythm of it with the sway of his body. At the murmured applause, he sang another of the same kind, and then a third, of a different type and timing, that set the head nodding and the feet tapping. Then, ending abruptly, he looked at Lachlan Mor. "*An fiodhal?* Let us have the fiddle?" he urged.

The old man shook his white head, but the chorus of acclamation swelled. "Dr. Graham may not approve?" he suggested, courteously. "Much of the Kirk does not love the fiddle. Mr. Keith names it the voice of sin."

"What nonsense!"

"Myself, I see no harm in it—but every man to his own opinion." That was mildness itself.

When Ewan had fetched the fiddle, Lachlan Mor laid it down carefully, felt in his pocket and produced a lump of resin which he applied slowly, lovingly, to the horse-hairs of the home-made bow, up and down, up and down. He was very deliberate. No one spoke. Aeneas did not have to glance round to perceive the air of expectancy. This, apparently, was an occasion. Perhaps he should feel honoured?

The patriarch was in no hurry to start. His eyes fixed on the glow of the peats, his veined hands ran over the smooth age-blackened surfaces of his instrument, lingeringly. Almost he seemed to have sunk into a trance, but none of the men that waited for him urged him on, or proffered any suggestion as to what he should play. It was with a long sigh that he raised the fiddle, a sigh that was curiously echoed by the company, tucking it under the side of his jaw where his beard did not interfere, and plucked a few strings. Then, with a single downwards stroke of the bow, he drew out a long searching chord, pure, flawless, fluid, and somehow anguishing, that faded and died but left its echo throbbing in the silence of the room, quivering, until it was cut short, as with a knife, as the bow leapt up and swooped.

What he played, Aeneas did not know, but that it was sorrowful and very lovely and utterly hopeless, was almost agonizingly apparent, as that it was superbly played. There was passion in it, and aching beauty, pain and tears and grieving, and the refinement of remorse that was beyond all these, intense, inevitable, and the sobbing strings ran together and fused, and rose to a single swelling note, persistent, ultimate, and so, suddenly, were still. There was no applause, no stirring, no sound, only a silent waiting.

Again the music commenced, this time a haunting melody, oft repeated, that gradually altered, not its tune but its tone and emphasis, as it seemed, from the wistful longings of childhood, through the unbalanced turbulence of adolescence and the sweet dreaming and fierce emotion of young love, to the strong steady flame of manhood, the even tenor of middle-age, the sudden fears and back-looking of declining years, and the quiet resigned acceptance of age. Truly, exquisitely, the music expressed each and all, with a masterly certainty, that questioned and sighed and raged and laughed and moaned and wept, before accepting, finally, fatally, for ever.

The old man's eyes were closed now, and, almost without a pause after that last quavering note of age, he slipped into a traditional lament of the West, full of infinite pathos, stern and melting by turns, and, in the climax, almost unbearable in its poignant sorrow; and from thence to a bitter scalding elegy of treachery and defeat, desolation and despair, woven into a pattern wherein the keening of women and the shouting of men lifted against a background of the roar of surf and sea and storm, rose but did not prevail. The sea prevailed, and the storm.

Lachlan Mor was playing more quickly now, and breathing more quickly. Aeneas, beside him, glanced sideways, and wondered. The man was leaning forward, crouching almost, rigid, eyes tight-shut, and the lean fingers that gripped the bow quivered, but not weakly. The whole fashion and method and tempo of his playing was changing, too. Hitherto there had been beauty in all that he had given them, weary, sorrowing, languorous, sublime, desperate, beauty—but always beauty. But now the beauty was fading out of his playing, the melody had gone and the harmony was going. Out of the storm of the last rendering, only chaos and violence had come, searing, clashing, jarring.

And yet, despite the crouching and quivering, the fiddler had by no means lost control of his instrument, that much was apparent. Rather, it seemed as though the man were in some sort of trance, carried away by the power of his own music, so that what he was driving, tearing, grinding, out of his fiddle now might be almost involuntary, subconscious even. But wild, violent as it was, Aeneas sensed something, some direction perhaps, some purpose, behind the harsh jangling strains. There was something in it, some motive, he was sure. . . .

Uncomfortably, he looked around him at the circle of dark faces—darker than they had seemed before. They were intent, all of them, staring transfixed at the hunched figure of the fiddler—but not in surprise; expectancy, fascination, fear even, but not in surprise. They confirmed Aeneas in his disquiet.

And then, out of the rending conflicting medley of sound, he perceived vaguely, as from a distance, a trend, a theme, not of a tune or refrain, but rather of design, a frantic pattern of disharmony, that recurred and persisted through the babel. Yes, there was no doubt about it. It was growing, advancing, inflaming, a profane unnatural chorus of discord, born out of turmoil, thriving on confusion, mounting towards destruction.

61

And it was horrible.

The effect on that crowded room was fierce, electric. Aeneas, perturbed, did not have to look about him to know it. The tension could be felt. They were moving, swaying, tight-packed as they were. The old man was gasping, with more than the violence of his exertion, his breath hissing between clenched teeth. The bow was jerking in his hand like a mad thing, faster and faster. The sound was shattering, now, agonizing, like a saw rasping into the brain, rising and rising into a crescendo of fury, always in the same malefic pattern, repelling yet somehow alluring, compelling, till a sudden corporate groan burst from the ranks of the listeners, swelled and continued. Lachlan Mor was on his feet now, still crouching, the fiddle alive, convulsed, in his hands, the noise intolerable, surging to a shout. And then, abruptly, piercing, a scream split and rent the uproar, shrill and high and sustained, a woman's scream.

The fiddle rasped to silence. The old man gulped for breath, seemed to paw the air with his bow and choking, sank back into his chair. The crowd of men turned slowly, dazedly, to stare at Mairi Macgillivray, where she stood by an inner door, white-faced, wide-eyed, her hands to her ears, her mouth open still. Blinking, shuddering, swallowing, they moved, shuffling shame-faced with one accord towards the outer door and the shroud of the night. Ewan Beg stumbled to his wife.

With a long breath, Aeneas Graham released his grip of the arms of his chair, and got to his feet. Climbing the steep stair to his room, he wiped the sweat from his brow.

## 8

A ENEAS presented himself at the Manse door early next morning; he found the atmosphere within the farm-house of Ruaigmore a little difficult, strained, and a thin drizzle that was falling damped his ardour for a time-filling walk. And, despite her tendency towards gloomy imaginings, he was glad to see Frances MacBride.

She seemed nowise displeased herself at his early arrival. She was dressed today, on his account maybe, rather more conventionally, in a noticeably longer dress of some fine-woven stuff, colourful, shapely, and quite admirable. All the same, he preferred her yesterday's less adequate but entirely sufficient garb. "Come away in, Dr. Graham," she greeted him. And, with a smile: "Is it your breakfast you want, and Mairi Macgillivray starving you?"

"Oh, no. I had it hours ago—at least, one hour ago, anyway. She's not so bright this morning, nor her husband either."

"Indeed? What is wrong with them?"

"We had a musical evening, last night!"

"Oh—a *ceilidh* was it, already?"

"I don't know if I'd call it just that. Your friend Lachlan Macgillivray came, and gave us a—a recital on the violin. They haven't got over it yet."

"Lachlan Mor—so soon!" She seemed surprised. "I must congratulate you, Dr. Graham. Lachlan Mor does not play for everyone. You must have made quite an impression."

"M'mmm. Not half the impression *he* made on me!" Aeneas said.

She had brought him into a pleasant apartment, part-kitchen, part-sitting-room, wherein a cheerful fire of birch-logs flickered, on blue delft against the dresser, gleaming metal-ware on the walls, and the polished planking of the rug-strewn wooden floor. The brightness of the room struck him forcibly, after the dark caverns he had become accustomed to. The windows were larger, of course, and the ceilings higher—the house having been rebuilt along with the church—and the walls were cream-coloured instead of smoke-blackened, a refinement that was not possible in the croft-houses with their fireplaces set in the centre of the floor. But Mairi Macgillivray's house had its fireplaces built into the walling, and yet was no patch on this. It must be the sparkle and polish with which everything seemed to shine, he decided, approvingly. Aeneas Graham had seen but little of gracious domesticity in these last years.

"Finlay was fortunate in his housekeeper, I see," he mentioned, perhaps a trifle heavily.

She did not answer that. "You found Lachlan's music to your taste, then? He is a very expert player, I know."

"Expert, yes . . ." Aeneas moved across the deer and sheep skins of the floor to the fireplace, on which he turned his back and stood wide-legged, a typically masculine attitude that the girl had not seen in that house for a long while. "I don't know about being to my taste. It was a peculiar performance . . . and somehow, I've got the notion that it was not intended, not for me, anyway. I don't mean the first part, which was straightforward enough, and fine fiddling, though melancholy to a degree. But after that, he seemed to drift into a strange mood, a sort of daze, and his playing changed completely. It got queerer and queerer, just a mass of discords—you never heard such a noise. He worked himself up positively into a frenzy—I don't believe the fellow knew what he was doing, or where he was. But there was something behind it—you could sense it, somehow, through the discords. It was a weird proceeding—'pon my soul it was. And it had a weird effect on the men, too—quite a lot of them had come in during the evening. Eventually it set Mrs. Macgillivray off in hysterics, which finished the whole business—perhaps just as well. And she's still something subdued, this morning."

Frances MacBride was eyeing him intently. "Discords, did you say? I wonder . . . ?" She came alongside him, to stare into the fire. "Some time ago," she said, "I heard the same sort of

64

thing coming from that house, Mairi's house. It was strange, hateful. And there was a sort of moaning, too, along with it—obviously there were a lot of people there. I tried to get in, but the door was barred—a thing I had never known before. The windows were covered, too, and I could not see inside. I spoke to Mairi about it in the morning, but she would not tell me anything—she said that they had just been having a *ceilidh*, but she wasn't at it herself. What can it be . . . ?"

At the agitation in her voice, the man became reassuringly masculine. "Just some sort of emotional nonsense, I suppose, that one would have to be educated up to to appreciate. I don't wonder you were not wanted as part of the audience—it is not the sort of thing they will be very proud of. As I say, I don't think it was done for my benefit, either, last night—I got the impression that Macgillivray more or less drifted into it, got carried away by his own playing, as it were . . ."

"It is more than that," the girl averred. "I know it. And it is all part of whatever it is that is wrong here. What happened after Mairi's hysterics?"

"Nothing—nothing at all. They all went away—sheepishly, too. Old Macgillivray more or less collapsed in his chair—and I took the opportunity to go up to my bed. I had had enough emotion for one night." He looked away, and changed his tone, advisedly. "So this is Finlay's home. He spoke of it often. He used to say that the view from his room so distracted him that he had to write his sermons elsewhere."

"Yes. This is his room, through here—I have kept it just as it was." She led the way across the lobby to a book-lined chamber in the end of the house, floored comfortably with a worn carpet, having a great desk in the centre, supported by two or three well-used deep-seated chairs in dark leather, and, above the tiered books, a few oil-paintings, a portrait and landscapes. And though it was a student's room, obviously it was still more definitely a man's room, with antlers of stag and roe-buck on the walls, a model-ship sharing the mantelshelf with a brass lantern clock and a case of birds' eggs, and a fishing-rod and musket occupying a corner near the door. The view, obscured now by the thin curtain of morning rain, would be much the same as that from the room Aeneas occupied in the farm-house, and needed no recommendation.

For a few moments they stood in silence, and then, abruptly, she turned away and left him there. He moved about, glancing at the books, which were mainly theological and philosophical, and no doubt had in the main belonged to the Reverend MacBride, senior. The portrait over the fire-place might be the same gentleman—though more likely a generation or two earlier; a grandfather, probably, and of the clergy also. The birds' eggs took him back to his own childhood, nesting amongst the rocks and links and modest cliffs of Fife. The model ship was presumably Finlay's own work—he had been useful with his hands. Aeneas was examining the flint-lock musket, a fair piece, delicately wrought and chased, and reasonably modern, when the girl returned, composed.

"That is Finlay's gun—he was very fond of shooting with it," she told him quickly. She gestured towards the antlers. "All these deer he shot himself, here on the island. Some people thought that it was not very suitable in a minister, I'm afraid. You are interested in such things, Dr. Graham?"

He nodded. "Very—though it has been wild-fowl and such-like that I've shot, never deer, like this. I have an old fowling-piece at home . . ." He stopped, and smiled wryly, ". . . or I should say, at my brother's house. But it is nothing so fine as this."

"Yes. Lord Dunalastair gave Finlay that—he was very proud of it. I have kept it oiled and clean. Once I shot a hind with it, myself . . . at least, I pressed the trigger, though Finlay got me to it, and did everything else, I think!" She laughed, briefly, uncertainly. "But . . . it is not usual, I know. Perhaps you do not approve of a woman doing such a thing Dr. Graham?"

He was looking at her, thoughtfully. "On the contrary," he said gravely, and sounded as though he meant it.

"Well—" The girl flushed, and looked away. "Will you . . . I would like you to have it—the gun—Dr. Graham."

"Me . . . ! Oh, I can't do that. It is far too much, too good . . ."

66

"Please. Finlay would have liked it, I know. You were his friend. Who better could have it? There is powder and shot in the bottom drawer of the desk, there. Please!"

"You are very kind, Frances MacBride," he said then, slowly, deep-voiced. "Thank you."

Hurriedly she swung about, and led the way back to the kitchen. "The rain is lifting, I think. Would you like to go and have a look at the church . . . ?"

Walking down the wet sand and gleaming quartz gravel of the track, that was cut into so many tiny channels by the overnight rain, it transpired that they would have to visit Lachlan Macgillivray first, before gaining admittance to the church. "Since Finlay left, the door has been kept locked," Frances explained, "—and he keeps the key."

"A church locked is no church," the man observed, a trifle sententiously.

"So I have pointed out," she agreed quietly.

He glanced at her, out of the corner of his eye. She would, too, if she felt that way. Her chin, without being prominent, was amply firm. He could just see the point of it now, and the small tip of her nose, beyond the hood of the cloak that she had donned to protect her from the rain. It did no detriment to her beauty, either, that hood, framing her face—not that she required any such enhancement, of course. . . .

Whether or not he had seen them coming, Lachlan Mor was standing at the door of his house when they arrived and greeted them with his customary unruffled civility. He mentioned that it had been a wet night but that he thought that it would clear. Also hat he hoped Miss MacBride was as well as she looked, and that Dr Graham had spent a comfortable night in his new quarters? If Aeneas had looked for embarrassment, discomfort, or any other reaction or reference to the previous evening, he was disappointed. The old man's equanimity was unshaken.

Frances informed him that they would like to visit the church, and could they have the key.

"The church—of course, the church." He nodded, after just a moment, conformably. "Yes, indeed. It is just here, the key, behind this door. I will come with you, my own self, and let you in."

"There is no need," the girl said quickly. "We will manage perfectly, thank you."

"Ach, it is no trouble, at all—a pleasure, indeed," the patriarch insisted, and came along forthwith.

It was Lachlan Mor that made the conversation. In an hour it would be a fine day, he thought, and what wind that was in it veering south. It would quiet the water, too, which was a good thing for the boats, and them going out that evening again. They had had the luck with the fishing yesterday, and could be doing with it, too—the fish had been scarce of late. It was bad when they could not get the fish. The new fishing ground they had found was far out—farther out than he liked. But it would move, always they moved—and it might move nearer, God willing. And this was the church, then!

Through the irregular scattering of gravestones and out-crops and little grass mounds that constituted the church-yard, they had come to the low squat building crouching on its knoll. Macgillivray turned the key in a lock that creaked loudly, and ushered them in. It was almost as modest within as without, naked stone, plain windows, and natural wood, and it was cold, with the heavy damp air of disuse. But the impression was nowise harsh; austere, perhaps, simple, sincere. Bare forms did duty for pews on a stone floor that was part flagged, part living rock, the communion table beyond was unadorned and inno-cent of paint or varnish, as was the low square-panelled pulpit, and the font was a rough-hewn boulder, hollowed like a quern. Only the lectern on the pulpit, carved in the form of an eagle with wings outstretched, supporting the great Bible, made any gesture towards the ornate, together with three vases of autumn leaves, two on the table and one by the font. And the quiet of the place could be felt.

They stood for a space, silent, and let that forsaken sanctuary speak for itself. And it spoke so very clearly, of one man's faith and courage, of hope and doubt and fear, of high endeavour brought low. The pity of it all brought a quiver into the girl's sigh and something of a lump into Aeneas Graham's throat. What it brought to Lachlan Macgillivray was not to be known. He said nothing, but his expression was strange.

Frances MacBride was the first to speak. "Those leaves," she jerked. "I should have changed them before this. Dying leaves are *too* much."

Aeneas followed her up the aisle, and was much aware of the noise his feet seemed to be making. He relieved her of two of the vases, and moved over to inspect the strong sweeping lines of he lectern eagle.

"Finlay carved that himself," the girl informed, and, coming closer, whispered, nodding towards the old man at the foot of the church. "He *would* have to come with us." Her companion was surprised at the concentration of feeling in her voice.

At the door, she turned to Macgillivray. "You could leave it unlocked, Lachlan. I will get more leaves this afternoon, and put them in later." And, with an incipient toss of the head: "No need to lock it, anyway. No one's likely to come near the place, more's the pity!"

The other stroked his beard. "Just as well locked, maybe, Miss Frances," he said, mildly firm. "A pity it would be if any harm was to come to the church. If there is to be a new minister in it, he will expect to find it in a good state." He turned the key in the door as he spoke, and pocketed it. He bowed courteously. "It will be no trouble at all to fetch it up to you again, afterwards."

He obtained no response to that.

At the churchyard gate, he turned to them. "If you are for up to Camusnacreagh today, I'm hoping you will be successful with Peig Macleod. It is a great thing for her, to be having a real doctor at her. If a small dram or two of the whisky would be helping her with her pain, you are very welcome. I will send it up to Ruaigmore."

"You are very kind. It would be useful, I admit. Thank you."

"Ach, it is nothing at all. I have known Peig since the night that she was born." His eyes went expressionless, and seemed to look past his companions to some distant contemplation of his own. At their good mornings he made no answer, still staring, and they were a dozen yards up the track before his voice, gently modulated but distinct, came after them. "God guide you both, whatever," he said.

Frances looked at Aeneas in the direct way she had. "So he knows that you are a doctor!" she said.

He frowned, in the way *he* had. "Yes. He seems to get to know most things, hereabouts. Though, I must say, he is fairly straightforward in his methods of finding out! He put me through quite an inquisition last night—before the music started."

"He would. I expected that—though hardly so soon, perhaps. That is why I warned you to be careful what you said."

He shrugged. "I suppose it is natural enough. A stranger coming to an out-of-the-way place like this is bound to arouse curiosity. And old men, like old women, are notoriously inquisitive."

"I wouldn't just call Lachlan Mor an inquisitive old man," she returned, almost grimly.

Aeneas changed the subject. "I liked the church," he said. "It was just what one would expect Finlay's church to be like, except, of course, for the unused feeling. Is it so seldom used, now?"

"Never," she said.

"But I thought Macgillivray still held services of a sort . . . ?"

"Yes—but not in the church. He'll hardly let anyone into it. None of the island people ever go near it. You see how he will not let me in, even, without being there to watch. Every time I change the flowers or leaves, it is the same. I think he hates the church!"

"But that's absurd. He's the Elder, isn't he—and seems a God-fearing sort of man?"

She laughed shortly, but said nothing.

Troubledly he eyed her. Erismore and its remoteness seemed to be getting too much for Finlay's sister. Things were getting out of proportion. Easy enough, perhaps, for a lonely young woman, so far removed from her kind. Mairi Macgillivray was right—this was no place for her. The sooner he got her away back to Edinburgh, the better. And yet, she was a Highland girl herself, brought up only a few miles away. . . .

"Don't you think, perhaps, that we are thinking a little to much about that old man?" he suggested judiciously. "A pity to let him get on our minds."

A retort seemed to spring to her lips. "As though *you* . . ." But she cut it short. "I have said the same thing to myself many times, Dr. Graham," she went on, then, quietly. "And still I say it. But it is not so easy to convince oneself, when every sense one has says differently. He is a very strange man, is Lachlan Mor. I think, if anything drove Finlay from Erismore, it was he."

"But, surely not. He never so much as hinted at it, anyway, even in his delirium. He would never have let one man do so, anyway. . . ."

"I dare say not. I don't suppose he knew it, himself. I didn't either, at the time. It is only of late that I have begun to see it, to feel it."

"But wasn't Macgillivray his assistant, his helper, here? He would not have made him Elder and Catechist, if he had been in any way hostile, surely?"

"Lachlan Mor was all that before ever Finlay came . . ."

"But he says he still keeps on Finlay's work, in some measure. He does still keep on the services and the catechizing . . . ?"

"Yes—but *what* services?" She turned to him, urgently. "Dr. Graham—I have been on this island, now, since Finlay went away, for months and months, all told. And I have never been at a religious service yet—except once when Mr. Keith came over to bury someone. Mairi and Ewan Beg were not married here—they went across to Eorsa—and that was Mairi's doing, and against Lachlan's wish, I believe. Oh, he holds services, all right, I know—but where? I believe he holds them frequently enough, but I have never got to one. I have tried to find out in advance where they are to be, but never succeeded. But I did find out that, before I came back, he held them regularly in his own house—but never once there since I returned. Why? Obviously there is some sort of conspiracy to keep me away. Why? And, remember—I told you that once I heard a noise like you

71

described, discordant music and moaning, from a locked house? Well that was on a Sunday . . . and I found out afterwards that there had been a service that day!"

"I see," Aeneas said.

In silence they walked on. "If you will tell me what I have to do, about this afternoon . . . ?" the girl said, at length.

## 9

THE operation on Peig Macleod went quite as well as could be expected, thanks to the woman's own courage and almost dog-like trust, Frances MacBride's tight-strung usefulness, praiseworthy dispensing with squeamishness, and deft obedience, and Lachlan Macgillivray's excellent whisky. Aeneas Graham had worked in worse conditions than these, many a time, as well as with less competent assistance, and though the abscess was recto-vaginal and chronic, it might have been worse located. Light had been the first essential, and so the wondering children had been banished to the hillside, not to return till called for on pain of terrors unknown, and the business had been carried out in the effective if unseemly daylight of the cottage doorway. Only the one cry had the patient uttered, though a groan or two escaped from between tight-clenched jaws, kind Nature, as well as her own spirit and pride and the potent whisky, aiding her, for though she bore the incision, she fainted away at the extraction of the pus, and the man, nodding his satisfaction, had been able to work quickly and get most of the stitching done before she came round again. More of the whisky had acted as an antiseptic wash, and with Peig safely in her bed, the small rest of it had gone down the throats of the surgeon and nurse—the latter however only because the former commanded it.

"I could have done with you by my side a hundred times, these last years, in the Low Countries and Austria and Spain," he told her. "You are a good nurse."

And though she had become very pale, after the surgery, she flushed again, then. But that might have been the effect of her mouthful of whisky.

"Finlay used to help me, but he had not your woman's touch, and . . ." he smiled, "I think he used to be quite indignant with me for the pain I had to give. He was not so obedient as you. Will you be all right, now?"

"Me? Yes, of course. But what about Peig? Will *she* be all right?"

"Yes—she should have no trouble now, if she takes care. She must rest as much as she can, for a few days, and eat nothing more solid than milk and gruel. Tell her I will come to see her again, tomorrow."

They had called the children back, and Frances had done what she could about the house, while Aeneas helped the small silent boy to carry in a stock of peats from the stack over at the bog.

So they had taken their leave of that lonely croft.

It was only mid-afternoon, and though the sun, which the prophets of the morning had foretold, had already left the floor of that deep valley, the higher slopes were still bright in its brittle radiance. Frances MacBride, with only a few steps taken on the homeward track, paused.

"Would you like to go back a different way—over the hill?" she suggested. "We have time enough. The view is very fine from up there, and I think there may be a sunset tonight."

"Delighted," he said. "A good idea. But are you properly dressed for hill-climbing?" He glanced down at her ankle-length skirts.

"And what is wrong with my clothes?" That had a hint of the ominous about it.

"Nothing—quite the reverse," he assured hurriedly. "But it would be a pity if you were to get anything spoiled."

"I don't have anything, on Erismore, that the heather will spoil, Dr. Graham," she returned.

"Even silken stockings?"

She looked at him with something between a frown and a smile. "You are observant, sir—but not observant enough. I took those off before we set out, this afternoon."

"Ah!" he said. "M'mmm. I beg your pardon." And then, at her glance, since attack is said to be the best method of defence. "Anyway, you were better clad for the hill when I met you yesterday; your skirts would be unlikely to catch in even the highest heather!" And that even surprised himself.

And she had nothing to say in answer, then, at all.

They did not start climbing right away but, turning, walked back up the glen, by the reeds and pebbles of the loch-shore, where the oyster-catchers flitted and piped. There was no wind in this sheltered basin of the hills, and the heavy scent of the bog-myrtle hung like an incense about the dark mirror of the still peat-stained water. It was marshy here, and the girl, leading, skipping from tussock to tussock, showed a nice lightness of foot that the man did his best to emulate. Also, he noted that she was right about the stockings, silk or otherwise.

Where a stream flowed in through mosses and bog-cotton, Frances turned left-handed to follow the alder-lined bank, across the narrow strip of haugh-land and up the quickly-mounting brae-side beyond. The slope was steep, but the burn had cut for itself therein a channel of steps and stages, a rocky staircase wherein the nimble-footed might mount more readily than on the bare hill-face without, wind and limb permitting. And the young woman's wind, and undoubtedly, her limbs, very much permitted. The man, following, was fully employed in keeping even a discreet distance behind her, and, moreover, keeping his eyes fairly consistently fixed on what he was doing.

So, up the cleft of that tumbling stream they clambered, between the dripping ferns and tiny rowans that sprouted precariously from its crannies, dodging the spray, slithering on moss and slimy stone, using toes and knees as well as hands, and Aeneas cursing the bag he had to carry, containing his surgeon's tools—but beneath his breath, all of that precious commodity being required for current purposes. And the valley and the loch sank and dwindled below them, and the world lightened about them as they drew out of the shadow, and the ferns and rowans faltered and failed and only wiry shoots of heather found root-hold in the cracks and crevices. And, presently, the angle of their assent lessened and eased, and the trough of the burn shallowed and opened, and they were out on to the shelving heather, with the steep gut of the glen behind them and the swelling breast of the hill lifting before them in sweeping folds and waves to the corrie-scored buttresses of the ultimate summit, etched sharply against the westering sun. The girl, flushed and smiling, her breathing only attractively deepened, turned to him. "That was good," she said. "The best way out of there."

"Dare say," he gasped. "'Fraid I haven't been doing much climbing lately." For very shame, and with a mighty effort, he gulped, and swallowed his respiratory agitation. As his eyes fell, he confirmed that she had kilted her skirts up, by means of her girdle, quite considerably. But he was learning wisdom, and made no comment.

They set off side by side on the long tramp upwards towards the ridge. The going was rough, but not difficult; shortish heather, blaeberries, deer-hair, and occasional peat-hags amongst the outcropping rock. They walked in silence, once Aeneas had controlled his breathing, no strained lack of words now, but an easy quiet in tune with the quiet all around them. And it was very quiet up there, with the hush of the high places like a benison about them, and the intermittent calling of the sad curlews, the whisper of prevailing waters, and the soft sigh of air over heather, no more disturbing it than they did themselves.

They would be more than half-way to the ridge when they saw the deer, the girl spotting them first, and clutching her companion's arm in a highly natural fashion, jerked him to an unceremonious halt. "There!" she pointed. "Over by the edge of that corrie. No—not that one. To your left—higher up."

"Who . . . where . . . ?" the man floundered. "I don't see anyone . . ." He found himself forced down on his knees nevertheless.

"Stags—deer," she whispered. "Don't you see! Quite a herd, too—a dozen of them, at least. See that cluster of big stones . . . ?"

"Deer, is it . . . ? Is that all? I made sure it must be old Lachlan Macgillivray again, at least, to get you so excited! Yes, I see them now."

Quickly, abruptly, she got to her feet, and strode off. Aeneas, head a-shake, followed on. Now she was offended it seemed. He had almost come up with her when he noticed her pause in her striding, and her head lift, gazing. The deer, perhaps six hundred yards away, were off, russet shadows that drifted over the rugged face of that tumbled land, swiftly but with no more illusion of hurry or effort than the sailing clouds above them. In an easy wide arc they spanned the great shoulder of that hill, swung in at a deep corrie, turning their white rumps as at a given signal, and were gone.

The girl frowned. "We could have got quite close to them, there," she said, and there was accusation in every tone and line of her as she marched off again resolutely.

Her companion shook his head once more, wordlessly, and hastened after. And the silence of their earlier progress descended on their walking again—but it was not the same silence, at all. Aeneas Graham sighed. Women were utterly unpredictable, and confoundedly difficult.

The summit of Beinn na Drise, like that of most other hills, was coy in revealing itself, behind its series of false sky-lines. The man, at least, found it infuriatingly so. There had been no need, of course, to climb right to the top of the hill, with their ultimate destination well over to the left, but Frances MacBride was not the one to fail thus cravenly to meet the perpetual challenge of that proud summit. So eventually, sufficiently breathless to make the silence between them quite noticeably less burdensome, they reached the wind-swept gravel and scoured naked rock, and saw no further ridge lifting before them. Indeed, they saw little at all that was terrestrial in the crimson blaze of glory that met and overwhelmed them there.

The mountain sloped away more sharply on this far western side, swooping down steeply over perhaps a couple of thousand feet of broken rock and scree and bare red earth, to a bold clearcut terrace that was the crest of the great cliffs of the northern cape. And after that, nothing. But this foreshortened foreground, fierce and striking as it might be, had no power to hold the eye, now; it no more than framed the splendour that the sea and sky made out of the obsequies of the dying sun. An ocean of blood they spilt as sacrifice, and a heaven ablaze as funeral pyre, with billowing livid clouds as incense and streaming molten gold as offering. The flooding vivid extravagance of it was almost more than the eye could bear or the senses accept. Too much beauty—if beauty that flaming magnificence could be called—breeds disquiet, perturbation. The man and woman stared at it, and knew the need for modest matter-of-fact speech, common-place and comfortable.

"I *thought* that there would be a good sunset tonight," Frances said. "It is quite a climb up here, but it is the best place to see it from. This is the second-highest point on the island." Her pique seemed to be dispensed with.

"I well believe it," her companion acceded, soberly. He nodded towards all the resplendency before them. "Very colourful," he mentioned, purposely inadequate.

"Isn't it. We are rather proud of our sunsets, here."

"I don't wonder. Quite a display."

"Yes, quite."

Their poise restored and self-possession reasserted in the face of the challenge, they moved on slowly along the ridge, leftwards, southwards. "You ought to be able to see Barra and South Uist from here, but the glare is too strong tonight," the girl told him. "Earlier, to the north, we could have seen Skye too, and Rhum and Eigg, and the mainland hills of Moidart and Morar and Knoydart. We keep along the crest, this way—there is an easier way down farther on. That great mass of rock down there, thrusting out into the sea, is the flat-topped headland you saw last night, Rudha nan Altair—the Cape of the Altar. Because of its shape, I suppose—or maybe there was a church or a cell there once. There were many cells on Erismore in the old days. . . ."

So they went, more companionably, with one eye to their going and only the other for the spectacle of the sunset, and presently they began the long descent, moving slantwise down the face of the hill towards the curve of the great bay. And as they dropped, the red faded gradually from the land, and purple shadows welled out at their very feet and spread around them and enfolded them. And through the twilight, so much more peaceable, more friendly, than the previous garish brilliance, they walked equably.

But Aeneas was not entirely at ease. Perhaps his conscience pricked him. He coughed. "About old Macgillivray," he began, "I didn't mean to be offensive. It is just that I feel that you—that we—ought to try and treat that fellow as more of a joke, instead of making a sort of bogle out of him."

"Lachlan is no joke," the girl rejoined, quickly. "If you think so, you are the only one on the island who does!"

"Maybe. Perhaps it is just that he would be a joke anywhere else but on Erismore. Such a remote place, and him the apparently undisputed leader. He's just a little bit crazy, I think."

"I dare say. I've often thought so, myself. But that doesn't make him any the less to be reckoned with. What he says is practically law, on Erismore."

The man nodded. "Yes, I see that. He certainly seems to wield an influence over everybody, ridiculous in such an old done man. Why, I wonder? "

She shrugged. "I don't know—I wish I did. But they are all afraid of him, I do know that—even his big surly son, Duncan Og. I know some of the things that have helped to make him what he is, of course. He is the only tacksman on the island, as well as having the best farm, and he is of the old blood of the chiefs, which is important here where the clan-spirit is still strong. And he knows so much more than the others—he was away from the island as a young man, for years; why, and what he was doing, I never found out, but he learned a lot, undoubtedly."

"That will account for his good English. I had wondered at it."

"Yes, he is proud of it, but he has taught only Mairi and Ewan Beg. I have often wondered why. There are other things too, that have helped to make him so much the leader. He was enormously strong when he was younger—quite a giant. The stories of the things he has done have become legends here—and he does not let them die, either, for he is the island's *sennachie*—

story-teller—and that is a source of power, too. And, of course, he is the Elder. But it is more than all that that gives him his grip over them, I know—more even than his personality. It doesn't account satisfactorily for his hold on the people's wills . . . they are all under his thumb. Even Mairi . . ."

"Why, *even* Mairi?"

"Well, it is not easy to explain—like a lot else. But Mairi is different, somehow, from the others here, though she is his granddaughter. Her father, Lachlan's eldest son, was drowned just the night after her birth, along with two of his brothers and a cousin, Ewan's father. It was a terrible storm, and a terrible tragedy. Lachlan was quite stricken for a while, they say; if he is a little mad it may well date from then. Mairi's mother was greatly affected too, of course, and became a changed woman—but she had no sympathy for her father-in-law, nor he for her, I think, whatever he said. She would not have him in her house, even. She was not an islander, of course, coming from the mainland, and she never took much to the island ways. So she brought up Mairi differently from the other children . . . till one day she was found, not far from here, at the foot of a cliff, with a broken neck—Rudha nan Altair, there, it was. Poor soul, I suppose life had become too much for her. . . . Then Lachlan Mor took charge of Mairi—she would be about ten, then—and brought her up. But I think that she has never liked him, and sometimes I've thought that despite all his looking after her, he transferred his hatred of the mother to the daughter all those years ago. It doesn't make sense, I know—he is attentive to her, he married her to Ewan, whom he intends to make his heir, I'm sure—for he had only one other son left, Duncan Og, whom he never loved . . . but it is just a feeling I have. . . ."

"He sent me to her house, speaking well of her," the man pointed out. "And you admit that he taught her English."

"I know." She shook her head with feminine positiveness. "But I don't think I'm wrong, nevertheless. . . ."

Suddenly Aeneas laid his hand on her arm. "Somebody coming," he said. "In front, there."

"So there is. A woman, too." The girl peered into the

gathering gloom. "Who can it be, I wonder, out here just now?"

Till then, Aeneas had scarcely noticed that they were on quite a well-defined path. "Where does it lead?" he queried.

"Just along the top of the cliffs, and round the coast. It is quite a popular walk . . . but hardly at this time of day."

As they approached, despite the dusk, it was possible to sense the woman's embarrassment, reluctance to pass them. She walked with her head down, and at the extreme edge of the path, almost off it, in fact, and she pulled the plaid which was around her shoulders up over her head. She carried a large basket over the crook of her arm.

Unnecessarily wide passage she gave them, stepping off into short heather, as she came up with them. Frances, slowing, spoke in the soft Gaelic. The woman answered quickly, breathlessly almost, and far from slackening her pace, accelerated it.

Staring after her, Frances shook her head. "That is Seana Macvicar—a single woman who lives alone, down near the pier. She says she is going to Ardmenish—there is a croft there, away round the headland. But it is a strange time to be going. And I did not know that she was friendly with the Campbells there."

"She must be," the man commented. "That was fish she had, there, and a fine basketful for somebody. I could see a great tail—cod, I suppose—sticking out from under the cover."

"And old Art Campbell one of the best fishermen on the island, himself! I wonder . . . ?"

"Courting, maybe . . . ?" her companion suggested, but only doubtfully. And he got no answer.

The scattered twinkling lights of the little township glimmered before them as they descended the last steep slope to the shore, and they walked in the soft sighing of the ebbing tide. Sea and land and sky were quiet now, wan, with all the colour drained out of them in the toneless half-light. Despite that sunset, the night was calm for the fishing, as Lachlan Macgillivray had said.

81

## 10

IN the days that followed, Aeneas Graham had no reason to complain of the apathy, the weariness of spirit, that feeling of being out-of-touch and out of sympathy with his fellows, that had dogged him ever since he finally had put off his uniform and returned as just one more soldier to a war-weary homeland. On Erismore, indeed, he lost his preoccupation with disillusion, with the years of war, and his lack of accord with those who had not known them. Erismore neither ignored him, resented him, nor condescended to him; it accepted him, not passively, supinely, but awarely, heedfully, as someone to be reckoned with—and would he have had it otherwise? Not that he consciously considered his situation thus, nor in such terms. He did not. He had other things to think about.

And he did not find time hang heavily, as might have been expected. The weather was, on the whole, kind; no Indian Summer, but with a fair percentage of breezy cold sunny days, with rain only incidental, and no storms such as had heralded his first approach to the island. With Frances MacBride he explored Erismore, climbing its hills and admiring its views, reconnoitring its woods and visiting its every croft, scaling its cliffs and investigating all the legion of the bays and inlets and lochs of its rugged and indented coastline. Nor could he fail to admire what he saw; the more he saw the more he admired—and that applied to his guide as much as to her island. He had never met a woman like this, and hesitated to consider what polite society would think of her—though, of course, in polite society she might well be all that polite society expected. But he was not unappreciative. It was a pity about her abstraction with the metaphysics of the place, and Lachlan Mor Macgillivray.

He had to try out Finlay's fine musket, too, that the girl had given him, sometimes with its donor as his companion, preceptor, and competitor, but more frequently alone. He shot at many things, and hit some few of them—rabbits on the machars and sand-dunes, wild-ducks amongst the reeds, blue-hares up in the heather, black-cock and pigeon amongst the birch-woods, even at the grey seals basking on the rocks. Indeed, he aspired to stalk the lordly stags up among the high corries, and though he shot none of them, and got bruised and soaked and humbled for his pains, he enjoyed the attempts and may well have been the better for it—for what man is not? And the fruits of his prowess were in great demand.

Also, on two occasions, he went out with Ewan Beg to the fishing, and renewed boyhood memories of another seaboard, taking his prentice-hand at the sweeps and the nets, and thrilling once again to the electric jerk of a taut line and a taken hook. And if the conversation, necessarily, was restricted, he had sensed no lack of goodwill.

But all this was but the one side to his activities. He was not entirely on holiday. He had to visit Peig Macleod, and her continued betterment did not go unnoticed. Gradually, furtively almost, by round-about means in which Frances MacBride was usually involved, others began to seek his aid. This he had become prepared for, inevitably, but hardly for the circuitous, all but guilty, manner of their approach. Frances said it was because Lachlan Macgillivray was against them coming—but then, Frances would. For reason, she could only suggest that the old man was jealous, having himself been the sole healer on the island hitherto. But in his meetings with the patriarch—and he seemed seldom to go out without meeting him—Aeneas always found him most kindly assiduous in his inquiries after such sufferers as had solicited his services—as well as remarkably up-to-date in his information thereof. So he attended on a variety of complaints, from teeth to tumours, and broken bones to blood-poisoning, for though on the whole they were a healthy folk with the simple ailments of simple living, there were three-hundred-odd inhabitants scattered over the island, with too large a proportion of middle-age and over and their work was apt to be hazardous. Frances MacBride, to whom visiting the sick had been a regular habit anyway—as well as constituting an excellent excuse for prolonging her stay—Frances MacBride then was his constant attendant as nurse and interpreter, and, he had a suspicion, positively solicited patients for him.

So there it was. The shortening days passed quickly, and the lengthening evenings pleasantly, sometimes by the fire in his own room, sometimes downstairs in Mairi's kitchen, but more frequently in the cheerful parlour of the Manse—for he was beginning to learn the Gaelic in a tentative sort of fashion with Frances as rather distracting tutor. Indeed, in all the foregoing, it will appear that Frances MacBride was apt to be prominent and much in evidence—and not unnaturally so. Perhaps then, it was also not unnatural that, being a normal healthy young man—and she being by no means unattractive—he should begin to take an interest in her, unconnected with the fact that she was Finlay's sister, and a pleasure in her company that was more than could be ascribed to mere duty. Nor might it be altogether unnatural, therefore, unfortunately, that the pair of them began to become the recipients of knowing looks and sly smiles and smirks, from the people they passed and visited, the provokers of little nudges and titters, human nature being what it is. Frances was the first to notice such—and once noticed they became rather evident—but she said nothing, even though the man was thereafter aware of a slight strain in her attitude, an undefinable coolness that he was at a loss to account for. It took Mairi Macgillivray to open his eyes, when, one evening, as he set off for the Manse, she mentioned to him, all smiling confusion, that she was glad that he had taken her advice about Miss Frances, that it was a man that she had been needing for a while indeed, and it was a good day for her that he had come to Erismore, whatever. She hoped they would be very happy with each other, and all the island hoped the same, she was sure! Aeneas, going out rather abruptly, had passed the Manse gate and taken himself for a long walk in the dark instead. He had been still very thoughtful when he came back and went to bed. Thereafter, he began to note things, likewise.

It was two nights after the evening referred to, and something like three weeks after the man's arrival at Erismore, that a rapping at the door of Ruaigmore farmhouse revealed Frances MacBride demanding Aeneas.

The girl was agitated, obviously. "It is Anna Maclean," she cried. "She's gone . . . and her pains on her!"

The man stared. "You mean the young woman down the road, there, who's going to have a baby? What do you mean—she's gone?"

"She's disappeared. She's not in her house—the house is shut and dark. But she was there an hour ago—less. I went down before, knowing that she was near her time, and when found that her pains had been started for a while, I hurried back to the Manse to get ready some things for her—you know how little they have, there. I was going to take them down, and then come for you. But she's gone. . . ."

"But this is crazy—moving her just now." Anna Maclean was an unmarried girl, living with her widowed mother, in a hovel down near the pier, a pleasant friendly creature if a little bit lacking, mentally. Aeneas had seen her once or twice, on Frances's urging, on account of her recent fainting fits, and had perceived that she was going to have a very difficult delivery owing to her build and the abnormal position of the child. He had promised to attend her. "Can she have been taken to some relative's house—or the midwife's . . . ?"

"No. I went to Kirsty's—nobodys there. And she has no relatives this side of the island."

"The father, then . . . ?"

She shook her head "It might be one of two or three. And the men are mostly away at the fishing, tonight." She turned to Mairi Macgillivray. "Have *you* any idea where they can have taken her."

"No. No," that young woman said quickly, definitely.

Aeneas shrugged. "Well, we'll have to find her," he said. "That young woman is going to need a doctor before the night is out, I'm afraid."

"Is it so ill she is?" That was Mairi, despite herself. "If she has Kirsty . . . ?" The implication that other babies had managed to get born on Erismore without a doctor, was not difficult to perceive.

"It will not be a normal birth," the man said shortly.

"Your midwife may be entirely competent, but she can't have the tools that will be needed. I have not, myself—but I have some that may serve."

"She is in danger, then—Anna?"

"Yes."

"Where would she go, Mairi? Have you *any* idea?" Frances looked at her keenly.

The other shook her head, wordlessly.

"Well, we'll just have to go from house to house till we find her" That was Aeneas, his professional ire aroused. "She can't have gone far in that condition. I'll get my bag."

He came down the stairs three at a time, to follow Frances across the berry-bushes of the front garden. Behind them, from the doorway, Mairi's voice came, uncertainly. "My uncle, Duncan Og, did not go to the fishing tonight. Maybe if you were to be trying at his house . . . !"

"Did you hear that?" Aeneas demanded, as he came up with Frances. "Duncan Og . . . ?"

"Yes," she nodded. "I heard. I was just thinking. It could be, perhaps, you know . . ."

"But isn't his house that one away along the shore, to the south—the last one? Not very convenient, surely?"

"Not convenient for *her*, perhaps—but it might be quite convenient in another respect, perhaps. Too convenient altogether. . . ."

Thoughtfully they hurried down the track towards the pier.

Pausing only to glance in at the miserable mud and turf cabin that the girl Anna and her mother inhabited, and finding it still dark and deserted, they turned left-handed along the path that twisted parallel with the shore. On the landward side they passed half-a-dozen cot-houses amongst their stone-dykes, with the pale light of fish-oil lamps gleaming from their small windows, and from most of them the whirring sound of spinning-wheels came to them on the still night air. By mutual consent they stopped at none of them, but pressed on to the last, a slightly larger house and set some distance beyond its fellows, under the lee of a bold rocky knoll.

"It is years since I entered this house," the girl said, as she led the way up to the door. "Duncan Og's path and mine seldom cross. Listen!"

From within they heard the murmur of voices, and through and above them, a groan of pain, low but unmistakeable. At their knocking, the voices stopped abruptly—but the moaning continued.

It was at the girl's second imperative knock that the door opened, and a tall spare stooping figure stood framed within the rectangle of light. "Ah, is it yourself, Doctor Graham—and Miss Frances!" Lachlan Mor greeted them, politely. "A very good evening to you—will you come inside—and welcome!"

Within, three people eyed them differently, but with a common discomfort that was in notable contrast to the old man's amiability, two women and a man. The fourth, on the dark bed let into the far wall, was past considering them or anything else but her own agony. Duncan Og stood near the door, big and silent and sullen, and his heavy stare and brief muttered words held no hint of welcome. The midwife, Kirsty Cameron, a bustling red-cheeked woman, with up-rolled sleeves, seemed redder than usual, and, after a darting uneasy smile at Frances and a frightened bob at the doctor, more bustling likewise. The other woman Anna's mother, a poor shilpit creature, crouched beside the fire in tearful abjection, spiritless and bleary-eyed— though whether the tears and bleariness derived from distressful circumstances, the steam from the boiling cauldron suspended over the fire, and billowing reek from the blown peats, or from the whisky of which the room smelt strongly, was a matter for doubt. She emitted a wail at the sight of the visitors, and that was all.

Aeneas strode straight to the bed, ignoring them all, to stoop over the moaning sweating girl, eyes and knowledgable hands busy. He shook his head and swore, quietly, briefly.

Lachlan Macgillivray was talking, seemingly to Frances, but since he spoke in English, perhaps it was meant for her companion. "Poor Anna," he said. "A bad time for her, indeed. The burden of women—but the Lord's will, it would seem. But we do what we can, little enough as it may be, for sure." He shook his white head. "We thought that maybe she would do better here, in a bigger sort of house, where the beasts and fowls were not just in the same room with her, at all. 'Tis the least I could do—my own son's house, forby . . ."

"She should not have been moved," Aeneas broke in shortly, without turning round. He was stripping off his coat.

"Indeed, now—is that so? And Kirsty and myself thinking a small bit exercise a good thing! The great thing it is, the book-learning . . . !"

"Your midwife must know perfectly well that this is not a normal birth. The child is in the wrong position."

"Is it not, indeed? Poor Anna—an unfortunate thing, whatever." Lachlan Macgillivray sounded only moderately concerned, and with small trace of the defensive about him.

"You could have told us, at least—let Dr. Graham know?" That was Frances MacBride.

"Och, but we must not be always bothering the Doctor with our bit troubles—and him on a sort of holiday, as he tells us. Too much bother he has been already, indeed, Miss Frances, for just a visitor!"

The girl's hazel-brown eyes met those of the old man, palely blue and unwavering, met and considered. She said nothing.

Aeneas throwing his coat across a table was rolling up his sleeves and demanding water to wash his hands, as well as his instruments. "Going to be a pelvic presentation," he said, to Frances. "Can you translate that to the midwife? And she's been giving the girl whisky. That must stop."

Kirsty Cameron, on being informed, was loquacious in her defence, her whole attitude a strange mixture of awe and defiance. "She says Anna's thirsty—and the whisky helps her to bear her pains." Frances told him.

"Of course she's thirsty—but water will do her very well.

Whisky dilates the blood vessels—and there's a big enough risk of hæmorrhage as it is."

"Will she be long, now?"

"I don't think so—but it's difficult to tell, with this kind. Have to use forceps."

"Is there much risk . . . ?"

"Naturally." He turned back to the patient, and moving her a little, began a careful feeling and massaging. Anna gave a cry and started up, staring, having some difficulty with the focus of her eyes. But his smile and quick confident nod seemed to reassure her, and she sank back. He worked on.

The woman Kirsty fetched hot stones from the fire, replacing those already arranged about the girl's blankets for warmth. When Anna cried her thirst, Frances brought water from a barrel near the door. The others waited, silent.

Presently Aeneas turned to Frances. "The forceps," he said. "I'll have to try and turn the child—nothing else for it."

She handed them to him, from out of the water, without a word.

"Try and hold her—like this. Over this way. And the midwife, this end. This damned bed—you can't get near her! She'll struggle. You'll both have to hold her. Now . . ."

The man stooped, tight-lipped. Anna jerked, and screamed, screamed again and again. The women held her, as best they could, Frances white-faced and tense, Kirsty gulping and breathless. Aeneas worked steadily, twisted uncomfortably, mouth open now, his eyes blank, turned inward as it were, his whole concentration in his hands, in the tips of his forceps. Then suddenly the screaming and jerking stopped, as the girl swooned and went limp. With a sigh of relief he altered his position, worked more freely. In a minute or two he straightened up, sweating, himself.

"That's as much as I can do, just now," he said. "Thank God she fainted. Tell the midwife to watch her—the waters will break any time now. So help me, it's hot in here!"

Washing himself again, near the fire, Lachlan Macgillivray spoke to him, pleasantly. "Strange work this will be, for you,

Doctor," he suggested. "Little practice at childbirth you'd get in the army, I'm thinking?"

"On the contrary. Camp-followers are notoriously prolific. When we were not fighting, they provided me with the bulk of my work."

"We are fortunate indeed, then," the old man said, and his eye strayed towards his son. "We are grateful, I'm sure. Will you have a dram of whisky, Doctor Graham?"

"Not now, thank you. Not while I'm working."

"Of course."

Another woman had come in, ill-favoured and elderly, apparently Duncan Og's housekeeper. Aeneas was unused to having a sick-room cluttered up with people, like this; it was unsuitable, even dangerous, but he did not see that he could do anything to remedy it—he certainly could not order them out of their own house. All this smoke and steam, too—as well that he had trained in a hard school.

"This difficult child of Anna's," the patriarch was saying. "Will it be all right, and will it live, think you, Doctor?"

"I hope so. It's lively enough just now, at any rate. It will be a bit bruised, of course, but otherwise I hope it will be normal."

"Is that not excellent! And Anna . . . ?"

"I will do what I can," the other said.

"It is in God's hands, then."

The midwife called out, and Aeneas hurried to the bed again. "The waters, she says," Frances cried. "Is this . . . it?"

He nodded grimly, and went to work.

Time, whatever the clock says, is not always constant, to be measured in seconds and minutes and hours. On occasions, stress and tension and action, emotion even, are better bases of reckoning, more truly interpreting its passing and duration. The half-hour or so that followed, in that smoky ill-lit crowded room, might well have represented a different space of time for each of the individuals who laboured and suffered and watched and waited therein. For Anna Maclean, undoubtedly, it was eternity itself.

At last Aeneas straightened up, wiping his brow with the back of his wrist, to leave a bloody smear thereon, and signed to the midwife, to take over, leaving a red-and-blue bundle of feebly stirring humanity beside the prostrate mother. His face was set in lines of anxiety and strain and even weariness, but he smiled as his eyes met Frances's. "She'll do, I think," he said. "A girl—bruised a bit, but otherwise all right."

"And Anna?"

"She's very weak—but we've avoided a hæmorrhage. With warmth and care she'll be well enough . . ."

"A girl, did you say?" That was Lachlan Macgillivray, urgently. "A girl, is it—and living?"

Surprised, Aeneas looked at him, nodding.

Frances turned, to convey the news to the others, in their own language. From Anna's mother, still beside the fire, a great cry arose, lamenting obviously. "*Och, ochan! Nuise'n duigh. Nighean . . . !*"

Lachlan Mor turned on her, swiftly. "*Co'ar sinn! Ciod so?*" he silenced her, authoritatively, almost fiercely. "*Mo naire, cailleach. Bi deas!*"

In wonder, Aeneas looked at the girl. "What is it?" he demanded. "What is it all about?"

Frances MacBride was looking almost as perplexed as he was. "I'm not quite sure," she began. She seems to be distressed that it is a girl . . . !"

"Well, I'm damned!" Aeneas said, and with sincerity.

"A foolish woman—and the whisky gone to her head," Lachlan Macgillivray suggested. "It is grateful she should be—like the rest of us, I'm sure."

The younger man looked from him to those others that watched him there, and back to the patriarch. "Um'mmmm, he said. "Yes, quite."

With the after-birth dealt with, Anna made as comfortable as might be, and detailed instructions left as to the care and treatment of mother and child, Aeneas and Frances took their leave.

"I will see them again tomorrow," the man announced.

"You are very good," Lachlan Mor said. "Too good, indeed. You do more than ever we could have expected—too much, perhaps. It would be a pity if you did too much, Doctor Graham—and Miss Frances, too!"

"Too much for whom, Lachlan?" the girl wondered coolly.

The old man, considering her, did not answer that, directly.

"The two of you have more to be doing, than running about after the folk here," he suggested equably. "A young man and a young woman have their own affairs to look to. Myself, I was young once, and I know. This sort of thing"—and he gestured back towards the bed where Anna lay—"is kind indeed, but not just seemly for young folk that should be at the courting themselves. An old woman's job, it is, the nursing. Time enough for it, Miss Frances, when you are married and bedded your own self. Leave you it to Kirsty here, and be a woman to the Doctor, and not just an assistant, whatever!"

"Goodnight!" Aeneas said tersely, and plunged out into the dark.

They had walked some distance along the track, the man half a pace ahead of his companion, and going strongly, before he spoke. "He's an old fool!" he announced suddenly, and with some vehemence.

Frances MacBride said nothing.

He glanced back at her out of the corner of his eye. "They're stupid—all of them," he asserted strongly. "The whole island—ignorant stupid folk."

"Yes," she acceded quietly.

Still he strode on, and still she seemed to keep a shade behind him—which, of course, was ridiculous. He even slackened his pace a little, but still that did not bring her up level. Where their path joined the main track mounting from the pier, he turned. "Look here, I'm sorry about all this—this, nonsense," he said, and his frown was blacker than the night. "I hope you will not let it, er, affect you. It is the last thing that I had intended. . . ."

"No," she said.

"I mean, it is all so childish, parochial. Believe me, nothing of the sort even crossed my mind. I may have been a little indiscreet, but in the circumstances . . . ?"

"Quite," Frances agreed.

He shook his head helplessly. She was being confoundedly silent and unresponsive. What more could he say? "If you think that we ought to be more, h'm, more cautious . . . ?"

She made no answer to that, at all.

He was no good at this sort of thing—and she wasn't being very helpful, herself. Evidently she did not want to speak about it. Damn Macgillivray, and all the rest of them! It took him another hundred yards marching, and Anna's cottage past, to change the subject, awkwardly. "It was a strange business, that—why that girl should have been moved away along there, tonight? I can't see any point in it. Can you?"

"There was point in it, if Lachlan Mor had a hand in it!"

"But why? That house—so far away. And it was not so much better than her own. If he was so keen that she should have better conditions, why not take her into his own house—or up to Mairi's?"

"Perhaps Duncan Og was the father?" Frances suggested.

"Yes—I thought of that, too. But still that doesn't seem to account for her having been taken away along there, and at the last moment . . . ?"

"Because they didn't want us to know where she was—because they didn't want your assistance, I imagine."

"But why, if they were so thoughtful for the girl, suddenly?"

"Perhaps they did not want the child to live!" she said, almost defiantly.

He turned to look at her. "But surely old Macgillivray would hardly lend himself to that . . . ?"

She shrugged. "It might not be beyond him. I don't suppose he wants an illegitimate grandson . . . nor, perhaps, any more trouble with Anna Maclean! He is a proud man, Lachlan Mor."

Aeneas took a little while to digest that. "You have not a very high opinion of your Elder and Catechist," he said then. "That would be as good as murder."

She raised a significant eyebrow, but made no comment. It

was she who led the way, now, for the remaining short distance to the Manse.

At the door, they paused, and stood for a moment, uncomfortably silent, while a thin chill wind eddied about them, bringing to them, gustily, the ceaseless sighing of the restive sea. From somewhere out of the night an untimely dog was barking, remote, wearisome, and there was no other sound, at all.

The girl drew the plaid that she wore around her shoulders closer about her, whether at the cold or the dog or at some thoughts of her own. "You will not come in, then?" Her head was turned away from the man, and it was hard to tell what expression her voice held, if it held any at all.

"No—better not." Aeneas shook his head. "Not now—but thank you."

"Well," she said, and her sigh matched the sea's. "It is late . . ."

"Yes—yes, it is late. And cold," he agreed uninspiredly. "You must not get cold. Best to go straight to bed."

"Yes. Goodnight, then."

"Goodnight." He was surprised at her sudden darting within the doorway. He could not see her now, in the dark shadow. "Goodnight." He turned away, but he had not heard the door shut, so she must still be there. "All this nonsense that MacGillivray was talking—about ourselves," he jerked. "This attitude of these people. . . . Do not think any more about it—please. It is quite unimportant."

All the same, he thought about it quite a lot, himself, that night.

## 11

IT was not so many hours before Aeneas Graham was back at the Manse door, despite the lateness of his bedding, and the protracted thinking that had followed before finally he slept. In fact, it was the results of that deep meditation that brought him, drove him, to the Manse thus early, his decision strong upon him. He was not one for off-putting, with a decision taken—especially a decision that had required as much reaching as had this.

Frances, looking a little tired, greeted him subduedly. Perhaps she had been thinking in the night, too. "Come in, and wait, will you?" she suggested. "I'm hardly ready to come with you, yet." The visiting of Anna Maclean and child had been arranged for the forenoon.

The man cleared his throat. "Well, I was hoping we could have a talk first, anyway, Frances."

She glanced at him curiously, as she led him within. That was the first time that she could remember him having called her by her first name.

In the parlour, she turned. "I'm sorry about the fire," she mentioned. "I'm afraid I was rather late up, this morning. Are you not going to sit down?"

"Thank you." He did not sit down, nevertheless, but took up a commanding situation on the hearth-rug with his back to the despondent fire, perhaps with a subconscious recognition of his need. The girl made to take a chair, and then, with an upraised eyebrow at her guest's attitude, remained standing, likewise.

"Is anything wrong?" she wondered.

"No. Nothing. On the contrary." He coughed, realized that he was frowning again, and endeavoured to smile instead, with only partial success. "The fact is . . . well, I was wondering if you would marry me?"

She gasped.

"Forgive me if I've startled you," he went on, hurriedly.

"It is very sudden, I know—but it seems an excellent idea—at least, *I* think so . . ." and his voice rather tailed away.

Still she stared, and with more emotions than wonder apparent in her hazel eyes. Evidently, he had surprised her.

"I had half-thought that it might have occurred to you, as well," he said. "It seems almost the obvious thing to do. And," with a pause, "and it would make me very happy, if you would do me the honour, Frances."

"Would it?" She did not sound entirely convinced.

"Indeed it would. I have never considered marriage before, but—well, I could hardly do better, I'm sure. And, while I do not flatter myself that you could say the same, at least I can assure you that it would be my earnest endeavour to make you a good and considerate husband."

She was looking away from him, out of the window. "And suppose I want more than that?" she said, her voice catching.

The man frowned again, uncertainly. "I cannot offer you more than I am, and have. You would not lack for anything. I have a little money, and a doctor is assured of his living, anywhere. . . ."

"That is not what I meant." Frances shook her head. And in another voice: "Is this all on account of what Lachlan Macgillivray said last night?"

"Well, not altogether. That brought it to a head, perhaps—that, and the way the people here are behaving. I cannot let my coming here injure you in any way, your reputation. . . ."

"I can look after my own reputation," she interpolated, swiftly.

"Yes, I know—but my presence *has* affected the people's attitude towards you, obviously. I should have realized that it might, perhaps, before I came. It never occurred to me . . . but it is not only all that, Frances. We have so much in common—work, outlook, interests . . . and we are both very much alone in the world. You have taught me much, while I have been here—opened my eyes to a lot—and I have learned to think much of you, to admire you. . . ."

He glanced up, to find her eyes fixed on him, now, strangely, with an air of waiting, of expectancy almost. He thought that he understood. "And you are Finlay's sister," he added, then, gently.

Her breath came out in a prolonged sigh, and slowly she turned away from him. "Yes—I am Finlay's sister," she nodded. "You are a very dutiful friend, Dr. Graham—Aeneas. And I am grateful, sensible of the honour you do me, sensible of all that you have done in the name of your friendship with Finlay. But I am sorry—I cannot marry you."

She spoke with a finality that brooked no argument. He said nothing.

The girl moved about the room, touching a plate here, straightening a rug there. "Don't think that I fail to appreciate your motives, and the—the advantages it would offer. I recognize that the situation is difficult, embarrassing—what Lachlan and the others imply . . . and that it can't go on. I agree that something will have to be done but not a marriage of convenience, please. That is too much, too big a price to pay for—for appearances! I am sorry, but that is how I feel."

"I see," the man said, tersely. "In that case, there is nothing more to be said. Think no more of it, please—and forgive me if I have upset you or hurt your feelings." He straightened up. "I will go down, now, and see that young woman Maclean. No need to come with me—I shall not require any interpreting, this time. No, there is no need. I think that will be best."

"You are sure . . . ?"

"Yes. It is only a routine visit. They should be all right. Those stitches that I put in—I will have a look at them. That is all—won't take me five minutes."

"As you will, then."

Sombre-eyed, she watched him stalk to the gate.

His frown now given full scope, Aeneas marched down the track between the dotted croft-houses, and no fawn-eyed children playing thereabouts received the cheerful greeting that they had come to expect from the doctor. To describe his feelings as mixed would be an understatement—yet, undoubtedly, mixed they were. For, amidst all his vexation, his sense of frustration, and the injury to his masculine pride, was just a hint of relief, only part-acknowledged—some small sort of consolation. He was a free man, yet.

Down at the pier, two of the boats, early returned from the night's fishing, were being emptied of their catch amidst a screaming circling concourse of gulls. It was a stirring, animated scene, on this bright cold morning, but the man had no eyes for it, and turned to the left along the path that followed the shore southwards. Lachlan Macgillivray and his son, from the pier-head, watched him go.

A third boat was coming in. A shoal had been met with, just to the west of Eorsa, and the boats of the two islands had had a successful night, with both net and line. Three more cobles could be seen beating up towards Maclean's Gate through the skerries, Ewan Beg's scarlet-prowed *Eala* leading. That they were all coming back thus early was an excellent sign. Almost, the watchers could imagine that the boats were sailing lower in the water with the weight of their catch, and the escort of gulls that followed each of them was a heartening sight. The work went merrily at the pier, men and women, young and old, participating, and Lachlan Mor presided over it all from an upturned barrel, with something of the air of a general benefactor. From each basket of fish he received a quota, making his own choice. Nor was it grudgingly offered. The young woman, Seana Macvicar, whom Aeneas and Frances had met with that evening near the cliff-top, stood by him and dealt with the fish that he selected. Nearby, a line of half a dozen women and girls were busily gutting and cleaning, joking with the men as they brought them the glistening herring and whiting and flat-fish and cod, and singing as they worked, despite the cold. It was, indeed, a matter for rejoicing when the catches were good, at this time of the year, with the winter almost upon them; it would make a big difference to the islanders when the storms of January and February kept the boats land-bound. Already the fires in the curing-shed were smoking copiously.

Aeneas Graham was not long in returning along the track from Duncan Og's house, walking swiftly, and his frown unabated. This time, he saw Macgillivray amongst the others at the pier-head, and came down long-strided.

Lachlan Mor rose from his barrel to greet him. "A very fine day for the time of the year that's in it, indeed, Doctor Graham . . ." he began, when Aeneas interrupted him, bluntly.

"That child, Mr. Macgillivray," he said harshly. "It's dead!"

The old man nodded, calmly. "Aye, that is so. It is a great pity, whatever, after all your trouble. The poor bit creature, and it with no strength, at all."

"It had plenty of strength. It has died of cold—inflammation of the lungs."

"Is that so, now! I am vexed, indeed. An ill thing, that, to be having so soon. But God's will be done."

"I don't know about God's will." Aeneas gave back grimly. "The trouble could only have been caused by lack of attention . . . or exposure!"

"Do you say that, Doctor Graham! Ach, that is bad. And me thinking they would both do fine and well there, in my son's house. A draught of air, maybe—a gliff of cold . . . ? A cold night, it was."

"A fierce draught it must have been!" the younger man commented. "It was more than that, I'm afraid. Obviously the child has been neglected—and that is putting it charitably."

The patriarch shook his head. "These women . . . !" He sighed. "That Beathag Maclean—she is weak, weak, and feckless with the drink in her. . . . A bad business it is, altogether—but maybe it is as well, too. The child born that way . . . And Anna not that strong in the mind. They're poor stuff, the Macleans . . ."

"And vastly convenient for the father too—whoever he was—don't you think?" Aeneas interjected, significantly.

"Who knows!" Macgillivray shrugged. "There could be more than the one in it, God forgive them. What a woman offers freely you will aye find men to accept—the pity of it. You will have found that your own self, Doctor!" In significance, that might have been as good as he got.

The younger man's brows rose. "What do you mean?" he demanded sharply.

The other smiled his gentle smile, stroking his white beard. "Ach just what you'll have seen in your travels, and in the Army, Doctor. That is all, whatever. Men are alike, I'm thinking, in most parts—and shame on us all that it is so!"

Aeneas considered him for a moment, level-eyed—and found those pale eyes unfathomable as ever. He drew breath to say something, hesitated, and changed his mind. Instead, he nodded briefly. "Good morning," he said, and turned away. His interviews with Lachlan Macgillivray seemed to be apt to terminate abruptly.

Up near the Manse again, Aeneas paused. His impulse, automatically, was to go and tell Frances MacBride all about this matter of the baby. But why should he, after all? The child was dead—there was nothing that she could do about it. She would hear of it soon enough, no doubt. No need to go running to her. . . . The man pressed on, to his own lodgings, his dignity intact.

All the same, he told Mairi Macgillivray about Anna's baby, seeing no harm in that. And if he sought to produce an impression, he was not disappointed. Mairi was more than distressed, he recognized—she was worried, frightened even. Of course, she was expecting a baby of her own, in three or four months.

Aeneas, with the urge for independent action upon him, went fishing for brown trout that afternoon, in a fair-sized stream that drained the rough hills to the south and east. He took a rod and flies of Finlay's that Frances had lent him, and walked and fished and pondered, till the dark and his hunger and a purposeful wetting rain sent him stumbling homewards over a land become suddenly drab, unsubstantial, and inimical. And, whatever the results of his pondering, he had fished to some purpose; without being giants, it was a basketful of speckled beauties that he presented before Mairi Macgillivray, and the half-dozen, fried in oatmeal, that he demanded for his own supper, no more than his share. "And I think that we can spare a few for Miss Frances over at the Manse," he suggested, as an afterthought. "Will you send them over, later?"

"You will not be taking them, your own self?" the young woman wondered.

"No," he said, and yawned excessively. "I'm tired. I did not sleep much last night. After supper, I'm going straight to bed"

He did, too, despite the doubtful glance she gave him

In the morning, after a preliminary peep at the driving rain, Aeneas slept late. By the time he did get up, the sun was shining in sparkling brilliance, in the way it has in the west, and all the morning reproached him. His hostess, too, seemed somewhat similarly inclined, though she did not say so. Indeed, she said very little, and the man ate his breakfast in a rather uncomfortable silence that was not usual. He was nearly finished, when, from over at the window, Mairi spoke suddenly.

"There is Miss Frances away up the road, by her own self," she reported. "And her with her basket, too."

"M'mm. Indeed," Aeneas observed, and went on with his eating.

She looked at him curiously, and sighed.

He reached for another oatcake.

"It's all of us will be missing her, and her the kind one," she said, then. "Erismore will not be the same, at all."

Munching, he raised his eyebrows politely.

"That will be herself away up to say goodbye to Peig Macleod, likely."

"Goodbye . . . ?" The man sat up. "What do you mean—goodbye?"

"You will know, surely—she is for going away, leaving the island, tomorrow."

"Tomorrow . . . !" Aeneas was on his feet, now. "Surely not. That can't be right. Who told you that?"

"Her own self—last night. Ewan is to put her over to Eorsa in the morning. My grandfather was up to tell him. . . ."

But her lodger did not wait for more. Ramming on the

military-style cocked-hat that he still affected, he was off up the glistening road forthwith.

Frances MacBride was no dawdler, and she had nearly reached the birch-wood in the mouth of the glen before he caught up with her—he had a shrewd suspicion, too, that she had caught sight of him fairly early on, at one of the bends in the path, and had by no means decreased her pace thereafter; though perhaps he misjudged her, there. When she could no longer pretend not to hear his footsteps on the track behind her, she turned, but even then she did not actually stop to wait for him.

"Good morning, Doctor Graham," she said. "You seem to be in a great hurry?"

"Morning. Been chasing you all the way up," he jerked. "Deuce of a hurry, yourself!" He probably did not intend to seem so abrupt as he sounded in his breathlessness. *Her* voice had sounded so confoundedly even—and she'd started doctoring him again!

Her chin lifted, just a degree. "Is anything wrong?"

"No . . . or rather, yes." He frowned. "Just heard that you are talking about going—leaving the island. And soon?" He never was one for beating about the bush.

"Yes," she nodded, without looking at him. "I have arranged to sail tomorrow."

"Just to Eorsa? To the Keith's?"

"Oh, no. I am going right away. That is the first stage, of course."

"But why . . . ?"

"Because I think it best."

She sounded so irritably cool about it. "But this is absurd!" he cried. "No need for any such thing. I suppose this is all because of what Macgillivray said . . . and my suggestion, yesterday? If so, it's quite unnecessary."

"I don't think so, Doctor Graham."

"But it is. You can't let the prejudices and stupidity of a few ignorant folk, peasants, chawbacons, affect you like this, force you into taking such a step . . . !"

"They're not ignorant chawbacons!" she exclaimed, with some spirit. "They're my own people, the people I've grown up amongst—cultured folk compared with your southern rustics. And their prejudices forced *you* to take the grim step of offering marriage to me!"

"That was quite different," he announced, with dark-browed dignity.

"I don't see why. Anyway, I had been thinking of leaving—before all this happened, before ever you came. I did not come to stay permanently—only to settle-up Finlay's affairs. . . ."

"You told me that you didn't want to go, that you felt that this was your home—that you would even stay on as housekeeper to a new minister! Here, it was, in this very place, the first time ever I spoke to you!" They had indeed reached the spot in the wood, within the jaws of the valley, where first he had met her.

It was the girl's turn to frown. "Well," she said tartly, "I've—I've changed my mind."

There was silence between them for a few paces, and each walked at the extreme edge of the track, with no eye for the slender beauty of the naked birches, or the rich red of the flaming junipers, or any of the russet and gold carpet of the wood's loveliness. Then, the man spoke slowly.

"It comes to this, then—that you do not wish to stay on the island any more . . . because of *me*! It is me, my presence here, and its consequences, that has changed your mind? Of course it is. So it is obviously me that goes, not you."

She shook her head. "No. It is the last thing that I intended—to drive you away from Erismore . . ."

"Nor will you. I did not come to stay, either. Already I have been here longer than I had expected. I just seemed to get involved in the life of the place. It has been very pleasant—but it is time that I went, now."

"But you weren't going, before. If I had agreed to you, to your suggestion, about marriage, you wouldn't have gone? You have found work here, and interest—though little profit, perhaps. You were content to stay."

He did not answer. He was wondering, asking himself just

what it was that made him want to stay on this island. It was strange, that he had never really thought about it. Almost, he had drifted here, and gone on drifting. It had been a haven, a refuge, he supposed, after the unsettled and unsettling life of the Army. He had been unwilling, unready even, to settle down, to start the new sort of life that seemed to be indicated, amongst the folk that he should have called his own but found it hard to. And then this had come as a stop-gap, a sort of stepping-stone, and he had been content, happy almost, happier than he could remember having been since he was a boy by the sandy Neuk of Fife. This place had a fascination, of course, and the people had seemed to need him—which was more than he had felt elsewhere, b'Gad! And this girl, too—Finlay's sister—had seemed to need him, too, for a time. It had been a good feeling. . . . But she did not need him now, it seemed—she did not!

He turned, to find her looking at him with something like urgency.

"I would have stayed, yes—for some time, anyway," he told her heavily. "But not now. Time that I was on my way."

She turned away, and her pace seemed to quicken. "You will go, if you want to, then," she said. "It is no business of mine. But *I* am going, anyway, whatever you do."

"But that is foolish, surely . . . ?"

"I have made up my mind. I could not stay here, now."

"Then I will come with you. We'll both go . . ."

"I would rather go alone, if you please, Doctor Graham." Her voice was very cold, decided. "Besides, you can hardly just pack up and go, like that, can you? What about Anna Maclean's stitches, and Colin Stewart's leg, and the Macmillan child's plaster? You can't just leave them as they are, surely?"

That was true. He would have to see to these people. He had let himself get involved, as a doctor, and now he was not entirely a free agent. He could not just drop patients in mid-treatment, with nobody to succeed him. It would take a little time to disentangle himself, undoubtedly.

They had come almost to Camusnacreagh. "There is Peig's house," the girl pointed out unnecessarily. "I am just going to have a last talk with her. There are other people I have to say goodbye to, afterwards. So . . ."

He accepted his dismissal, stiffly polite. "Very well. I will walk back over the hill. I'm sorry. . . . I will see you, before you go. If there is anything I can assist with, please inform me. Good morning."

He was half-way up that steep exacting brae-side, and going hard, when it occurred to him that he had not told her about Anna's baby. He had meant to tell her. Though she probably knew already—Mairi Macgillivray might have told her last night. It did not matter much now, anyway—except to Anna. . . . He kicked an inoffensive but convenient piece of stone with sudden violence, and eyed its headlong career downhill, scowling. "Damn all women!" he cried.

It was cold, next morning, down at the pier, and grey, with a soft dismal rain soaking a colourless land and flattening a leaden sea. Quite a crowd had assembled to see Frances off, in which Lachlan Macgillivray was much in evidence—indeed, if Aeneas Graham had thought to have opportunity for a last talk with the girl, alone, he would have been disappointed, so attentive was the old man. Ewan and his three colleagues were already in the boat, and the girl's baggage was being handed down to them.

"We are all of us sorry to see Miss Frances go," Macgillivray announced genially. "It is a great loss to the island. But it is the wise thing, whatever. Erismore is no place for a young lady like herself to be passing her days, especially in the winter. If you had been going with her your own self, Doctor Graham, I would not have blamed you, at all!"

"Quite." Aeneas nodded briefly. "I have some matters to attend to here, yet, before I can leave."

"To be sure, yes. But it's wearying you must be for the civilities of the South."

The last of her luggage stowed, Frances moved to the head of the worn stone steps above the boat, with Aeneas close behind her. "There is nothing you want me to do for you, then?" he demanded, just a little aggressively.

"I don't think so, thank you. I have left everything at the Manse ready to be moved out at short notice. My own things are packed, and Finlay's are stored in his own room. Mairi has instructions as to what to do should the factor arrive suddenly, wanting the house cleared. There is no use in my taking all those things with me now—I have nowhere to put them, meantime. They are as well where they are, ready." She sighed a little. "Mairi has the key, too. If you want anything, just ask her for it."

"Everything will be quite safe, you may be sure, Miss Frances." That was Lachlan Mor, reassuringly.

"Thank you."

Aeneas frowned.

"We will be seeing you again, one day, likely?" the old man suggested.

"I suppose so." For that young woman, she sounded listless indeed.

"Ach, yes, indeed. And it's welcome you'll be, too."

"Liar," commented Aeneas beneath his breath.

"Thank you," she said again, automatically. "Goodbye, then. . . ."

"*Beannachd leat. Na h'uile la gu math duit.* Goodbye, and may the good God go with you."

The girl turned to Aeneas to find him close at her back almost pushing her down the steps, indeed. She acceded to his obvious design, and moved on slowly down the stairs, he all but treading on her heels.

"He is as good as a shadow, that old hypocrite," he muttered." Can't get away from him. This is just victory for him!"

She glanced at him, surprised. "So you recognize that, at last, do you?"

"Of course. He has worked for this. He has got you away now—when I go he will be triumphant."

Troubledly she looked down. "I didn't think that you'd ever come to see it, to feel as I felt." They had paused, half-way down the stairs, just out of ear-shot, they hoped, of Lachlan above and Ewan below. "I told you that he got his way on this island."

"Then why are you going!" he demanded. "Why play his game for him? Why not stay, and fight?"

Frances shook her head. "I have fought for too long—and got nowhere. I have been struggling with that man for years, and always he wins. And I am no wiser than when I started. I do not know, yet, what it is that I've been fighting *against*—except that it is evil, I'm sure. But I cannot go on . . . I am only a woman, and, and . . . oh, I don't know, but I have had enough of it all—I can't go on any more. It is no use. . . ."

"But with myself to help you . . . ?"

"You haven't helped very much, Doctor Graham!" Bitterly she said it. "I did better before you came, I think."

She stopped. "No—that is not fair. I am sorry. You have been very good, kind. Forgive me! But I must go, I must get away. I am going because I must. Please try and understand I cannot stay any more. . . ."

She ran down the remaining few steps, and into the boat, where Ewan Beg waited to hand her in. Aeneas, perplexed, thought that he glimpsed tears in her eyes; certainly emotion was apparent in her voice, her actions, the evident heaving of her bosom beneath the plaid she wore about head and shoulders as protection from the weather.

He followed, slowly, to the last step. Already the rowers were getting out their oars. "I am sorry," he said, then, and with his own difficulty. "I wish that it could have been otherwise, Frances. But—well, I wish you very well, wherever you go." He held out his hand. "I shan't forget you, believe me. And I am glad that I came, despite all—very glad. Goodbye . . . and God bless you—always!"

Her grip was tight, convulsive. "Goodbye, Aeneas. And thank you. Try not to think hardly of me, please. I just couldn't, you see . . . not like that! Try and understand . . ." Abruptly she turned, and sat down, facing away, out to the grey rain-shrouded sea. Ewan pushed off with his oar, and from the little crowd above swelled a chorus of farewell.

It was some little time before she twisted round, in the stern sheets, to wave, and it was a handkerchief with which she waved. She looked extremely small and forlorn and lonely, in the stern of the black coble, and the inadequate feminine handkerchief did not help. Up on the pier-head again, the man watched, and after an initial wave, did not raise his hand again. But he frowned his blackest, and went on frowning. So he stood, till the boat was only a blurred smudge on the dreary uncertainty of the waters. Then, with a final sudden gesture, part valediction, part salute, he swung on his heel, to stride hugely.

Lachlan Macgillivray bowed to him gravely as he passed.

The land seemed even drearier than the sea.

## 12

MANY times in the wet and weary weeks that followed, Aeneas Graham almost packed his bags, and approached Ewan Beg for a passage for Eorsa or Coll. There were many and obvious reasons why he should, and few cogent reasons why he should not. It was the sane and logical course, the course that he must follow sooner or later, inevitably—as well as being rather evidently expected of him. Though that last, it might be, was a factor calculated to keep him from going, being the man he was.

There were other factors, of course, however seemingly inadequate. There was his doctoring, which was apt to get him, and keep him, involved. There was Lachlan Macgillivray, whom it had become a matter of conviction to circumvent, and whom he was assured wished him gone. There was a certain stag up amongst the high corries of Beinn na Drishe, with a proud head, too keen a nose, and a scornful way with him, that he had stalked once or twice already and with a growing grudge; he would like to have that brute before he went—the more so as Frances MacBride had been only a little less scornful than the creature itself about his chances. And there was Mairi Macgillivray, estimable young woman, whom, he was just beginning to get a notion, was less anxious than her grandfather to see him go. And there were other things, too, less adequate still, one or two that he did not admit even to himself.

But they were weary weeks, for all that, and whatever it might be, it was not contentment that kept him on Erismore. The weather was grey and dispiriting, the place was grey and lifeless, and he himself was greyest of all, dissatisfied with himself and all else. It might have been his stomach.

He missed Frances MacBride, of course—no harm in admitting that; it would have been strange indeed if he had not. Not that he let himself moon about her, needless to say; he flattered himself that he was man enough not to make any such fool of himself. But he was apt to be reminded of her by so many things—places, associations, contingencies, people. Indeed, she had left so many traces of herself, her vivid personality, about the place, that there was no escaping her. And she had always been someone to talk to.

Mairi missed her, too, he was left in no doubt, and, after an initial period almost of estrangement, with that young woman apparently blaming him uncharitably for the other girl's departure, she seemed to be drawn closer to him, in consequence. She talked about Frances increasingly as time went on—such small encouragement as he gave her, was only fitting and polite—and he learned quite a lot about Finlay's sister that he could have done with knowing when she had been present. Mairi, a warm partisan by nature, may have been biased, of course; perhaps she exaggerated a little. But the picture that she painted was credible as it was creditable—and Aeneas, in this instance, was not disposed to criticise. And, according to Mairi, Frances loved Erismore too much to stay away from it for very long, of choice—which was a contention worth considering.

Concurrently, too, he learned more about the island and its people—though Mairi was much more noticeably guarded as to what she said in this respect, and quick to recognize and resist any judicious pumping. But, inferentially, Aeneas gathered that Frances had been right in imagining that Mairi did not love her grandfather—more, that in some way she went in fear of him; that all was far from well with Erismore, in some respect not divulged; that church services, Finlay MacBride's work, and religion generally, were no subjects for discussion; that sometimes, despite their fine farm and fine boat, Mairi wished that Ewan would take her away from Erismore altogether, to some other island, or even to the mainland itself. Also, he perceived that she was preoccupied, not to say frightened, about the baby that was to come, much as she longed for it, and twice she asked him if there was no way of telling whether it would be a boy. This was natural enough, perhaps—though not altogether in keeping with the girl's character, as he assessed it—but the rest was vague, indeed, indefinite, and therefore irritating. Aeneas Graham

110

was not a vague person himself, and did not like vagueness.

But when, presently, something quite definite did occur he was not entirely pleased, either.

Aeneas Graham was having his mid-day meal in the big kitchen of Ruaigmore farmhouse, two Sundays after Frances MacBride's departure, when Lachlan Mor came in, accompanied by a young fisherman.

"Ach, it's the Doctor himself I want to see," he told Mairi, "—if he'll forgive us, and him at his dinner? It's maybe important, or I'd never be troubling him."

Mairi darted a quick glance between her grandfather and her lodger, and shook her head. But Aeneas nodded. "Go on, Mr. Macgillivray."

"I thank you. This is young Seumas MacIan from Altdruie, across the island, there. He is just after coming in his boat to say that his father is taken bad again, and would the Doctor be so good as to be having a look at him, maybe?"

Altdruie was a remote croft on the far north-eastern coast of Erismore, and Ian MacIan an old man who had had a shock some time before, and whom Aeneas had attended once already.

"When was this?" he demanded. "How bad an attack is it?"

"Just this morning," Macgillivray interpreted. "And it was bad, he says—bad as the last time."

"It couldn't have been," the doctor commented, "or his father would not have lived through it!" He pushed back his chair. "All right—I will come."

"That is kind, indeed," the old man acknowledged. "But you can be finishing your dinner, surely?"

"Oh, I've had enough. And the sooner I see him, the better. How long will it take to get there?"

"It's a fair distance, whatever. But it will not take that long, if you go back with Seumas in his boat. Quicker it is by the boat."

"No—not the boat!" That was Mairi Macgillivray suddenly. "Better across the hill," she jerked, flushing at their stares. "It is only a little boat, Seumas has—there could be danger in it.

Doctor Graham could have Ewan's garron—the pony."

"*Thoir toigh, a bhean! Cha bhuin sin duitsa!*" her grandfather said shortly. "There is no danger to it, at all. A small boat it is, yes—but it is big enough. Wasn't Seumas after coming himself in it? The sea is quiet, and there's little wind in it."

Mairi, closing her lips tightly, turned away.

The old man shrugged. "She means it kindly, the girl, Doctor," he said. "And you will please your own self. But it is an ill road for a horse, over the hill—and more danger in it from a broken neck, I'm thinking, than in the boat, whatever. And Seumas will be taking the boat back, anyway . . ."

Aeneas nodded. "I'll go with him," he said. "I'm used to small boats." And, with a half-apologetic glance towards the girl's back, "—more used than I am to climbing mountains on ponies! I'll fetch my bag."

There was no sign of Mairi Macgillivray when he came down again, and the three men set off forthwith to the pier. "She has a fear of the sea, that one, and her father drowned in it," Lachlan Mor explained. "We'll not can blame her too much."

"No."

The boat was not so small as he had imagined, and adequate for the journey in that weather. Seated in the stern-sheets, with his many-caped coat about him, he nodded to Macgillivray, standing on the same steps from which he had said farewell to Frances MacBride a fortnight before.

"I hope you find MacIan better, Doctor," the old man said. "A voyage of mercy, indeed. See—" and he reached into one of his capacious pockets. "Here is a drop of the spirit. Take it with you. You will maybe be cold, and it a help." And he handed over a black bottle.

"You are very thoughtful," Aeneas acknowledged. "Thank you."

Rounding the pier, Seumas turned the boat's prow northwards, rowing with short strong pulls that sent the squat little craft forward in a series of jerks. There was comparatively little sea running here, within the breakwater of the skerries, though from seaward the boom of breakers was constant, as indeed always it was, where Erismore's rocky outriders fought their unending battle with the long Atlantic swell. There was no great wind, as Macgillivray had said, only a steady breeze, and the boat rolled only moderately. But it was cold out here, sitting still, and soon, before they were half-across the great bay that scalloped the west coast of the island, Aeneas had his heavy coat off, and had taken an oar from the acquiescent Seumas, pulling stoutly. They made good time.

With the great cliffs that culminated in the cape of Rudha nan Altair towering in front of them, young MacIan kept directly on the course, not swinging seawards as his passenger had expected. The line of the skerries came very close to the headland here, and when they had passed by both MacLean's Gate and Beallach nan Partan, the Pass of the Crab and the more northerly of the two channels through the reef, Aeneas had wondered how they were going to circumnavigate the point. But Seumas pulled as though straight for the base of the beetling cliffs, where the sea broke awesomely in foam and spray and a hollow booming. The roar of the waves pounding on the skerries was very loud now, too, and ever increasing. But the stroke oar never faltered, and Aeneas could do no less, and the little boat crept right under the giant wall of rock. Soon they were both pitching and rolling ominously in the onrush and backwash of waters, and rising and falling alarmingly with the swell's ebb and flow, that lifted and sank against the sheer face of the cliff a good dozen feet at every surge of the tide. The noise was thunderous now, on both sides, and also, it seemed, from above, where the clamour was caught and amplified and thrown back at them by the rock-face as by a sounding-board. The nearmost edge of the skerries was no more than thirty yards off on their left, and the black streaming precipice of the cape less on the right. Apparently there was a passage between the two, around the headland. Aeneas had to assume that this MacIan fellow knew what he was doing, for, when at length, he glanced over his shoulder at him, enquiringly—he hoped not anxiously—the other grinned cheerfully. But if it got much narrower than this . . . or, worse, if the line of these skerries failed them, even for a short space, and let in some

113

of the great swell, unbroken, it would be the end of them; they would be smashed against that cliff like an egg-shell. Moreover, there was no great depth of water underneath them; when they sank to their lowest in this see-saw business, he could just make out the shadow of weed-covered rock below. This channel would be impassable at low tide, he imagined. But it was more than half-tide now, and still making. However, his escort and pilot was a fisherman; presumably he was not a fool. Perhaps this was what Mairi Macgillivray had been warning him about?

But when, presently, they rounded the westernmost point of the cape, and saw the skerries stretching away at a tangent to their left, and the calm water of a series of narrow bays ahead, Aeneas recognized that there had been indeed no danger at all, however portentous-seeming their passage. It was a perfectly practicable route for a shallow-draught boat, in moderate weather, at half-tide or more. In different circumstances, of course, it could well be a death-trap.

Pulling easily now, with the south-west wind directly astern, they followed the indented coastline, cutting across the mouths of half-a-dozen small coves and creeks and bays, scooped out of the soaring plateau of the island. Giving a wide berth to a jagged peninsula of low weed-grown rock whereon grey seals were basking, they turned sharply southwards, proving it to be Erismore's northern extremity. And now they were protected from wind and swell by the bulk of the island, and it was straightforward rowing, till a gap in the wall of cliff and rock seemed to indicate some sort of inlet. Towards this Seumas pulled, and presently they found themselves in the narrow mouth of little Loch Druie, half-way along the crescent-shaped mile of which, the croft of Altdruie stood. Two children stood awaiting them on the shingle, in giggling wordlessness. Stiff a little about the legs, Aeneas disembarked, and strode up between the drying nets towards the cottage.

Seumas MacIan said a word or two to the children, and followed on, but leisurely.

Aeneas frowned, and stared from the old man on the bed to the old woman by the fire and the younger woman working rather busily at a spinning-wheel. Seumas had disappeared behind the partition, into the cattle's part of the house. "There is nothing wrong here, that I can see," he said slowly.

The old woman gazed blankly. The younger did not look up from her spinning.

"This fit . . . ?" He spoke sharply, and rather more loudly. "Just when did he get better?"

At the complete lack of response, the doctor's frown grew darker. His Gaelic lessons had commenced too late for this sort of thing. He pointed at the old man, who was eyeing him from the bed with a smile of child-like innocence. "*Am bodach . . . tha e . . . cha*, er, *tinneas . . .*" He paused, helplessly. "*Cha tinneas . . . ciod . . .* Oh, damn and confound it!" Lifting up his voice, he called, loudly: "MacIan—James MacIan!"

Seumas came, but slowly, as with some reluctance.

"Look here—can you speak *any* English?" He did not wait for an answer—possibly because he did not wish to hear the expected reply, or the lack of it. "Your father doesn't look to me as though he had had a shock. He seems perfectly well. He's drunk, that's all!"

The other shook his head. "*Am bheil fios agad. . . ?*"

It was only for his own satisfaction, because he had to say something, that Aeneas spoke on. "He shows no signs of shock. Heart, pulse, temperature, eyes—they show the reverse, stimulation. He's drunk—otherwise normal. There was no need to fetch me all this way to see a drunk man! What is the meaning of it?"

Whatever was the meaning of it, it was obvious that it was not going to be explained by any of the MacIans. The old woman launched into a stream of eloquence, certainly, defensive-sounding, but entirely unintelligible. Seumas eyed his boots, heavily, and the young woman took the opportunity to slip out of the door. Stalemate appeared to have been reached.

The visitor glared at them all, baffled. Then he stooped, closed his bag, and picked it up. "Nothing for me to do here," he said. "*Mi theid . . .* the boat . . . *an bata . . .*"

115

Seumas came to life. "*Stu tha cabhagach. Uisge beatha . . . ?*" From a shelf he lifted down a bottle, and his mother produced a dish of oatcakes.

Aeneas shook his head at both of them. "No, thank you . . . *Cha gabh.* I will go back, right away." He bowed, briefly, to the old woman, and strode to the door.

Seumas came out, hurrying, talking volubly, as in protest, with a new fluency. His hearer could make nothing of it, however, and walked on, down towards the beach, the other following. Then, gripping the doctor's arm, and letting out a cry of dismay, Seumas pointed. The boat floated, some hundred yards out on the loch, obviously adrift.

Aeneas swore, and MacIan gabbled profusely. He gestured towards the two children, now playing on the beach some distance off, and shook his fist. Evidently he blamed them for loosing the boat. Then he turned, and shrugged, and nodded back towards the house again, smiling invitingly.

But his guest dissented, and with vehemence. This was crazy. Surely the fellow was not just going to leave the boat—let it go? Of all the useless ineffective idiots, these MacIans took the prize! The tide though nearly full was still making, but the boat was not drifting in, but up-loch, parallel with the shore. There was another larger boat, an ordinary fishing-coble, drawn up on the shingle above high-water mark, and upturned. Aeneas pointed to it, inquiringly.

MacIan shook his head decidedly. He went to some length to announce, presumably, why this craft was unuseable or immovable or unseaworthy. He tapped it with his foot and sighed over it, and walked away from it, eloquently. He drifted back towards the house, with Celtic resignation.

Aeneas Graham, being no Highlandman, was neither so philosophical nor so easily defeated. He hurried after him, and gripped the fisherman's arm, and produced with staccato exasperation every word that he could think of, in doubtful Gaelic, that might indicate that he wanted to go, to travel, back, home, to the village, to his house, to Ewan Macgillivray's house, now, at once, straight away, not in the vague future. The other listened, nodded, looked apologetic, shrugged, and then pointed with a fine wide gesture, over the hills and away.

The doctor stopped, and with darkly knitted brows, considered. It would be a long walk, and he would certainly not get back before dark—he would not, anyway, now, but he did not relish being benighted on the hills this side of the island, which he did not know well. It was going to rain, too, and the hill-tops were already mist-covered. It would be early dark. If he could get over the watershed before all the light was gone, he would probably find his way well enough . . . But what a devilish nuisance! He glanced out at the boat again indignantly, and then suddenly, speculatively. There was a spine of rock and seaweed stretching out, along there, a little way up the loch-shore . . . ? He started off, hurrying.

Stumbling over shingle and tangle, he reached the rocks. Behind him Seumas MacIan came, without enthusiasm. The drifting boat would not ground on the little peninsula, but it would pass near it—within a dozen yards or so. Jumping from rock to rock, slipping and slithering on the slimy weed, clutching his instrument-bag, he ran. Once, he missed his footing, and plunged one leg almost to the knee in a pool. On the last rock, or at least, the last uncovered, he halted. The boat, floating slowly, was nearly level, and no more than eight or nine yards off. If only he had a rope, or something! It was tantalizing—so near and yet so far. He looked about him. This ridge of rock he was on, went further; but under water. He had got one foot, and leg, wet already, hadn't he! Well, then!

Onward he stepped, into the cold water, gingerly. He could not leap from stone to stone now, but must feel his way with an exploratory toe. He could see through the water, of course, but the swirl of the tide lifted the weed on the rocks and it was hard to tell what was weed and what was solid. It was cold, too. If he had had a stick of some sort. . . . Precariously, in imminent danger of capsizing, he crept and stumbled and staggered along. The boat was level with him, now, and only nine or ten feet away.

Then the rocky spine ended, abruptly. Swearing, Aeneas

stared down into the pale silvery-green that betokened sand. How deep was it? He looked at the boat and he looked at the water. Well, damn it all—he wasn't made of sugar! He was not going to be beaten, now. Throwing off his heavy coat, forward and down he plunged.

It took him almost up to the waist, but the sand was firm and even, and wading on, he reached the boat without difficulty. He turned back to pull it towards the rock, the more easily to clamber aboard, and to regain his coat. Seumas MacIan stood on the beach, eyeing him with gloomy disapproval. "A fine fisherman, you!" Aeneas yelled derisively.

Fortunately, the oars were still in the boat, and he rowed her back to the landing-place near the cottage, MacIan walking abreast along the shore. But when the doctor had run the craft's stem up on to the shingle for Seumas to climb in, the other hung back. With much wordiness, he indicated the house and his return thereto; presumably he wanted something, had left something behind. Cursing him, Aeneas waited.

It was cold, sitting there in his wet trousers, and presently the doctor was out on the shingle, marching up and down. At first he took short turns, to and fro, but gradually they got longer. And still the fellow MacIan did not reappear. Heaven knew what he was up to! Some more striding, and Aeneas hallooed loudly. But without result. The croft of Altdruie might have been deserted. He would not give him much longer, sink him! It was deucedly cold, and raining now, into the bargain. Then he remembered the bottle of whisky that Lachlan Macgillivray had presented to him—bless the man! He took a couple of mouthfuls of the potent stuff, gratefully. The old scoundrel made good whisky, whatever else he did. But what in the devil's name kept that James MacIan? Loud and long he hailed, hand to mouth. Should he go up, and rout him out? Be damned if he would! He'd put up with enough from these crazy MacIans today, already. The fellow was dead lazy—just wanted to put off the journey back, no doubt, Well, he could get back without him, b'gad!

Aeneas waited no longer, but clambered into the boat, and pushed off.

The voyage back was neither pleasant nor rapid, but at no time did Aeneas Graham regret his starting it alone, nor envisage any other than a successful outcome. Perhaps the whisky helped, there—but the man had been used to rowing and sailing since childhood, and if the sandy shores of Fife was a very different proposition to this iron-bound coast, at least he felt at home in the boat, and confident in his ability to manage her. Also, the pulling kept him warm, and his indignation with the MacIans helped to counteract the fact that he was out of practice.

The first part of the trip was simple enough, with the mass of the island to shelter him, and, with the tide now full in, he was able to cut it finer round the foreland where the seals had been lying. But once beyond the most northerly point, he had to turn and pull slap into the wind and tide, and it was heavy work, admittedly. But, with the rain, the breeze had dropped a little, and there was still light enough to see where he was going and to avoid snags. The boat was handy enough for her size, but he seemed to spend much time and energy in beating up to the great cape, with the roar of the waters ahead of him beckoning him on only doubtfully. Strangely enough, when he did make it, the noise was not nearly so daunting as on the outward journey, with the high tide more fully covering the skerries and producing less broken water, and the whole passage between cliffs and reef less disquieting therefore—though hard enough work, in all conscience. In places the swirl and undertow tossed the little craft this way and that, and whirled it round in alarming fashion, almost jerking the oars out of his grasp, and once or twice he was driven so near the cliff-face as to be wet with the spray thrown from it. But he grit his teeth and pulled with all the strength and steadiness that was in him, and presently he won out of that heaving quaking corridor and into the wide sweep and comparative quiet of the great bay of Erismore. After that it was just steady rowing, though the boat rolled unpleasantly now, with the swell less broken by the submerged skerries. He had another gulp of the whisky, to celebrate, and even mustered some bars of a tuneless song.

It was quite dark before the mass of the pier materialized

before him, and Aeneas, aching and sore and just a little bit light-headed, climbed out on to the steps, and tied the boat's painter. But he would not have reached even the summit of the first ridge of hills by this, had he had to walk back—which was a satisfactory thought. But what an afternoon! He was ready for his supper, anyway.

The man stalked stiffly up the track. When Ruaigmore farmhouse loomed up, it was black, its windows unlit. Mairi must be out somewhere—she might not be expecting him back so soon, of course. But as he drew nearer, he became aware that the house was not empty. He stopped in his tracks. Faint as it was, he was not likely to mistake that sound, eldritch, spine-chilling. Lachlan Macgillivray was giving another recital. But why the darkness! Frowning grimly, he moved forward to the door, slowly.

But there was more to it than the violin, this time. Dimly, he could hear a kind of moaning chant, punctuated now and again by a high yelping noise, that would have been more pleasant could he have thought it animal. Twice he heard some sort of prolonged screaming, and after it the loud roar of many voices. And through and above it all, the fiddle jigged and screeched and sobbed.

Aeneas lifted the door-latch. The door held. He shook it. It rattled, but did not yield; indeed he could feel the weight of the bar behind it. He was locked out. He hurried round the house, to try the back-door, in the steading. It was barred likewise. But here he could see a thin pencil of light from the side of a window. They weren't in darkness inside, then—only the windows were covered! He moved up to the window-jamb, peering.

It was only the narrowest slit that was uncovered, the merest splinter of a view. All that he could see was a man's back, moving, swaying. He tried another position, twisting his head round, with no better result. The light inside was not strong, either, and he was wrongly placed to gain advantage of it. If only he could open the window a little, and lift whatever the curtaining was aside an inch or two. But these windows were not made to open.

120

What a fiendish noise! Whatever sort of performance was going on in there, they were putting plenty of gusto into it. And he could see only that man's back, and . . . was that an arm waving, a woman's bare arm? He could not see. . . .

Aeneas Graham saw a blinding flash, knew a jarring sickening jolt and a red roaring, and saw and knew no more.

## 13

THE curious pale formless blur in front of him, that expanded and contracted, drew near and receded, disconcertingly, steadied and took shape, and resolved itself into a face, a man's face, Ewan Macgillivray's face. It seemed to be anxious, concerned. He appeared to be speaking, too, but he couldn't be sure what. It was hard to concentrate. His head was reeling, and splitting open at the same time, it seemed. To use his eyes, to try to make them act in concert, was a trial, an agony. Aeneas Graham did not feel disposed to go to further trouble in the matter.

There was the man again. Could he not leave him alone? What was that he was saying? "Is it better, at all . . . is it, at all . . . better is it . . . is it, at all . . . at all . . . ?" Why couldn't the fellow speak English! How could it be better anyway—and what?

"No," Aeneas announced, quite clearly, he was sure, and once and for all.

But the man persisted. What was this—water? Aeneas moistened his lips. Better up in his room, this Ewan fellow was saying. Where was he, then? He peered about him with extreme penetration, but could distinguish nothing. That was because his eyes were not open. With a supreme effort he opened them again, frowning fiercely to keep the top of his head in place. He seemed to be in the kitchen, the kitchen of Ruaigmore. Should he be there? Why not? He couldn't remember for the moment. Better upstairs in his own room, though, undoubtedly. He could get peace there . . . on his own bed. Bed was the place.

He found himself getting to his feet—though whether that was his own doing or Ewan Macgillivray's, he was not sure. His feet, which appeared to come down extremely heavily on a curiously uneven floor, seemed to connect directly with that opening and shutting split in his head. Unpleasant. It might well be difficult to get up those stairs.

It was—especially with the steps rising and sinking, and Ewan Beg with them. But at the top, in his own room, he spoke more lucidly, nevertheless. "What happened?" he asked.

"Ach, it would be just a fall you had," Macgillivray told him. "Easy enough done, it is."

Aeneas sought to consider that, sitting on the edge of his bed. "No," he said at length, carefully. "Don't think I fell."

The other suggested that he should get his clothes off; they were very wet, especially the trousers. Better get into his bed, right away.

The doctor conceded that. "I do not think I fell," he announced again.

"Ach, well—don't you be bothering yourself about it, just now, at all," Ewan soothed, helping to take off the soaking breeches. "Get you into your bed, now, and Mairi will be after fetching you up some porridge, to put the heat into you."

"Yes." He listened to the other clumping down the stairs, and each step was like a hammer blow in his aching brain. With extreme care he raised a tentative hand to touch and feel that head. Shrinking from the pain of the contact, he grimaced. There was a great lump on his crown, big as an egg, and sticky too. A monumental fall, indeed! As thoughtfully as he could, he stared up at the flickering firelight on the ceiling.

It was Ewan again, not Mairi, that brought him up his porridge. "Take that inside you, and you'll be sleeping in no time, at all," he advised cheerfully. "A great thing, the porridge."

"Thank you," Aeneas murmured. "Where did you find me?"

"Ach, just at the door, there. A right hard knock you gave yourself, whatever."

"M'mmm. How would I give myself a knock on the top of my head, Ewan?"

"Ach, it would be easy enough, and you falling. Dark, it was."

Aeneas started to shake his head, but stopped incontinently. "I couldn't have fallen on the top of my head," he protested, but more weakly than he had intended. "I can't just remember. Let me see . . . ?"

"Ach, wheesht you," Ewan ordered urgently. "Sleep's the thing for you. Sup you that porridge." He made for the door. "I'll be up again, after. Do not be troubling your head just now, man."

Though he had an idea that perhaps he shouldn't, Aeneas was inclined to feel that that was good advice. He couldn't just remember . . . it was so hard to think, with that great hammer beating in his head. Later, he'd think about it. . . . The porridge was good, but eating was a trial. He'd finish that later, too . . . when Ewan came back, maybe . . .

He slept.

Aeneas awoke, with the impression that someone had just gone out of his room. It was broad daylight. He started up, and fell back with a groan. His head—Lord! Of course—he remembered. Last night—he had been peering in at the window—that horrible noise. Somebody must have given him a clout over the head—a thundering clout! And then, he'd been in the kitchen, and Ewan Beg had said that he must have had a fall. A fall, indeed! He raised his hand. There was some sort of a bandage round his head. That would be Mairi. Kind of her . . . a pity it hadn't been Frances, though! He frowned.

Mairi would be able to tell him. He sat up, warily. His clothes were gone. They would be wet, of course; she would have them downstairs, drying. He lifted up his voice, to shout for her—and ceased almost before he had begun. What a head he had! He leaned down, and knocked on the floor.

For some time he waited, and then knocked again. There was no response, though he could hear movement below. This would not do. They need not think that they were going to get rid of him so easily as that. He had more clothes than those, and he was not going to be bed-ridden, broken head or none. He had some inquiries to make! Making only a token toilet, he gingerly donned his best suit, and made his unsteady way downstairs.

Though she must have heard him coming, Mairi Macgillivray

had disappeared into the back premises by the time that he had got down, and was an inordinate time in reappearing. When she did, she professed great surprise, almost shock, to see him there.

"Doctor Graham," she cried, "what are you doing down here, at all! It is your bed you should be in, with the head you've got on you."

"Haven't I been trying to attract some attention this last half-hour?" Aeneas counter-attacked strongly. "It's long past breakfast-time, isn't it! I want my breakfast." He eyed her, significantly. "And how did I come by this head I've got, I'd like to know, Mairi Macgillivray?"

She glanced quickly away. "I couldn't tell you that, Doctor Graham." Promptly she made for the door. "I'll fetch you your breakfast, then."

His breakfast was long in coming, but when she arrived with it, the man went on, inexorably: "I want to know what happened last night—I intend to know. You might as well tell me now as later."

The girl shook her head. "How can I tell you?" she answered. "I do not know, at all. I was not here when—when they fetched you in."

"Look here." Aeneas frowned. "I was attacked outside your door last night, and carried into your house some time later— and you say that you know nothing about it! I thought better of you, Mairi Macgillivray!"

"Attacked . . . ?" She looked at the floor, unhappily. "They told me that you had fallen . . ."

"Fallen!" the man snorted. "Do you think I could give myself a blow like that, by falling—and on the top of my head? And why should I fall, anyway?"

Mairi was twisting a cloth round and round between her fingers. "They said you had the whisky in you—that it would be the whisky. There was whisky all over your coat. I had to wash it . . . the smell of it was strong . . ."

"And you believed them? Have you ever seen me the worse for drink, woman? If there was whisky on my clothes, it was put there by some of your friends. I was no more drunk last night

125

than I am now."

Mairi sighed. "I do not know, I do not know, at all. I was not there, my own self." She busied herself at his table.

"Your breakfast, Doctor Graham," she said, almost pleaded. "Cold, it will be getting."

Aeneas sat down to eat, but continued, doggedly: "There was something very queer going on here, last night—you won't deny that? All that noise and moaning and fiddling . . ."

"It would be just the *ceilidh*." She did not look at him. "Singing and music, that they have. I was not at it, myself. I was in my own room—I was not there, at all."

"*Ceilidh*—nonsense! A devilish queer kind of *ceilidh*, that, as you know very well. You would have been there yourself, if it had been only that, wouldn't you? And the doors were barred, and the windows covered! Is that usual at your *ceilidhs*? I had tried the door, and was trying to see in through one of the back windows, when I was struck down. I wasn't meant to see, that is obvious. Why?"

But Mairi had no answer for him, beyond her own agitation. She seemed to be about to take refuge, once more, in some other portion of the house, when her glance lighted on the window. "Here is my grandfather," she announced, not without relief.

"Is it indeed—I had hardly expected him," Aeneas said grimly. "But it saves me a walk. I want a word with Mr. Macgillivray!"

"Ach, is that yourself, Doctor Graham!" Lachlan Mor greeted him. "And you sitting taking your breakfast as pleasant as you like! Here's me coming to ask for the invalid whatever."

"I have a hard head, Mr. Macgillivray."

"You must have, then. That was an ill dunt you gave yourself, last night."

"An ill dunt, yes—whoever gave me it!"

The old man smiled genially. "No need to ask if you are feeling better, Doctor! Myself, I was a small bit anxious for you, last night."

"You are vastly kind," Aeneas said sarcastically.

"No, no. But it is our concern, you see, to get you away from our rough island, back to your own place . . . none the worse for being in it!" There might have been just a gleam in those strange, washed-out eyes, there.

"Indeed. I wonder why I should be so much on your . . . conscience?"

"Aren't you the stranger within our gates?" the patriarch wondered. "And the friend of Mr. MacBride, as well."

Aeneas could only stare at him.

"It as a great pity, last night, though," the other went on, equably. "I blame my own self, too, in a kind of way."

"I'm interested to hear it."

"Yes. I should have warned you, maybe, that the whisky I was giving you was that strong—stronger than you will be used with, at all."

Aeneas Graham pushed his chair back from the table, abruptly, and its scrape on the stone-flagged floor was harsh. "See here," he announced distinctly, "—let us be clear on this matter, once and for all. I was not drunk last night, nor any degree the worse for drink. Let that stand!"

Macgillivray smiled deprecatingly. "Ach. Doctor Graham, nobody is blaming you, at all. 'Tis a thing that could happen to any man, indeed. The spirit is strong, yes—and on an empty stomach, maybe . . . ?"

"Damn it, I was not drunk, I tell you!" The younger man was on his feet. "I was as sober as I am at this minute. And I did not fall, either—so you need not produce that story!"

Mairi stirred uncomfortably, and began to tidy up the breakfast dishes. But her grandfather only stroked his beard, imperturbably. "But you had drink taken, surely, Doctor?"

"Only two or three mouthfuls, during the afternoon."

"Why not," Lachlan Mor agreed. "But the bottle that I gave you was empty when they brought you in!"

"That's nonsense. It couldn't have been. Or if it was, someone else had emptied it when I was unconscious. It was two-thirds full when I had my last sip." He turned to Mairi. "The bottle was not broken? And yet you say that my coat was soaking with the stuff. Down the front?" And at her nod: "The bottle was in my coat-tails pocket. It is quite obvious what was done—and why!"

The old man shrugged, smiling still. "Ach, well, Doctor—say no more about it, at all. What is a drop of whisky on a cold night. . . ."

"But I'll say quite a lot more about it, so help me! There are quite a number of things I want to know, about yesterday's happenings—and I think you can tell me all of them! Why was I sent on a wild goose chase to Altdruie? There was nothing wrong with Ian MacIan. And why did they attempt to delay me there, to the extent of turning the boat adrift, so that if I had not as good as swum for it, I'd have had to walk back over the hill? And what was going on in this house when I got back? What sort of performance were you up to, with your moanings and shoutings and screechings, that the doors and windows had to be barred and covered? Tell me that!"

Lachlan Macgillivray shook his white head in sorrowful bewilderment. "This is strange talk, Doctor Graham—indeed it is. Strange wild talk. I do not understand you, at all."

"I think you do. I was got rid of, to the most distant part of the island, and delayed, so that you could indulge in whatever sort of horrible proceeding you were doing, without my seeing. But when I came back, sooner than you expected, and tried to get in, and see in, to this house, I was knocked on the head, and made to look as though I'd been drunk." Aeneas paused. "What is going on, in Erismore, Macgillivray?"

The other inclined his head, with grave sympathy. "It is your bed you should be in, Doctor—I was thinking that you were up too soon. A nasty dunt it has been, yes—your head must be sore, indeed. Sleep is the thing, whatever. Sleep you, and these foolish dreams will be gone, for sure. It's not myself that needs to tell you that the head is a kittlish part . . ."

Aeneas struggled with his temper, if only for Mairi's sake. "Sink me, man, do you take me for a complete fool! Let's have no more of this damned hypocrisy . . ."

"Ach, it's just exciting you I am. See that the Doctor lies down on his bed, Mairi. Quiet is what he needs, yes. I'll away now, and hope I find you better, soon. Good morning to you, Doctor."

"I'd rather you stayed and answered my questions." That was flung after him, but the old man made no pause, and closed the door behind him. Aeneas took a step after him, halted, and shrugged helplessly. He turned to Mairi, standing motionless by the table, and man and woman stared at each other for a long moment, wordlessly.

"It's no use," she said at last, wearily, finally. "No use, at all." And picking up his breakfast dishes, took them away.

## 14

IF anything could have been calculated to prolong Aeneas
Graham's stay on Erismore, it would have been the happenings of that Sunday, such was the man's nature. Where, previously, he had been only moderately interested in the curious
state of affairs that seemed to prevail in the island, now he was
vitally concerned. He had been assaulted. They had gone to
some trouble to hoodwink him and get him out of the way. They
had tried to make him look as though he could not carry his
liquor. They wanted him to leave the island. It was obvious that
he must stay.

His head gave him little trouble, beyond a few headaches; his
cocked hat and his thick hair had taken the worst of the blow.
He did not let it interfere with his activities, and neither it nor
any of the day's doings were referred to by any of the islanders,
by word or look—save only Lachlan Mor himself, who made a
point of asking after the injury, with much civility, on each
occasion that they met. By no other sign did Macgillivray make
any allusion to the incident, nor allow it to affect his manner or
urbanity—despite the younger man's coldness and scarcely-
veiled hostility. It was a ridiculous situation. Aeneas began to see
the island as populated by hypocrites, and himself beginning to
turn into one, in sheer self-defence. No normal man can live for
any time in a state of open enmity and warfare with all his
neighbours; surface civilities, at least, are an essential. He
should have gone, of course—the obvious, and, no doubt,
looked-for solution. But as we have seen, Aeneas Graham was
not that sort of man.

His relations with Mairi Macgillivray were peculiar. While
she showed clearly enough that she was not going to discuss
with him the cantrips of the weekend—nor any of the strange
on-goings of the island—and thus her manner towards him held
an undeniable reserve—he could not feel that she was out of

sympathy with him; indeed, rather the reverse. Somehow, he gained the impression that she would have liked to confide in him, but could not. Also, though she indicated more than once that it might be better for him to leave Erismore, he was sure that she did not want him to go. For his part, the man, recognizing something of her difficulties, sought not to be too critical, and to meet her at least half-way. He was glad enough to have one friend on the island, however helpless she might be to aid him. Also, she was a friend of Frances MacBride, and, with certain other subjects of conversation difficult, found this one the more congenial.

So Aeneas went about his affairs, his doctoring, his fishing, his campaign against the stag of Beinn na Drise, much as he had done before, only less casually, more watchfully. He was waiting, now, for he knew not what, but waiting quite definitely.

He was fairly busy, too. Erismore was visited with what almost amounted to an epidemic of stomach troubles—the colic, according to the islanders, a form of enteritis by the doctor's diagnosis. It was not the first time that this had happened, apparently, and it was put down variously to the water, to the effect on the milch-cows of the change from outdoor pasture to winter feed, and to the increasing percentage of salted and smoked fish that the deteriorating weather was forcing on to the dietary. Whatever it was, it gave Aeneas scope for much practice. Also, there were two advanced pregnancies in which he was interested; on neither had he been specifically consulted, but in both cases the women had been smitten with this enteritis, along with the rest of their households, and Aeneas, fearing complications and premature births, kept an eye on each of them. His vigilance was justified, for one, the mother of three children already, did have an untimely delivery. Fortunately, thanks to his attention, both mother and son survived, though for a little while it was touch and go. The other, Jean Cameron, the young second wife of the elderly crofter of Drumbeg, got over her sickness and carried her child to the allotted time without further trouble, to the doctor's relief. She was by no means a robust girl, and this was her first child. Aeneas had been anxious.

His relief, however, was short-lived. He was not summoned to the birth, was not informed, indeed. But he was summoned two days later, to a half-demented woman and a febrile prostrate child. The infant, a well-developed girl, was in the last stages of pneumonia. Aeneas did what he could, but it was a hopeless struggle from the first. The crisis came that same night, before a frenzied mother, a silent father, and a sullen midwife. The child did not survive it. At once, the doctor had to turn his attention to Jean Cameron, striving to pacify her wild raving, but with little success. There was more than inconsolable grief here, or even hysteria, he knew, but he could not understand a word that she said. He had an idea that she was trying to tell him something, in an intermittent incoherent fashion, indicating her husband and rejecting his approaches, threatening the midwife and another woman who was present, and cursing all and sundry. Aeneas was in fear that she would go into a fit, when Lachlan Macgillivray arrived. The effect was extraordinary. After a single piercing scream and a dramatic pointing at the newcomer, she was silent, trembling, limp. Her eyes never leaving the old man's gently-smiling face, she suffered herself to be carried through to the back portion of the house. When Aeneas saw her again, she was palely composed, and as silent as her husband.

Wondering greatly, the doctor left them there, with only Macgillivray's courteous thanks and regrets ringing in his ears.

Mairi and Ewan Macgillivray had retired to bed by the time that Aeneas got back, but hearing him, Mairi arose, with a plaid around her, to show him the bite of supper that was left, and to ask his news.

The man was very tired, distraught, and puzzled. Also, he was somehow angry. But that did not excuse his thoughtlessness, as he admitted afterwards.

"There seems to be a curse on your island—like Finlay MacBride said!" he told the girl, harshly. "Jean Cameron has had her baby—and I was not told. Two days ago. Did you know?" He did not wait for an answer. "But it is dead, now. The lungs again—cold, exposure. And the girl is mad, or next-door to it. Lord, it is sickening, infuriating . . ." He flung away from her, and then, suddenly, spun on his heel and darted back. He was just in time to catch her in his arms, as she swooned.

As has been said, he blamed himself, sharply. He should have remembered that she was going to have a child herself.

## 15

WITH a volley of invective that paid eloquent testimony to his army service, Aeneas Graham got to his feet, and shook his fist. He had crawled and grovelled, he had striven and struggled, he had sweated and shivered, with a single-mindedness and whole-heartedness and patience, comparable only with the discomfort he had suffered. And now—this! Observed at last, spurned distantly, and most contemptuously left. It was too much. The man's pent-up eloquence poured out of him in a spate of profanity, as the great stag and its satellites drifted up and up and over the skyline and away.

It was useless to think of further pursuit. In another hour the light would be gone, and the short January afternoon swallowed in the long January night. Besides, he had had enough for one day—for always, perhaps. The brute was not for him, it seemed. He could have shot other stags, some of them fair-enough beasts, and many hinds. But it was not other stags and hinds that he wanted; their meat was of little use at this season, he was assured. It was only that great brute with the arrogant head, that Frances MacBride had laughed at him for so much as consider-ing, which he coveted—the more fool he! Well, it was gone now, after leading him a fantastic dance, up rushing burn-channels, over treacherous bogs and quaking peat-hags, across slithering screes and streaming aprons of naked rock, bent back-breakingly most of the time, on his knees when he was fortunate, on his belly more often. So be it, then—let it go . . . and let Frances MacBride smirk. What use was a pair of antlers, anyway! Soaking, mud-covered, and aching-backed, Aeneas Graham strode off downhill, disgustedly.

He was fairly high on the north-westerly flank of Beinn na Drise, for his sins—not far, indeed, below the spot where Frances and he had paused that day, so long ago, to admire the sunset. That was the worst of this island, it always was reminding him, one way or another, of that young woman.

Or not exactly the worst, perhaps . . . But very definitely she seemed to have stamped her personality on the place, as far as he was concerned, and somewhere, at the back of his mind, the man resented it. He had quartered Europe, from the Low Countries to Italy, from Austria to the Peninsula, and managed to see places as they were, to observe mountains and forests and plains and towns as just such, to admire or to deplore them according to his taste, and to pass on. He had retained his perspective before St. Peter's in Rome, the naked grandeur of the Matterhorn, the Moorish splendours of Granada. And yet he had to see this miserable island only in relation to a troublesome slip of a girl. It was not as though he was in love with her, or any nonsense of that sort, thank heaven! But it was humiliating, when he came to think about it—like the business of this confounded stag!

He tacked left and right on his descent, with the land dropping away sharply before him, to the cliffs and the shore. There was no sunset tonight for Frances to miss, at any rate. The sea stretched grey and desolate, to merge imperceptibly with the grey desolate sky. He was very near the clouds, and every now and again the thin smirr of the skirts of one would drift across the face of the hill, chill as death. No doubt it would be raining soon, again. It was a damned cold wet miserable place, this Erismore, when all was said and done, and goodness only knew why he was still on it! Sometimes he was beginning to gain a suspicion that he was a bigger fool than he had realised.

He changed his course a little, trending farther to the left and south. Just below was that great headland that he had had rather too close a view of a fortnight, three weeks, ago, in MacIan's boat. What was it, Frances had named it—Rudha nan Altair? The Cape of the Altar. A grim spot. She had suggested that there might have been a chapel or a cell or something there, once, to account for the name. Or something to do with the shape of the hill. A curious place to put a church, then. It was down there, somewhere, that Mairi's mother had fallen to her death, too, apparently. Frances had hinted that there was something queer about that, as well. There well might have been—there was plenty of queerness about Erismore. Though Frances was apt to see things as queerer than they were, at times, perhaps; she was romantically inclined, that one—though not where he was concerned, b'gad! Damn it, there he went again—Frances, Frances, Frances! Confound the girl!

Of a sudden, Aeneas slackened his pace, halted. There was someone down there. A woman, too, he thought, moving southward, along the cliff-top, away from the headland, back towards the township. He drew out from his pocket Finlay's telescope, that he had borrowed for his deer-stalking, and sat down to focus it. Yes ... yes it was. History repeating itself. The light was poor, but it looked like the same woman that they had seen together that other day just thereabouts, and with the same basket over her arm—the woman that he had seen down at the pier handling Lachlan Macgillivray's share of the fish for him. Seana Somebody-or-other. Now, what the devil ... ?

He watched her, walking, a shadowy strangely-lonely figure, till a fold in the land hid her. From the way that she carried that basket, it was empty this time. He knew the lie of the land well enough now, to recognize that the only place she could have been to was the Campbell's croft of Ardmenish, a difficult mile-and-a-half further north. But what could she have been taking there? It had been fish, before . . . to a fisherman's house! Pensively he shut up the glass, and resumed his descent.

The man was not taking quite the same route that Frances had led him, and presently he found himself on a steep, almost precipitous, slope of water-rotted soft rock, that forced him somewhat out of his way, to the north. But he was not going to turn back and retrace his steps up that hill, at this stage; he would just have to make a detour, since he was not seeking a broken neck. And a detour he made, though a longer one than he had anticipated. He had to go right down into a sort of valley between the main hillside and the lesser slope that culminated in the bare summit of Rudha nan Altair, before he could turn back to his proper course.

He did not so turn, just then, either. A great hullaballoo was going on up there, round the top of the headland, the screeching raucous circus of hundreds of loud-mouthed gulls. Even as he watched, more were coming in from every direction. And not only gulls, either; there were larger birds amongst them—buzzards, could they be? On an impulse, he turned, and started to climb up that braeside. As he did so, a great bird swept down, almost on top of him, so close that the wind of it nearly overbalanced him. Aeneas stared, as it soared upward on wide-spread up-tilted motionless wings, along the hill-face. That was no buzzard. He climbed on.

On the flat summit of Rudha nan Altair, the man halted, astonished. He was in a bedlam of flapping, swooping, plunging birds, so dense that the fading light was almost lost behind the multitude of beating wings, the air was churned dizzily, and the noise was deafening. Every kind, and size of gull was circling and diving there, in a frenzied vortex—terns, kittiwakes, petrels, black-backs, ivories, skuas, herring-gulls, and the stink of them caught at his throat. But it was not at the gulls themselves so much, that Aeneas stared. They were whirling and fighting round a central point, a hub, which seemed to draw them, in baffled vociferous fury, like a magnet. What it was he could not see, for the milling press of them. He bent his head as though against a storm, and moved forward. And he seemed to recognize the din and clamour that beat against his ear-drums; it was the same horrible cacophony that he had listened to, once within and once without, the kitchen of Ruaigmore, with a crazy violin, there, as its interpreter.

Flicked and buffeted with wings, spattered with droppings, peering through the medley of threshing pinions, the man pushed his way. Then he saw it. Before him, out of the level summit of the hill, rose a great stone, or rather, a formation of steps and stairs of natural rock culminating in a flat top, like a table on a plinth, that was, indeed, the miniature and pattern of the entire hill. And on this tale, surrounded by the yelling eddying envious throng of the gulls, three great birds crouched, tearing at something that gleamed white, with cruel beaks and talons.

Gazing, Aeneas swallowed. They were eagles, obviously—by their white heads and streaked plumage and size, ernes, sea-eagles, not the golden eagles of the mountains. Fascinated, he watched them, intent on their snarling gobbling. Hunched, heads down, wings just slightly open to give them balance, they tore and gulped greedily, sparing a moment now and then for a savage lunge at any too venturesome gull, or even at each other. Three feet or more, they stood, with beaks like scimitars, and flat evil heads, and they hopped on their fierce yellow claws as they fed. Then, one of them, lifting its head to swallow, saw the man. With a harsh choking scream, evident even in that howling babel, it flounced awkwardly along that table of stone. There was a vast heavy beating of wings, a crescendo of noise, and the three huge birds were in the air, circling, spiralling upward, ungainly no longer. And each in its talons held a large fish, or part of one.

Almost before the eagles were in the air, the cloud of clamorous gulls had swept down to the remains of the feast, snatching and rending and battling. From the sky above, a lump of fish fell with a thud, to be pounced upon instantly by a score of distracted birds. Aeneas glanced up. One of the eagles had soared up and away, but the other two still wheeled and hovered, not more than fifty feet above. He did not like the look of those two, at all, great fierce brutes with talons like a yearling's horns and a wing-span of six or seven feet. The one that had dropped its cod seemed to be coming lower, menacingly. The man, deciding that he had seen enough, gripped his musket by the barrel for use as a club, if need be, and turned and ran.

So that was it! That was where the Seana-woman took her fish—Macgillivray's fish! That was the pattern for, the source of, Lachlan Mor's crazy fiddling. But why—why? What sense was there in it? What did the feeding of those foul birds portend? And there, in that grim spot? Cape of the Altar, indeed—a fishy altar. And where did the music come in? There was some connection, he was sure—something shameful, degrading. Some queer sort of ceremony, doubtless. But how could he find out? Nobody on the island would tell him, that much was certain. Even Mairi would not speak, he knew. This was the first real discovery that he'd made. If only he could talk it over with someone—with Frances MacBride. If only Frances were here! Why the devil did he have to go talking marriage to her, and scaring her off. She would have found something queer about this, b'gad! Perish and confound everything!

## 16

A ENEAS was right in his surmise that Mairi Macgillivray
would not discuss this latest development with him. When
he mentioned, tentatively, that night, that Rudha nan Altair
seemed to be a great place for the birds, it was met with a swift
glance, a widening of the eyes, and then a mask-like assumption
of disinterest, together with a prompt changing of the subject
and an early retiral. Ewan was present, too, and kept his eyes on
the fire and his mouth shut. And there was nobody else on the
island to whom Aeneas could speak, since, other than these two,
only Lachlan Mor had more than a smattering of English. And
there was no point in questioning that venerable individual; that
much was self-evident.

He had half-a-notion of going across to Eorsa and talking to
Mr. Keith. But on deliberation, he could see little profit in it, to
make the effort worthwhile—even if Ewan would be prepared
to take him and bring him back. What help could that elderly
leave-well-alone time-server be? Aeneas could imagine the
advice he would get. Better to stay where he was—wiser, too,
perhaps. These people must know now that he was more than
suspicious, and might well guess the object of his visit; if they
had been prepared to knock him on the head before, they might
well consider going still further, at any such move on his part.
It had begun to dawn on Aeneas Graham that he might
conceivably be in some small personal danger.

So he watched and waited, and kept his own council, and
outwardly, all was as it had been.

As it transpired, he could not have gone, if he would. For two
weeks and more, great storms of wind and sleet and hail lashed
that seaboard incessantly, and no boat left the island. Erismore
was the centre and focus of a wild battle of the elements,
cudgelled, battered, mauled, and deluged, isolated from all else
by cloud and mist and spray and the raging sea, and deafened by

the roar of the surf, with, through and above it, the wind's frantic howling. Human activity came almost to a standstill. The least travel or outdoor work was a travail and a weariness. Men, numbed with cold, dulled by the buffeting wind and the rain, found their firesides excellent places and their beds better still, Aeneas amongst them. Mairi, getting near her time, now, and busy with baby-clothes and the like, taught him how to card and spin wool, and Ewan showed him how to work the hand-loom, and how to concoct the vivid colourful dyes of the Hebrides out of lichens and bark and heather-roots and sea-weed. And often Ewan sang to them as they worked, keeping time to the clack of the loom and the tread of the spinning-wheel, and once Lachlan Mor struggled up to the farmhouse with his fiddle under his plaid, and played for them—but pleasantly, orthodoxly. So passed January.

When at length the storm blew itself out, there was much to be done, and few over-anxious to start the doing of it. Stock, roofs and buildings, boats and nets, dykes and ditches—all had to be attended to. Aeneas gave Ewan a hand with most of these, and after the first lazy reluctance, enjoyed the active labour. By the third day of comparative calm, the sea had abated suffi-ciently for the boats to go out, and the doctor, rather guiltily, set off on a borrowed pony to visit some of his neglected patients. There were one or two of them who might well have expected to have seen him before this. On the other hand, of course, had he done as seemed to be expected of him generally, and left the island altogether, they would not have seen him at all!

He was returning at dusk that afternoon, via the shore track from the south, and was turning his shaggy garron into what served as the main road of the place, when he paused, surprised. A stranger had just come out of one of the houses, with Lachlan Macgillivray in attendance. This was no crofter, no islander at all, wearing a cocked hat like his own, a long well-cut overcoat of broad-cloth, and Hessian boots. Wondering, Aeneas moved up to meet him.

Macgillivray introduced him, easily, composedly, as though the arrival of well-dressed strangers was an everyday occurrence

141

on Erismore. "Doctor, this gentleman is Mr. Mitchell, the laird's new factor, that is after paying us a visit in the way of business. This is Doctor Graham, that does be having some sort of a holiday on the island, whatever."

"Ah—yes. I've heard of Dr. Graham."

"Your servant, sir."

The newcomer was a greying-haired thin-featured unsmiling individual, with a long nose and chin, a calculating eye, and a tight mouth. He spoke with the clipped accent of the south-east. "And yours. It would appear that you have an unusual taste in holidays, sir!"

"A change is lightsome, Mr. Mitchell, so we are told. I find it so. You had a comfortable journey?"

"Damnable," the other said, briefly.

Aeneas inclined his head, slightly. "Possibly not the best season of the year to travel amongst the islands," he suggested.

"I believe you, sir. But I have my reasons."

"Quite. You have been particularly unfortunate just lately, of course."

"I have." That was grim. "We have been cooped up on that other island—Eorsa—for more than a fortnight, waiting to get across here. Just kicking our heels. A barbarous country, sir."

Aeneas looked at Lachlan Macgillivray. "H'mmm," he said. "Trying."

"You will have been anxious indeed to get here, for sure?" the old man mentioned mildly. "The great place it is getting for the visitors, Erismore."

The factor glanced around him, drew up his thin shoulders, and sniffed, fastidiously. "Personally," he said, "I'd rather be practically anywhere else, sink me. Curse me, if I can see what you, and that young woman, see in it, Doctor Graham. . . ."

"Young woman . . . ?"

"Miss MacBride—sister of the late incumbent here. Nothing would do but I must bring her back with me from Tobermory. . . ."

"She's up at the Manse this minute, Doctor," Macgillivray added, solemnly.

"Well, I'm damned!" Aeneas pulled the pony's head round, and in a single vault was on its back. "I . . . you'll pardon me, gentlemen? I'll see you later, Factor. Good day." And he was off, up the track.

"He's in a devilish hurry," Mr. Mitchell complained, his thin mouth turning down at the corners.

"That is so," the other agreed, genially. "That is the youth of him. He was a great friend of Miss MacBride's brother, you see, the Doctor."

She was not at the Manse. Though smoke was rising from a chimney, and the place had a welcome lived-in air about it again, there was no answer to the man's knocking. He hurried across to Ruaigmore.

Mairi, her soft eyes shining, admitted that Miss Frances was back—almost with an I-told-you-so—had been over to the farmhouse, indeed, but had been gone some time now. If she was not at the Manse, she must be away walking somewhere—the great hurry she was in to be out on the road! Mairi cocked an eyebrow at her guest. He might try the track that led up to the glen, if he was thinking of seeing her. She had mentioned to Miss Frances—just in the by-going—that she thought that he might be up that way. The man waited for no more, but turned the pony into its stall, and set off up the path.

Aeneas was well up beyond the peat-bog before he saw her, far off and coming downhill towards him. Involuntarily his pace quickened, but after a little, began to slow down again noticeably. What was he going to say to her? This might be a little difficult. He'd have to be careful what he said—keep strictly discreet and calm and so on. Nothing even faintly romantic, or anything of that sort, in case he scared her off again like he'd done before. Not that he was apt to be romantic, of course, not being that sort of man. A brotherly attitude was the thing—fraternal, that was the word. . . . He raised his arm to signal vigorously, in answer to her wave of recognition.

But now, instead of hurrying downhill, as before, she suddenly stopped, and sat down on an outcrop of stone at the roadside. Apparently she was going to wait for him there—a typically unfair, thoroughly feminine trick. There she would sit, cool as you like, enjoying the view, while he had to labour up the hill to her, puffing like a grampus, and feeling all of a fool, and not knowing where to look! Which was exactly the way it happened.

She rose, however, as he came up with her, a colourful pleasing figure in her short-skirted island clothes again, with a vivid tartan plaid about her shoulders and a kerchief around her head to keep her hair in order. Her eyes searched his face for only a moment and then flickered away, aside, down, anywhere. "Well," she said, and, having difficulty with the word, had to say it again. "Well. Here I am . . . back again."

"Yes," he agreed, heavily. "I'm glad to see you." If his own voice was a shade uneven, he had all his climbing to account for it.

"Are you?" That was a question, not a mere remark.

"Yes—very. I've missed you. I . . . ." He recollected his resolutions on the way up. "Not to be wondered at, is it, with hardly anyone else on the island able to talk more than a child's English!"

"Oh—I see," she said. "Yes, of course." Unaccountably, she lifted her chin a trifle. "Why did you stay, then?"

He frowned. He had intended to question, not be questioned—ask *her* why she had come back. "Why not? I was involved here, with cases, as you know. And we had a sort of epidemic. I had got interested in the island and its—er—problems. I was comfortable enough—and I had nowhere particular to go, elsewhere."

Frances nodded. "I see. I'm glad that my absence didn't affect you vitally."

There she went. Women were so touchy, unreasonable, took things so confoundedly personally. Almost, he scowled. "I missed you, anyway," he reiterated doggedly.

She relented a little—perhaps because he seemed so like a small boy when he scowled like that. "I missed you, too," she admitted. And, as he glanced up, added: "Though of course, I

144

had plenty of people to talk to!"

"Why did you come back, then?"

"I suppose I just felt that Erismore was where I belonged."
That was carefully said; she might have rehearsed it. "I was too
fond of it to stay away. And when I heard that Mr. Mitchell was
coming . . ."

"That's just what Mairi Macgillivray said. She said that you
were too fond of the place to stay away for long. We hoped that
you would come back—we talked about you, often." He
frowned again—at himself, for saying it. "In fact, that is why I
stayed, I think."

He heard her breath come quickly, and began to curse himself
for saying too much. "Was it, Aeneas? That was nice of you."
That came in quite a rush.

He cleared his throat, commenced to say something, and
changed his mind. "Er . . . how is Mrs. Munro, your aunt?" he
demanded.

She took a moment to answer him. "Quite well, I think," she
said, her voice less confident. "Her last letter seemed very
cheerful."

"Letter . . . ? You haven't been to Edinburgh, then?"

"No. No. You see, I only got as far as Tobermory. I . . . well,
I just stayed there."

He stared, but she was not looking at him. "You've been there
all the time—not thirty miles away!"

"Yes. You see, I have friends there, relatives . . ." Frances
shook her head. "I just couldn't go any further . . . from
Erismore . . ." and her voice tailed away. She looked at him,
quickly. "Shall we walk on?"

"Yes, of course. By all means."

And they started walking, but, curiously, not back towards
the village, but onwards, up the hill.

They went on in silence for fifty yards or so, and then Frances
spoke. "What has been going on in Erismore since I left? You
mentioned an epidemic?"

"That was the least of it," the man told her. "Enteritis—

nothing serious. But other things have been happening. Another baby has died—Jean Cameron's. I have been decoyed and assaulted. And I have discovered in your friend Lachlan Macgillivray an unusual passion for birds; he feeds them and uses them to inspire his music!"

"Assaulted—you? And birds . . . ?" she wondered. "Tell me."

He did, and it took him all the way up through the glen and the woods to do it. He had an attentive listener.

She was very thoughtful, when he had finished, disquieted. "This is serious, Aeneas," she said at length, uneasily. "I'd never have thought that they would have attacked you. It means that things are worse, far worse, than I had realised. You see, they are not like that, these people. They are not a violent folk—and hospitality to strangers is one of the essentials of their character. And pride. They are so very proud; you are a sort of guest on this island, and you've done so much for them—and yet they do this to you! It is against every instinct, every impulse, they have. I know them . . . and this is bad, bad." She turned to him, perturbed, as a new thought occurred to her. "If they're desperate, if they'll go that far, they might go farther! Perhaps it would be as well, safer, to try and forget the whole affair . . . ?"

Though it was pleasant to have her so evidently concerned over him, Aeneas Graham was obstinately inclined—moreover he had his reputation to consider. He had not campaigned from one end of Europe to another, to be put in a state of fear by a few Highland fishermen. "They have assaulted me without cause—without cause on my part, anyway," he maintained. "I'll find out why—and maybe make them wish that they hadn't—before I leave Erismore."

She smiled, if faintly. "So *that* was why you stayed!" she commented.

But Frances herself had not really considered any other course, in fact. After all, she was Finlay MacBride's sister. Her next remarks showed it. "But this astonishing feeding of the eagles—what can it mean? How can we get to the bottom of that? We must find out, somehow. I never had the slightest inkling of it—and yet it must have been going on for some time, presumably. I wonder whether I could worm anything out of Seana Macvicar? She always was a strange, secretive sort of creature. Others must know all about it, too, of course—possibly all of them."

"I've tried Mairi," he told her. "But she was like a clam. They'll never tell us. Obviously it's something that they're ashamed of."

"But what can it be? Witchcraft of some sort? Superstition? They are very superstitious, you know—we all are in the Highlands, of course. There are lots of strange beliefs that I know of—but there's no real harm in any of them. Things like those ropes you see hanging from chimney-stacks, for the little people to dance round, to stop them, may be, pulling the house to pieces. And the way we shun lapwings as being possessed by the souls of Jews who gloated over the Crucifixion. And favouring robins because they were supposed to have got blood on their breasts by trying to remove the nails from the Cross. Believing in kelpies and water-horses and so on. All that sort of thing. Though the Kirk is very much against all of it, Finlay used to say that there were much worse heresies. Do you think it is something like that—in a more extreme form, of course?"

"I don't know. It may be—probably is, I suppose. But if it is comparatively innocent, why all this secrecy? And why knock me on the head over it?" He shrugged. "Heaven knows what it's all about—but I am glad that you are here to discuss it with. I felt very helpless and defeated about it all when I had no one to tell, no one to talk it over with. . . ."

"How *I* felt, before you came," she interposed.

"M'mm. Yes, I suppose so. Anyway, I'm glad that you are here."

"Yes, I am too." She laughed a little breathlessly. "I should never have gone."

"No," he agreed carefully. "But it was my fault that you went." Involuntarily they had paused at the edge of the trees, looking out over Loch na Creagh and Peig Macleod's croft, to the tall mountains that stood guard about it. "I was thoughtless. It was my—my importunity that drove you away."

147

She shook her head. "No, it was my own pride that drove me away," she asserted. "I am proud, you know, like the rest of them—sinfully proud. However, I soon discovered how much my pride was worth—before even I left Eorsa! And, and . . . anyway, I came back."

The man frowned his uncertainty. "Pride? I cannot just see where pride comes into it. You went away, didn't you, because of the innuendos of the islanders about our—er—our association, and"—he cleared his throat sternly—"because of my unfortunate suggestion?"

Frances turned away, but only to a fallen tree-trunk nearby, on which she sat herself. "I went away because of my pride," she asserted, strangely. "And I came back, because I had got rid of it—that pride, at any rate. Don't you believe me?"

Aeneas stared perplexedly. "You know best, I suppose . . ." he said. "But I don't see it, I must admit. Not that it matters, really . . ."

"But it does—desperately!" Her hands clenched on her plaid as she said it. Obviously she was much affected by something. "Can't you see? Can't you leave me the last rags of my pride to cover me?"

He came over to her, and stood above her. "Forgive me if I am stupid," he urged. "I am, in many ways, I know. But I'm quite sure that you have nothing to blame yourself with. As I see it, you went away because you were embarrassed by the conditions that had arisen." He was speaking slowly, picking his words. "And you had every reason to be. I had put you in a difficult position, a modest and gently-reared young woman . . ."

"And yet I've come back. So what now?" she interrupted. "What of my modesty, now?"

Aeneas swallowed, and dug at a tree-root with the toe of his boot. "It is your kindness. . . . You are magnanimous. And you will not regret it—as far as I am concerned—I promise you. I cannot stop the people here from talking, hinting, but at least you will not be embarrassed by any further overtures on my part . . ."

"Oh, dear!" she cried, and jumped to her feet. "This is quite impossible! Let us say no more about it. Come along—it is quite time that we were getting back." One last word she threw back over her shoulder to her mystified companion. "I have still a little pride left, you see!"

He did not question that, at any rate.

Finding subjects for conversation to young women in the grip of uncertain emotions was no talent of Aeneas Graham's—especially when he was having difficulty with his own emotions, at the same time. There was so much that he would like to say, was bursting to say, that was prohibited, out of the question, that made mere idle talk unsuitable, impossible indeed. And sober discussion, however carefully considered, did not seem to be very successful. Why must it be like this, he demanded of himself, a shade resentfully. Why must all this be so damnably difficult?

Presently she did speak, however, at a certain bend in that woodland path. "It was here that I first met you," he announced suddenly, abruptly.

Perhaps she sensed a hint of truculence in his voice, because she turned to look back at him quickly. "Maybe you wish that you never had?" she flashed.

"Maybe," he agreed grimly, and they walked on.

But he was an honest man, at heart, and he could not let that pass. "No," he said, presently. "That is not true. I could never wish that. Knowing you has been too . . . important."

She said nothing.

He could not just leave it at that. "I had to know you—it could not have been otherwise. That was fated, it seems . . . and I would not have it different, whatever the—the . . ."

"—the cost?" she completed for him. "It has been at a cost, Aeneas?"

"Yes," he acceded, and in some detached portion of his mind he noted that she was calling him Aeneas now, quite naturally— it might be that she had been thinking of him as that, for some time? "Yes—at a cost. The greatest cost." He stopped. Why continue with this farce? She might as well know. He had a right to justify himself. They could not continue like this, indefinitely—*he* could not, anyway. It was too much of a strain. But he had promised, assured her that he would not embarrass her further . . . ?

"And this cost . . . ?" Frances persisted. She did not turn, this time, as she spoke.

The man shrugged at her back, with a queerly final gesture, almost of resignation. "It is just myself," he said simply. "Myself—that is what I have paid for knowing you."

## 17

FRANCES MACBRIDE had stopped her walking now, and turning, slowly, she searched the man's face. "What do you mean, Aeneas?" she whispered.

"I mean that I love you, adore you. I am sorry—I cannot help myself. It is too much for me. I am lost in the love of you, in the need of you. I had not meant to tell you, to say this. . . ."

"Dear God!" the girl breathed, and it was true praise as she said it. "What are you saying, Aeneas? Do you know what you are saying? Are you blind, blind!" Her hand reached out to grip him, almost to shake him. "Or am I crazy mad?"

"Yes, I know what I am saying . . ."

"Then say it again, in the name of pity!"

His wondering eyes fearful, unready, to believe what he sensed and saw, he stared at her, and speaking, his voice was deep and vibrant. "I say that I love you—love you with all that is in me. I think that I have loved you from the first day that ever I set eyes on you, in this wood, Frances MacBride . . ."

"Oh, dear!" The girl began to laugh, trying to stop herself with an effort that brought her to tears, and so stood, her eyes swimming. "Help me, Aeneas!" she pleaded, chokingly. And then, at the sheer marvel in his eyes, she threw herself at him, bodily, and her arms were about his neck, tight, and tightening. "My dear, my dear," she cried. "My love, my beloved. My dear foolish Aeneas . . ."

He let her say no more, blind, groping, happy Aeneas Graham.

They can be left there, in their sheltered wood—it is their lovers due, surely. Lovers' explanations are seldom coherent, and their methods dilatory and not for the onlooker. It was February, and chill, but they did not feel the cold. Neither did they hear the wood-pigeons that gossiped about them in the dark pines and bare birches above, nor the turgid age-old stream that laughed and chuckled at them on its way to the sea, nor any of the woodland things that watched them quietly. Why should they? They had so much to tell each other. The man was so late in the avowal of his love—four months late, at least. If he had told it— had known it—when he ought, the girl would never have left him, in what she named her pride, her baulking at a loveless marriage. He had time to make up, and Frances, who, woman-like had known and recognised her own love from the start, had months of disappointment and restraint and heart-burning to dissipate. And their lips were not their own. Leave them, then.

## 18

B OTH of them would have liked to be married in the little austere church of Erismore—Finlay's church. But this was not practicable, in the meantime, at anyrate. Frances was quite certain that Robert Keith would not consider leaving Eorsa while winter seas and winds prevailed, and Aeneas was not inclined to doubt her. And neither of them so much as contemplated waiting. What was there to wait for, indeed? If marriage had seemed a suitable procedure four months before, with love unprofessed, how much more to be commended now. Besides, they were young and virile, and far from cold-blooded, either of them, and could see no virtue in conventional delay. So, if Mr. Keith would not come to them, they must go to him. And the sooner the better. Three weeks would serve, for the banns to be called, and for Frances to make her woman's preparations. Three weeks was long enough, in all conscience, Aeneas asserted, and was not contradicted.

The news of their intention was variously received on the island. Mairi was delighted, unreservedly, even if her husband seemed less enthusiastic. Lachlan Mor, despite his earlier hints and suggestions, was far from pleased, they were sure—though his compliments and congratulations were eloquent and sustained. Many of the islanders spoke their felicitations to Frances, in their own tongue, shyly, formally, or waggishly, as became their several dispositions, but more made no comment—which might have been noteworthy in that mannerly people.

They had other matters on their minds, just now, of course, the folk of Erismore. Mr. Mitchell, the factor, had not come all this inconvenient way for nothing, or the good of his health. Indeed, he was very busy. With his man, a furtive-seeming Campbell out of Mull, he visited every croft and holding on the island inspecting, measuring, assessing, and surveying, and taking detailed notes of all he saw. He was a thorough individual, was Ezra Mitchell, however little he seemed to enjoy his work. The new laird wanted a great deal more money from Erismore than had his brother, it appeared. Uncollected rents were to be paid in full, on pain of dispossession, and future rentals were to be raised, in some cases more than doubled. There were to be no exceptions, no appeals. Those who did not like it could get out. The Canadas were waiting for them. The old days of sloth and indolence were past.

The Manse too, had to pay its way. The Estate was prepared to permit Miss MacBride, or others, to occupy it, till such time as it might be needed for the proprietor's purposes, but at a substantial rent; which rent was payable from the date of the late Finlay MacBride's decease. And there would be no lease nor guarantee of tenure. Mr. Mitchell's instructions were definite.

Frances and Aeneas saw rather more than enough of the factor during those waiting weeks. He had taken up residence in the Manse, as a matter of course, and was not backwards in matters concerning his comfort. A girl from one of the crofts was brought in, to help to look after him, but necessarily Frances was much involved and tied—when she fain would have been otherwise. Aeneas consigned the fellow to the devil daily, and maintained superficially civil relations only with difficulty. Any ideas they might have had of confiding in the man as to the curious happenings on Erismore, were quickly dismissed. Indeed, what with one thing and another, their sympathies were quite definitely enlisted on the side of the islanders, in their treatment by this soured minion of soulless authority. And then, of course, they were somewhat preoccupied with their own affairs; new-plighted lovers are not noteworthy for the catholicity of their interests. For the time-being, at anyrate, they were inclined to let bygones be bygones.

Even three weeks will pass, eventually.

If the waiting was protracted, the wedding itself was not. Indeed, it developed into a hurried affair, that the conventional might have accounted unseemly. Transit difficulties, and the weather, between them were mainly responsible. They left

Erismore early on a wet March morning, in Ewan Beg's boat, with Ezra Mitchell and his man, having finished their inauspicious mission to the island, as unwelcome fellow-passengers. It was not a conspicuously merry bridal-party at that hour and in that company, crouching under cloaks and plaids to shelter from the hissing rain. But the sea was calm—glassily so for that time of year—and Ewan and his rowers made good time, though the sail was little use to them. They reached the pier at Eorsa uneventfully, in time to permit the happy couple—and incidentally the factor, also—to have an early dinner at Mr. Keith's manse. The ceremony had been arranged for two o'clock, but Ewan and his colleagues, sniffing the air and shaking ominous heads, recommended haste. They did not like the look of the weather, they said, and the sooner they were on their way back to Erismore the better. So, immediately after dinner, Frances changed from her travelling clothes into the finest things that she had with her on the island, assisted and delayed by an excited Mrs. Keith, and repaired forthwith to the church.

The kirk of Eorsa was larger but more gloomy than that of Erismore, and damply cold. Mr. Keith would have preferred to have the service in the Manse, but the bride had been adamant that she would not feel adequately married unless in church, and Aeneas had supported her. So in the dim and draughty empty kirk they exchanged their vows, before God and two or three of the Eorsa folk and Ewan and his men, Robert Keith rubbing his thin cold hands unceasingly, and cutting the business as short as possible, and, with his congregation, keeping an eye on what the small windows showed of the weather, the while. Thus they were briefly but quite effectively pronounced man and wife. Some part of Finlay MacBride's charge had been most fully performed.

Outside, Ewan Macgillivray, in the same breath as his congratulations, urged an immediate departure. Weather was blowing up, he was sure, and he was supported by most of the men present. Mrs. Keith, lonely soul, suggested that the happy couple should let the fishermen go, and spend a few days on Eorsa as her guests—nothing would give her greater pleasure.

Her husband seconded her, though less eagerly, but Aeneas and Frances were at one in declining. They were anxious to be on their own; the boat was going, anyway; and who knew how long it might be before Ewan would come back for them again? Better to go now. So, taking time only for Frances to change back into her more serviceable clothes, and having their healths expeditiously drunk in the minister's whisky, they hurried down to the pier and the boat.

The rain had stopped, though the sky was still overcast, its leaden grey shot through with a curious browner tinge. A gusty moaning wind came and went, light as yet, and though the sea was still calm, it heaved quietly but ponderously beneath them, as though to the echo of a great swell. The rowers gave way with a will, but the boat slid forward only dully, sluggishly, as if the water was heavy, leaden as the sky. It was not warm, but soon the men were sweating. They sang no chant as they pulled.

Once out of the harbour bay of Eorsa, and turning north-wards, they did better. The brown square sail was run up, and the desultory south-west wind sent them onwards by fits and starts. But the sea was rising, noticeably—or, rather, the swell was growing steadily though the surface remained deceptively smooth. The *Eala* lifted and sank in great sweeping lurches, but with never a toss or a splash. Ewan, at the stroke oar, was obviously uneasy; he said that a swell like this *after* a storm was bad enough, but *before* one . . . ! He kept glancing over his shoulder, forward, and keeping the bows a few degrees westerly of their direct course. They did not want to get into the tide-race between the two islands, with that swell piling up on it. Aeneas and his wife nodded. They sat in the stern, rather evidently not huddled together, trying not to look as ridiculously lover-like and newly-wed as they felt.

The wind was rising rapidly, though still it came in gusts, squalls, that heeled the boat over alarmingly, forcing Ewan to shorten sail. The clouds were very dark and ragged, and the brownness more evident than ever. The craft was being headed due north-west now, at forty-five degrees to their direct course, with one of the port oars crossed over to pull starboard to help keep the *Eala's* head, against the pull of the part-lowered sail. They were half-way, at least, across the mouth of the sound between Eorsa and Erismore, and no one needed Ewan to point out the strong easterly drag of the tide. Not so far to the east, from the summits of the seas, they could glimpse the dead white of broken waters. Yet there were no rocks there, in the deep open channel. That was swell and tide at cross-purposes.

Soon crests were forming at the tops of the great rollers, and when the squalls struck them, the same crests were swept off in angry spray. The *Eala* was plunging deeply, sickeningly, now, and the sail was furled away almost to nothing. Aeneas, impatient at sitting still for so long, pleaded to be allowed to take an oar. Ewan nodded, and directed him to take the place of the single port oar, a middle-aged man, who was set to handle the sail—to keep it up, as far as was possible, between the gusts, and to dowse it completely as the squalls struck them. It was a difficult task, calling for a quick eye and a nice judgment, and was not uniformly successful, so that more than once a sudden blast found them almost capsized. After the third and most startling of such mishaps, with water shipped, Ewan ordered the sail to be brought down altogether.

More and more the *Eala* was pitching and rolling, as well as plunging, as she fought the cross-seas. But still Ewan would not turn her head towards Erismore. That he knew what he was doing, his passengers accepted, but Frances at least found it a nerve-racking business. Also, she felt undeniably sea-sick, for the first time in her life.

The full force of the storm struck them with a suddenness that was nearly the end of them. The boat heeled over violently, smothered in spume. The rowers tumbled head-long on top of each other. Aeneas, at the port, leeward, side, found himself half under water, his oar, wedged transversely across the wooden rowlock, alone saving him. Uncontrolled and part-full the *Eala* yawed and slewed and drifted. Broadside on and water-logged, the next great wave would sink her.

Ewan flung himself bodily over his floundering colleagues and stumbling, clutching, groping, found the flapping halyard and hauled up the sail. It was a desperate expedient, but it was that or nothing. The wind caught the sail immediately, threw the boat over again, but at the same time pulled her round, slowly, heavily. Barely in time. A great comber hurtling down on them, caught them before they were fully round and into the wind, and the crest of it came pouring in-board. The reeling weltering craft lurched and slid, down and down.

Paradoxically, it seemed almost as though their cumbrous heaviness saved them. The swift-running wave did not take them with it in its chill heart, but left them wallowing, all but awash. But they were stern-on now, at least. Furiously, Ewan shouted his orders, and brought the sail down again. They had lost two oars, but Aeneas and one other had hung on to theirs, and now got them out and pulling, somehow, striving heroically to keep the weighed-down intractable vessel under control and fore and aft to wind and wave. The rest bailed frantically, with whatever came to hand, Frances, who, owing to the narrow confines of her stern seat, had suffered least upset of them all, using even her shoe, for want of anything better.

Another wave, not quite so large, raced down on them, hissing its menace, but definitely, however inertly, the *Eala* lifted to it, and shipped only the frothing snarling crest of it. If they could keep her at that, and get most of the water out of her, they might manage—for the time being. Ewan took the oar from Aeneas, and the others bailed for dear life's sake.

There was nothing for it now, of course, but to run before the storm. Nothing beyond the very slightest alteration of course was possible. Aeneas, shouting, asked about the skerries and Maclean's Gate. Ewan Macgillivray shook his head grimly. They were half-a-mile too far south still, he told them. By no possible means could they make up that half-mile. MacLean's Gate, or any other, was out of the question. They were about a mile off-shore, half that from the skerries, and heading straight for the island.

What chance had they, then, the doctor demanded.

It was in God's hands, Ewan shrugged. There was nothing that they could do but keep the boat running before the wind—

if they could do that! There was a sort of a chance, that was all that he could say. The tide was high, and it was just possible that a big wave might carry them over the worst of the skerries. On the other hand, of course, if they came on the reef in the trough of a wave, then . . . ! The skerries had been crossed before, in a storm, at high water—himself, he had done it once, in his uncle's boat. He did not say how often the attempt had failed, however. The line of the skerries was not continuous entirely, of course, nor of an even height, and there were one or two places where the reef was very narrow—one near enough to the line they were on, he thought. Ewan looked away. The storm god might be kind. . . .

The urgent bailing kept them from the worst ordeal of inactive, gnawing, waiting. None had time for more than recurrent anxious glances ahead, through the murk and gloom of the storm to where the dark mass of the island loomed, rimmed with white. They had got most of the slopping water out, but they were still taking the crests of every other sea, and their labour was continuous. Ewan, at the port oar, eyed and traced and anticipated each breaker as it came, with unfailing desperate skill, and between each glanced swiftly over his shoulder at his land-fall. Aeneas, preoccupied as he was, could not fail to admire.

Suddenly, a shout from the starboard oar turned all heads in that direction. A curious wall-like sea was bearing down on them abeam. Frenziedly, Ewan backed-water, to his partner's anguished pulling, and the boat swung round to it gallantly. The wave took them half-astern, and carried them with it, only drenching them with spray. And there, roaring down both on them and on their side-sea, was a huge comber from the old direction. They swept to meet it, powerlessly, furiously as the rowers worked to wrench the *Eala's* head round again. Hopelessly they stared, as the two opposing seas rushed at each other. The noise of thundering waters was deafening now, above the shriek and shout of the wind. The boat was jerked round, spun like a top, and then lifted, up and up. Dizzily they rose, to hang, as it were suspended, motionless, for a breathless eternity, crazily balanced on the curling lip, with a long smooth glissade, veined with foam, ahead of them, and a vast yawning gulf behind. So they hovered and slithered, and then a great gust of wind struck them, blasted them, and flung them forward, onward, down that long smooth slope of waters, down, down the very throat of the sea. Out almost of a trance, Aeneas Graham roused himself, and hurled himself on Frances, to grip her tightly.

Out of a very welter of waters, out of a time unmeasurable by any of her passengers, the *Eala* lifted her weary prow, slowly, sluggishly, fuller than she had ever been. Huddled, dulled, numbed in spirit even more than in body, her people stared. Aeneas felt the girl shudder violently in his arms, and the hurt of it roused him, immediately. They were still afloat, which he had hardly thought possible. The starboard rower was slumped exhausted over his sweep. Aeneas lurched across and pushed him off his thwart unceremoniously, grabbing the oar. Ewan Beg, who had been almost subconsciously pulling, straightened his back again, and recommenced his grievous struggle. The others, spurred by example, groped again for bailers.

In quick succession the seas raced down on them, spurred them, and passed them. It took some time for Aeneas to realize that they were all from the same direction now, and possibly, assuredly, definitely, they were not so large. Also, the noise was less. Impulsively, he turned to Ewan. The skerries . . . ?

The other nodded, in the weariness of reaction. Yes, those were the skerries, back there. They were through.

Lifting up his voice, Aeneas yelled to the girl. They were through! They had crossed the skerries, God be praised! That great comber . . . that side wave . . . between them, had carried them over. He had not realized it. He shouted his relief.

But Ewan was not shouting. They had still to land on an iron-bound coast. Staring over his shoulder, he shook his head. There were one or two small beaches hereabouts, amongst the rocks and cliffs, but none were directly ahead of them. They could make out the most southerly of the houses now, Duncan Og's, the last of them, straight in front. And there was no shingle there. And even on the smoothest sand, with this sea, beaching would be a wild risk. But it was their only hope, nevertheless. There was one thing only he could try. Calling for another man to take his oar, Ewan struggled forward to the bows, and hauled up the sail, half-way.

Heeling, the coble answered to it, heavily, veering round a point or two to the north. It was not enough, though, angrily as the waves struck them aft. Aeneas and his oar was switched across to the port side again, to reinforce the other—a risky move. Immediately they were shipping water again, and the bailers had to work prodigiously. But each wave, each gust, brought them closer to the shore. The roar of the surf was loud before them. If they could keep the foundering craft afloat long enough, there was a small slice of bay just a little farther to the north.

They could see people on the shore, now, watching them. So near and yet so far. How much longer could they keep up this crazy struggle, with each sea looking as though it must be their last? Gasping, reeling, the bailers laboured, but more and more wildly, less and less effectively. The breakers now, nearing the land, were piling up and curling over more venomously, fearsomely. Each one left more of itself in the stricken low-lying boat. She was so heavy to handle, that the oarsmen's fiercest heart-tearing pulling made little or no impression. They were little better than a drifting hulk. And the black jagged rocks were so close, one moment grinning evilly, the next covered in seething white water and soaring spray. It was a matter of minutes and yards, now.

A great platform of weed-hung stone rose out of the streaming water half-ahead, and the *Eala* lurched towards it sideways on. They were almost on top of it, so near that Aeneas had to draw in his oar, before the back-wash of a wave dragged them back a little. Digging their oars in again, the rowers strove, and Ewan, shouting, jerked the sail higher, just as another sea hurled them forward. They swept past that rock so closely that their stern-post grated shudderingly on its cruel flank. But there were others immediately ahead, and the entrance to the little bay was still a hundred yards away.

Ewan was shouting again, and Aeneas suddenly found him beside him, helping to pull his oar. He had tied the sail up, trusting to the water-logged weight of the boat to keep her from otherwise inevitable capsizing. Another man had given up his bailing to assist with the second oar. This was the last throw, the last gamble. The *Eala*, waddling crookedly onward, crab-wise, was picked up and thrown violently, side-long. She scraped and slithered over a ledge, was caught and swept and dragged along a channel between two masses of rock, on an out-going flood, swirled round and tossed onwards again. They struck, with a jarring shock that threw the rowers flat, and wrenched the oars out of their grasp. Another breaker lifted the wrecked boat and carried her crashing on, over tearing rending rock, and flung her and her crew over and over, into deeper water. The *Eala*, smashed and broken and finished, had made the bay.

The happenings of the next minutes defy coherent description. As the coble turned over, Aeneas, winded as he was by the kick of the oar, heaved himself at Frances, gripping her anyhow, anywhere, and so hung on. Flung out and down, drawn on and back, struck by they knew not what, rolled and dragged, the man and the woman clung together. One moment their feet, their knees, were on sand, they were gasping air, the next the black waters were thundering down on them, roaring over them. Aeneas fought as he had never fought in his life, against pounding blows, smothering water, and the vicious undertow of the tide, with toes and knees and elbows and one hand, and all the breathless will-power that was in him, and somehow he held the girl with his other hand, tight as a vice. So they fought, both of them, blindly, faithfully, till a great comber spewed them up bodily on to the shingle, and willing hands gripped them and dragged them up, and laid them down, out of the reach of the ravening sea, still clutching each other.

So they lay, side by side, whom God had joined together.

## 19

ALL six of the *Eala's* people reached the shore, though not all without mishap. The most elderly member of Ewan's crew had a nasty gash where his head had struck a rock, and Ewan himself was half-drowned and unconscious. Aeneas, after he had recovered his breath, and been satisfactorily sick, was fairly fit. He found Frances shivering and exhausted but well enough, and gave thanks for her sturdy constitution. When he had seen her off, in a woman's care, to the nearest croft, he turned to see what he could do for the others, gratefully sustained by a couple of burning mouthfuls of the island's never-failing whisky.

The broken head he bound up as best he could—the man's home was near at hand, fortunately, and his wife present to look after him. The two other members of the crew seemed to have taken little hurt. On Ewan, Aeneas got to work, seeking to pump the water out of his lungs and to restore the circulation of the blood. It was hard work, but the exercise did him almost as much good as it did his patient. Soon his own shivering had gone, and Ewan's painful snoring had given place to an erratic but more natural breathing.

Aeneas, when he had time to think about it, was surprised to see no sign of Lachlan Macgillivray. It had become automatic now, to expect to see him to the fore when anything was toward on the island. There had been no large throng, indeed, awaiting them, and no English-speakers amongst them to give him any information.

Making signs for Ewan to be carried to his uncle's house, and to keep him warm at all costs, Aeneas made for the cottage where Frances had been taken, to find her wrapped in a couple of plaids, by the glowing peat fire. His heart went out to her, there, pale and dark-eyed and bedraggled, but she was cheerful enough and nowise lacking in spirit. Asking after the others, she nevertheless seemed most concerned over the necessity for getting Aeneas out of his sopping clothes, and insisted that he hurry off to the farm-house immediately, running all the way, to change at once, and then go over to the Manse and collect some clothes for her. After an initial very brief, but quite delightful, confusion, she told him fairly exactly what she required and where to get it. He would be finding out about these things soon enough, now, anyway—wasn't he her husband! Obediently he set off to do as he was bid—after an inadequate embrace under the interested eye of the woman of the house.

Staggering and buffeted by the gale, he was nearing the main track that led up from the pier, when he perceived the crowd down at the beach nearby. Wondering if they possibly could still be waiting for the *Eala's* arrival, he hastened down towards them. The people were in two or three groups, and though some were staring out to sea, leaning against the wind, more seemed to be more actively occupied. Murky as it was, he could make out Lachlan Mor's streaming white hair, and thitherwards he made his way.

As he got closer, Aeneas saw a wrecked and shattered boat down amongst the spume and spray of the water's edge. That told him what to expect. The *Eala* was not the only one. People were bending over the bodies on the shingle, working, chafing, staring. A little way apart, a woman sat on a boulder, her plaid completely covering her head, wailing, and by her side a dry-eyed child stood in stricken silence. Only snatches of the woman's keening came to him, weirdly, on the wind.

Aeneas made his presence known to the old man. But this was a different Lachlan Macgillivray, neither calm nor affable nor polite. Wild-eyed, gesticulating, he stared at the newcomer, shouting something in the Gaelic, and turned away forthwith. Beside him knelt his son, Duncan Og, hair and beard plastered flat to his head, as wet as was Aeneas himself. His boat it would be, probably. He was working to revive a fisherman who lay face-downward on the beach, bleeding from nose and ears. The doctor crouched down beside him, frowning.

It took him little time to make his inspection, and he straightened up, shaking his head. No human skill could save this man. Duncan Og glowered at him, and went on with his rubbing, dully.

Aeneas rose, and went across to the next casualty. Here he found a man already responding to treatment, and stirring. He stopped a woman from forcing whisky between the blue lips, and passed on to the third group, surrounding a youth who sat up, being violently sick, with an arm hanging limply. He made a sling and pad for the broken collar-bone out of a woman's kerchief, and left him to his vomiting. Duncan Macgillivray's boat appeared to have had quite as bad a passage as his nephew's.

Lachlan Mor was striding from one knot to another, stumbling in the squalls, muttering, shouting, staring out to sea and up at the lowering sky, occasionally raising his tight-clenched hands to heaven and shaking them, in a wild gesture, part threatening, part supplicating. Now and then his voice rose in a scream, above the screaming of the storm. Saliva was flowing down his beard. Aeneas made sure now that he was mad. The people obeyed the old man under lowered furtive brows, but none spoke to him.

Then a boy came running, waving his arm and pointing up, northwards, along the shore, and beckoning. Most of those watching, immediately turned to follow him, the patriarch amongst them. Aeneas, after a last look at the dying man, hastened after them. He could do nothing more, here.

The lad led them a good half-mile along the machar and rocks of the coast. Then he stopped suddenly, mouth sagging open. His outstretched hand, raised to point, fell back limply, so eloquently. Before them was only empty streaming beaches, tortured waters, and the ragged curtains of spindrift. Whatever the boy had fetched them to see, there was no seeing it now. The whole company stared at the angry, menacing sea, dumbly.

Two more children, running along the shore to them, gasping, fearful, told and pointed and gulped, and it required no knowledge of their language to understand their story. A boat there had been, out there—Nial Maclean's boat; near enough it

165

had been for them to see that. They had watched it come through the skerries by the Beallach nan Partan. They could point to the place it had reached, not far from the shore. And that was all.

Out of the upraised lament of women, the men hastened down to the tide's edge, but a search of the beaches and rocks revealed neither survivors nor bodies. A few of the people remained, to wait hopelessly, but most turned back to the township, Aeneas amongst them. Time that he was getting up to Ruaigmore—Frances would be wondering.

When he left them, near the pier, Lachlan Mor was leading the folk in some sort of monotonous chanting. One more boat, apparently, was still to be accounted for.

Mairi was nowhere to be seen when Aeneas arrived at the house, but before he had stripped and towelled and re-dressed himself, in front of the kitchen fire, she returned, with Ewan and Frances. She had been brought word as soon as they had landed, and with the aid of a couple of farm-women, had hurried down to the shore with changes of clothing for both the men, and some of her own things for Frances. She had a great pot of porridge boiling for them, and altogether was entirely adequate to the occasion—even to the extent of saying nothing abut the agony of her waiting fears. Ewan, though his condition was much improved, was still very shaky, and was despatched to bed forthwith. Mairi advocated the same treatment for Frances, but that one would not hear of it, maintaining that she was perfectly well, and insisting on accompanying Aeneas down to the pier again, when he put forward this intention.

They had heard about Nial Maclean's boat—news travelled fast in that community—and the tragedy of it was upon them all. Five boats had been out at the fishing. Two had drawn in early, and got back safely before the storm broke; Duncan Og's had managed to get through Maclean's Gate, but had struck the rocks as they were beaching it; Callum Ruadh Macgillivray's still was missing. There could be little hope, now.

It was dark, with the darkness of night added to that of the storm. Down near the pier a crowd still kept despairing watch, huddled under the lea of the drying and curing sheds, staring blindly seawards, unwilling to publicly, finally, disavow the hope that they had all inwardly given up, by moving away. It was a silent company, now, with Lachlan Mor disappeared, and woe heavy upon them. Five men were already dead, and four more most likely so.

The gale was blowing itself out, but the seas had not yet reached their climax, and the land shook under their hammer blows. It surely was evident to all that no open boat could hope to live in that maelstrom. There seemed to be little point in waiting there.

Frances and Aeneas were about to move away when a halloo from up the track turned all heads. A young woman came hurrying, calling for Anna Bain, and snatches of her shouting reached them through the gusts of the wind. Her man was safe. They all were safe. They were here, at their own houses. They had got ashore away at the east side of the island, and had crossed over the hills. The boat was not wrecked, itself. Even, they had brought some of their fish with them!

Aeneas had all this translated for him, amid a babblement of relief and thanksgiving and quick laughter. Belated congratulations were offered to Frances and the Doctor on their own escape. Ewan and the other casualties were asked for, the storm discussed, its duration prognosticated. Someone even put forward, tittering, that they had mismanaged things blackly, in not getting the factor drowned on them when they had the chance. Thus went reaction.

Aeneas and Frances walked up the road, arm-in-arm, in silence, busy with their own thoughts, private thoughts, thoughts that at last might be permitted, considered, savoured, out from under the crazy pressure of events. Then, suddenly, the girl pointed.

"What is that?" she wondered. "Over there. It's a fire surely? And . . . that must be up on the hillside—or on the cape, Rudha nan Altair."

"Looks like it," Aeneas agreed. Away to the north, high in the blackness above the black plain of the sea, a small orange glow flared and sank and flared again. "That is the headland, sure enough."

"That is strange." Frances frowned. "What can it be?'

"Lord knows! Perhaps it has been lit as a beacon, to guide in the missing boat?"

"But why there? Why not light it down here, if it was needed—or somewhere where a boat could land? There's only cliffs there. And there is nothing to burn up there, either, but wet heather...."

"Queer, I admit." The man shrugged. "Devilish queer, like a lot else about this island of yours. But I, for one, am not going to investigate—tonight." He squeezed her arm, strongly. "And neither are you. Do you hear?"

"Yes, Aeneas."

"Has it occurred to you that you are my wife—Mistress Aeneas Graham, in person? Have been for some seven hours?"

"Yes, Aeneas."

"And that this is our wedding-night?"

She gulped. "Yes ... Aeneas." He felt her tremble within his arm.

Swiftly he leaned forward, to peer into her eyes. "You are not worried, my dear—frightened?"

"No." She shook her head. "No."

"If you would prefer ... another night? It has been a trying day for you ... ?"

"No, Aeneas." Her voice was no more than a whisper, but it was nowise hesitant. "Tonight. I am just ... very happy." They had reached the side-track that led up to the Manse. Her hand reached out and gripped his, tightly, tensely, as she turned into it. "Come," she said, simply.

They were young and strong, like their love, and they had paid for their happiness out of pain and tears and striving and danger. Are they to be blamed that they lost themselves, as well as the tragedy and sorrow that surrounded them in that place, in their new-found joy? Surely not. They hurt nobody in their so private delight. No one sought aught from them that night—the reverse, indeed; the party that set out, later, furtively, into the blustering dark, northwards along the thundering shore, wanted anything but their company.

## 20

IT was surprising, to Aeneas Graham, how little the storm and its consequences appeared to have affected the life of the island. It might have seemed that Erismore would have crouched cowed under its blows, stunned at her losses—for apart from the sorrow of it all, five able-bodied men was no insignificant proportion of the island's man-power, and three large cobles a third of her fishing fleet—or, allowing for an access of spirit, defiant in the face of cruel fate and indifferent heaven. But Erismore was neither cowed nor defiant. The storm's handiwork was accepted. There had been other storms and other losses, and, no doubt, there would be more to come. With what seemed like a stoicism that was far from typical of their race, the islanders carried on as though little untoward had occurred. Bereaved households continued with the daily work of their crofts neither more urgently nor more lethargically than before. The repair of damaged roofs and dykes and the like was considered and sometimes put in hand, but without unseemly haste. Some part of the great banks of seaweed that the waves had piled up on the shingle, was lifted and carted for fertiliser, and was spread or stored or just left lying, as always. When the seas had abated, the remaining fishing boats put out once more, and plans were made to replace those that had been lost, but not in any hurry. Even Lachlan Macgillivray straightway became his urbane fair-spoken self again, felicitating the doctor and his wife on their wedding and their escape, deploring the unfortunate weather they had had for the occasion, and making neither explanation nor reference to his own unusual conduct of the same day. Aeneas, who had been prepared for some sort of general prostration, and something in the nature of an orgy of self-accusation, announcing that all that had happened was God's visitation upon them for their sins—after the fashion, in disaster, of the Gael that he knew—was disappointed. He had an idea that Finlay MacBride would have been disappointed, also.

Not that he was more than superficially concerned, it must be admitted. Aeneas and Frances were happy, happy with a completeness, an entirety, and a oneness, that was greater, finer, than anything that they could have imagined. They were absorbed in each other, self-sufficient, discovering in one another each day and each night fresh attributes and gifts and facets of person and personality, and with wonder at what they found. Themselves they took and accepted joyfully, wholeheartedly, unstintingly, as became them, a whole man and a whole woman, complemented and made entire in their union. It is not all who wed, who are thus married.

But a certain diminution of interest in the affairs of others, and in what went on around them, was inevitable. Were they to be blamed for that? Not by their neighbours on Erismore, so much is certain.

And yet it was their neighbour's need that aroused them, at last, and turned their eyes outward again. It required something like a cataclysm to jolt them out of their honeymooning.

It was mid-March, with lighter airs blowing out of the west, and the earth itself stirring sensibly to its annual rebirth, that Mairi Macgillivray's pains came upon her. With her time approaching, the girl had become increasingly nervous, anxious—strangely so, as Aeneas saw it, for she was a level-headed young woman and no physical coward, he would swear. But that she was worried was obvious, as was the fact that it was to the doctor that she looked for help. Not that she would put a name to her fears, beyond the generalities that she hoped that nothing would go wrong, and that all would be well with her son—she was determined on a boy, it seemed—and the repeated insistence that he, the doctor, must be present at the birth. Aeneas reassured her constantly; everything was in order. She was well-made for the task, and the child was normally placed; all pointed to an easy birth, insofar as birth ever was easy. But she must stop worrying—the mind was important in this matter, almost as

171

important as the body. She had let herself become affected by misfortunes that had attended one or two other births lately, the result of carelessness, ignorance, and folly. She need fear none of that. And he would be with her, he promised—yes, all the time.

Ewan, her husband, seemed to be anxious, too, though he made a point of not admitting it. But if he did not confide in the doctor, Aeneas more than once found him eyeing him with an impotent helpless appeal, that told its own story.

It was in the forenoon that Mairi's pangs started, and a girl came hurrying across to the Manse, demanding the doctor. A brief examination showed that it would not be for some hours yet, probably not until the evening, and he told her what to do and how best to bear the pains meantime, and when to send for him. She was in a highly nervous state, he was sorry to see, and did not want him to leave her. But to sit beside her all day would be ridiculous, and only pandering to her fears. He promised that Frances would come over to be with her, and that he would be back in plenty of time. As he went, she called him back to urge that he tell no-one as to her state—not even to send for Ewan, who was away dragging timber for the new boat.

Twice during the day he saw her, and each time she asked him if there was no way in which he could bring the child on more quickly. He assured her that it would be foolish to attempt any such thing when everything was so satisfactory; she must just have patience and be brave. He had never imagined that she would be so difficult. But she made no complaint about her pain.

In the evening, when he arrived, it was to find the house full. Lachlan Mor was there, with Ewan, and his uncle Duncan Og, and the midwife Kirsty Cameron. Mairi, her pangs regular now and working towards a climax, was verging on a panic. They must not come near her, she cried—none of them, not even Ewan. She would not have them in the room—only the Doctor and Frances. Aeneas advised Ewan that he would be wise to accede, and that anxious young man agreed unhappily. His grandfather was less easily convinced, talking about headstrong foolish lassies, unnatural conceits, and the price of inexperience.

172

The midwife too was much offended. But Aeneas was firm on Mairi's behalf, and the disgruntled visitors remained with the husband in the kitchen. Upstairs, in the glow of the peat fire and the smoky light of a fish-oil lamp, Mairi sweated and laboured and fought her own fight, in the company of her own choosing.

It was as Aeneas had foretold—as births went, not difficult. There was no complication, no undue delay, nothing that was not to be expected. In her actual labour, Mairi made an excellent patient, her fears and alarm apparently forgotten. She was quiet, helpful, and courageous, with scarce a cry out of her—till the moment when Aeneas stooped down over her relaxing body with the gently-stirring morsel of humanity in his arms, smiling.

"It is all right, now, Mairi," he assured "All over. A fine child—strong and healthy. See."

She opened her eyes, slowly. "*Brogach* . . . a boy?" she demanded.

He shook his head. "I'm afraid not. But she is a fine sturdy child. . . ."

Then she cried, a single piercing anguished cry, half sat up, and collapsed back, her eyes closed, her strength finished.

Ewan appeared at the door, agitated, with his grandfather and the others peering behind him. "*De tha tigh'n* . . . What is it? Is she all right?" he wondered. "We heard her cry . . . ?"

"Yes, she is all right. Everything has gone very well. It is a girl. She seemed to be very distressed that it was not a boy—that is all. That is what she cried out about . . ."

"A girl . . . !" Ewan's glance sank slowly to the floor, as he turned, and then lifted to meet that of Lachlan Mor. "*Caileag* . . . !"

The old man was staring, with a strange almost exultant look in those colourless eyes. "A girl, indeed!" he said. "Why not, then," and he laughed, a short quavering laugh, so old, that stopped as suddenly as it had commenced, and the only laugh that Aeneas ever had heard out of him—or wanted to hear.

For a space there was silence in that upper room, to be broken by the thin sound of the baby's crying.

"Do you not want to see it, then—and her?" the doctor demanded, his voice grating.

They came in, then, all of them, Ewan to the bed where his wife lay in a swoon of exhaustion, the old man to the child that Frances held in her arms, the midwife following. She made to take the baby from the younger woman, but Frances shook her head and drew it closer, wordlessly. There was little joy and felicity in that birth-chamber.

The doctor drove them all out after only a few moments. He had work to do yet. The afterbirth had still to come away. If Mairi wanted her husband, he would send down for him.

When, half-an-hour or so later, Aeneas and Frances tiptoed downstairs, it was to find Ewan crouched over the kitchen fire, alone with a bottle of whisky.

"She is asleep, now," the doctor told him. "I had to give her something to help her over. Don't disturb her, and she should be all right for the night. Sleep is what she needs."

Ewan, just a little drunk, nodded, unspeaking.

Aeneas coughed. "She should come round presently—be herself again—in her attitude to you, I mean. Be kind to her, make something of a fuss of her. . . . She seems to be vastly disappointed that it is not a boy. You, too, I think? That is foolish, surely?"

The other only stared into the fire.

"Never fear, Ewan—she loves you dearly," Frances told him, in the Gaelic. "She is not quite herself just now—and little wonder, indeed. You will both be very happy with your baby, I know." She touched his bent shoulder lightly. "If you should need me—a woman—do not hesitate to send for me."

At the door, Aeneas looked back. "And I would keep your grandfather away from Mairi for a bit, if I were you," he advised significantly. "He seems to have an unfortunate effect upon her!"

Ewan Macgillivray, on his stool, did not even turn round.

It would be three or four hours later, and after midnight, that Frances sat up in their bed, and gripped and shook her

174

husband's arm. "Aeneas—wake up !" she cried. "Listen!"

Drowsily he heaved himself up on an elbow. "Somebody at the door," he announced profoundly. "Ewan it will be, maybe . . ."

"No—that's not Ewan. There was a woman's cry, sobbing, I'm sure. There . . . !"

There could be no question of it. And the knocking at their door was a wild uneven banging. Man and woman leapt out of bed, throwing a dressing-robe and a plaid about them, and hurried downstairs.

Leaning half-naked against the door-post, all but collapsed, was Mairi Macgillivray, panting, her hair hanging about her, her eyes wild. A flood of gasping Gaelic burst from her lips at sight of them. Aeneas, unhesitating, picked her up in his arms and hurried through to the Manse kitchen with her, Frances throwing her own plaid about her. And Mairi, broken-voiced, raved on.

"She says that they have stolen her baby!" Frances cried. "She says it is dead. Lachlan Mor has taken it . . ."

"But this is crazy! She's been dreaming, probably—her mind unhinged. How the devil she got here . . . ! She'll kill herself—a hæmorrhage . . . pneumonia . . . Where in God's name is Ewan . . . ?"

But Mairi was gripping him, fiercely, almost shouting in her frenzy, railing, urging, pleading. It was gibberish to the man, but Frances made something out of it all.

"She insists that it is true—they've taken her child. Ewan is gone, too. She says they locked her in—she had to smash a window and climb out . . ."

The man cut her short. "Let that be, just now. We'll have to get her warm, settled, or it will be the end of her. We'll put her in our own bed. Tell her I'll look after everything for her—tell her I'll find her baby for her . . . but she must come upstairs to bed. I'll carry her. Try to calm her."

Staggering, for she was a big well made woman, Aeneas carried Mairi, sobbing and moaning, upstairs. In their warm bed, she would not lie down, but crouched, swaying from side to side, muttering, as Aeneas and his wife threw on some clothes. They talked to her soothingly, rationally, the while, trying to assure her that all would be well, that she must take care of herself for her own sake and the child's sake. That the baby would be all right. Probably Ewan had taken it to show to some neighbours—he had some drink in him, and might not see the foolishness of it. He would bring it back, none the worse. Perhaps he had the midwife looking after it. Ewan would never let any harm come to the baby. . . .

But she would not listen to them, would not be comforted. Aeneas saw that the only way to calm her was to find the child itself. He would go across to the farmhouse himself, straight away. Frances should get in beside her—keep her warm. He would not be long.

He came back in a few minutes, grim-faced. Yes, it was as she had said. The doors were barred, and the house was empty. He had climbed in through the shattered window—how she had got out, in her condition, Heaven knew! There were no lights showing from any of the houses round about. This was stark madness!

Mairi was only semi-conscious now, and her snatches of talk were rambling and incoherent. "She blames us for leaving her—says we promised not to," Frances told him, horror in her eyes. "She says she knew that this would happen. It is Lachlan Mor. And she keeps talking about Rudha nan Altair!"

"Rudha nan Altair! Good Lord!" They stared at each other. "D'you think . . . ?" He hurried from the room, to a window at the other side of the house, and came back, tight-lipped.

"There is a light up there on the hill-top," he said harshly. The man squared his shoulders. "I am going there now."

"But, Aeneas . . . No, you must not. . . ."

"I must," he said fiercely. "It is time that this thing was looked into, high time."

"Then I am coming, too. . . ."

"No," he said, commanded. "You'll stay here. You can't leave Mairi—she's more important than the child. You must look after her. This is no ploy for a woman." She clung to him

176

now, and he kissed her gently. "I'll be all right. I'll be careful, I promise you."

"No, Aeneas—no! You must not . . ."

He put her from him, firmly. "I'm going. It is my duty, girl. And I will take Finlay's musket. . . ."

## 21

A ENEAS took the northward track, long-strided. It was a quiet night and mild, with only a faint air from off the western ocean to rustle the grasses of the machar and match the sighing of the ceaseless swell. Already the nights were losing the pitchiness of their dark, in anticipation of that northern summer that knows but little night at all, and he had no difficulty in following the contortions of the path, that wound its way precariously between the black hills and the wan pallor of the sea, now at the very margin of the making tide, now high up amongst the rocks and heather of the brae-side. Ahead, the dark mass of the headland reared itself starkly against uncertain sea and empty sky, with the fitful flickering gleam of fire at its summit, no uncertain beacon to draw him on.

The man's hurrying purposeful walking was no pointer to the variety of his emotions. He was angry, of course, that Mairi Macgillivray should have been treated thus, that the child should be so endangered, that his own work should be nullified and confounded—also, despite all the practise he had had in the wars, he reacted badly to being forced to get up from his bed in the middle of the night. But he was fearful, too, for the mother and the baby, and in some measure for himself as well—since he was no fool. And he was curious, intrigued, to get to the root and cause of it all, to uncover the secret of this island, and yet repelled by the nameless dread of what he might reveal. He was not unimaginative, the man, for all the sober habit of his appearance and conversation, and the certainty that he was dealing with a great evil was strong upon him. But that it was time that he came to grips with this thing, this mystery, this shadow on Erismore, this bogey of Finlay's, he knew no manner of doubt. So he strode, up and down, around the great sickle of the bay, his musket in the crook of his arm.

As he lifted upwards, on to the cliffs proper, the summit of

Rudha nan Altair, and the light with it—a fire, obviously, and similar to that they had seen on the night of the storm—was hidden from his view by the lie of that land. But his direction was unmistakable and his path well-defined, and he mounted steadily, till presently he reached that last hollow before the soaring crown of the cape, where he had first become aware of the raucous concourse of the seabirds that day three months before. He was nearer the cliff edge this time, however, than then, when he had approached it from the hills behind, and from far below him he still could hear the sough and murmur of the waves. And as he climbed, further, another sound came to him, tenuous and high and searching, quivering—not the screaming of gulls this time, but the thin strains of that crazy fiddle. The very hairs of his head lifted as he heard it.

Arriving thus from seawards, he reached the summit much more abruptly than he had done before, with the sheer face of the cliff dropping away dizzily to his left, north-westwards. Suddenly, then, he saw and heard, and halted, dumbfounded.

Two fires blazed on that benighted hilltop, one large on the ground, and one smaller, at the end of the great stone table, and by the smoky eddying lurid light of them a throng of gesticulating figures milled and pranced and gyrated. Up, above them, as it were on the steps of the altar, Lachlan Macgillivray crouched, tall but bent-shouldered, fiddling, and behind and around them a mass of onlookers stood and shuffled and swayed. And the shouts and screeching of the dancers, and the chanting and moaning of the watchers, rose and sank and surged around the horrible oscillation of the fiddle, that soared above and persisted, and dominated them all, barbarous, devilish.

It was at the dancers that Aeneas stared—if what they did could be named dancing. There would be a dozen or more of them, men and women, young and old, frenzied, lost in the delirium of abandon. None were fully clothed, and the women were bare to the waist, their skirts hitched high, and one was completely naked. They leapt and twisted and contorted themselves, stamping feet, waving arms, clapping hands, gesturing madly, obscenely, and yet with some system and pattern, some rhythm, under the urgent spell of that frantic discordant music. Round and round the rocky plinth they circled and capered, and even as he watched, one or another dropped out exhausted, to be succeeded by others from the ranks of the watchers, casting clothing from them as they danced and curvetted.

As his eyes became accustomed to the wavering light, the man perceived that there were not a few figures lying on the ground, many of them coupled, clothed or otherwise—but not all prostrate with exhaustion, by any means. Disgusted, he felt ready to vomit. Presumably these had recovered from the first stage of their exertions. Evidently this wild circus, this orgy, had been going on for some time, despite the pace of it. Lachlan Mor looked ready to drop, certainly, furiously as he still was fiddling. As Aeneas moved forward warily, nearer the circle of murky light, his boot kicked against an empty bottle, cast away thus, seaward. He nodded, grimly.

Beyond the mere awareness of some design, some theme, to their dancing, he could make nothing of it, nothing significant. But the other weird picture of that place, vivid before his mind's eye, of whirling, striving, screaming birds, milling about that same symbol of sacrificial rock, was not to be dismissed as irrelevant. And the noise was like enough, in all conscience. There was a parallel, an association, somewhere, meaning behind it all, murky as the light in which it proceeded. Those figures that darted constantly out from the throng towards the central altar, well might represent the gulls that braved the eagles' wrath . . . ?

And then, as a flare-up of the fire coincided with his advance, Aeneas saw it. There was something on the altar, as well as the blowing fire, something small but essential, isolated. . . . By Heavens, it was a child, a baby, naked, exposed—Mairi Macgillivray's baby! Merciful God . . . !

Aeneas Graham went berserk.

That none of the crowd perceived his approach is not to be wondered at perhaps, considering the darkness and their trance-like preoccupation, but even when he was pushing angrily through the jostling dancers he was barely noticed. It was Lachlan Macgillivray himself who, despite his seeming stupor of passion and exhaustion, saw him first—or at least, reacted to the sight. Almost as though it had been throttled, that violin choked into silence, as the old man stiffened and stilled, and though the dancers' skirling did not cease with it, at once, the watchers' chanting did, and quickly enough the last hysterical laughs and drunken shout died away, and a hush, tense and brittle, settled on that hilltop. The patriarch lifted an arm to point at the intruder, wordlessly, and the fiddle-bow quivered in his hand.

Aeneas, in his wrath, had not paused, even for a moment. Unmolested, he had reached the foot of the great table of rock. Now, in the face of that pointing, wavering bow and baleful glassy stare, he ran up the worn natural steps of it, and reached out for the child.

A single snarling scream rang out, rageful, commanding, and Lachlan Mor flung down the fiddle and rushed at him. Aeneas, in the act of picking up the baby, jerked around the altar, to keep it between himself and the other's onset. Even as he did so, he heard the beat of heavy running feet below him, and whirled about to meet the attack. It was Duncan Og, his coarse face contorted with fury, a bottle upraised as a club in his great fist. In his extremity, the younger man realized that he still clutched Finlay's musket in his arms, unprimed and forgotten. Quick as thought, he gripped it by the muzzle, and swung it, up and round and down. Its longer reach, and his elevated position at the top of the steps gave him the advantage. The musket stock crashed down on the side of Duncan Macgillivray's head with a sickening crunch, and the big man lurched forward with the impetus of his charge and fell headlong, the bottle flying out of his hand and splintering to fragments on the rock.

Surprisingly light on his feet, the old man was nearly upon him. Scrambling round, almost losing his footing on the narrow ledge, Aeneas managed to keep the breadth of the altar between them, his every perception keyed to sense the next assault from behind. Lachlan Mor was shouting now, in wild Gaelic, a

181

torrent of menace and imprecation. For a moment there was no movement in that evil place but the spasmodic flaming of the fires; whether out of reaction, momentarily stupefied by their excesses, palsied by the suddenness of it all, or regardful of what had happened to Duncan Og, no man stirred or lifted voice to add to the virulent stream of Lachlan's invective.

But the pause was only transitory. With a strangled gasp, the old man came at him again, and Aeneas, as he edged round, felt rather than saw the crowd sway forward, move in on him. The seconds were numbered now, he knew. Suddenly he stumbled and all but fell, and his weapon slithered away out of his grasp. He had tripped over the outstretched Duncan. Desperately he flung himself away, onward, with the other almost on top of him, only saved by the fact that Lachlan Mor did the same, tumbling over his unconscious son. Gripping the edge of the altar to pull himself round, Aeneas found his hand actually in the fire. He knew no pain, but his mind reacted to the shock. Violently he reached over with his left hand and grabbed the child, and, almost in the same motion, he dashed his right into that fire and swept it in a flaming shower directly in the face of his adversary. Almost overbalanced, he managed to twist round, to stagger and totter down the steps. And, head down, blindly, he ran, with the baby clutched to him, and his free arm swinging right and left wildly, cleaving a passage through the confused throng. Madly he struck and was struck. Ferociously he kicked and fought and butted. Somehow, he broke through.

Thus, he ran, slipping, stumbling, toppling, over bodies and stones and heather and he knew not what, in what direction he knew not, with only his purpose coherent in him—to get himself and the child away from that place, anyhow, anywhere. Heedless of all save that urgent need, he ran, and the ground heaved beneath him and fell before him and rose up and hit him, as he plunged onward.

He could hear the footfalls and shouting behind him, but he did not look back. Thirty, forty yards he went, and then an unseen hollow in the ground engulfed him and brought him down. As he fell, instinctively, he held the baby clear. And as he rose, reeling, a fearsome sight was upon him. Lachlan Macgillivray, leaping crazily, came bounding down at him, his clothes afire, his hair afire, his beard afire, shrieking, yelping, slavering. Straight at his unsteady quarry he launched himself, like some tattered thunderbolt, arms flailing. Throwing himself backward, Aeneas managed to avoid the full impact, and the old man fell head-foremost across his legs and feet. Furiously Aeneas kicked and squirmed and twisted. Even with the child to hold, he was on his feet sooner than the other, his young agility responding more swiftly even than the uncanny strength of Lachlan's madness. Gulping for breath, he hesitated. There were others coming. He could not fight with the baby in his arms. Breaking away, he lurched on.

And then, with the vehemence of utter despair, he threw himself down, on his back, slithering forward, downward, digging in his heels convulsively, grabbing, scrabbling at the soil and heather and rock with his one hand, seeking with every nerve and muscle to force his body backward, unnaturally, against the pull of gravity and his own momentum. With only inches to spare, he stopped himself.

And from behind, Lachlan Macgillivray came pounding. Too late he saw what Aeneas had seen, too late he sought to stop his headlong career. Blind with fury, distracted with pain, crazy, beside himself, his aged body failed him. Gabbling, he hurtled past, lunging at Aeneas in a last frenzy of malice as he went, on and out and over, into void. And the lost howl of him, as he fell, lifted high, quivering, discordant as his own fiddling, echoing back and back from the surrounding cliffs to end suddenly, abruptly, entirely, and for ever.

At last, as out of a dream, a nightmare, Aeneas got to his feet, and turned round slowly. Above him, at a distance, the mass of the people stood, in a half circle, silent, immobile. Wilting, limp, stricken, staring into the emptiness that had taken their Elder, their Catechist, their leader, they stood, while the man at the cliff-edge stared back at them. Then, even as he watched, the solidity of the mass began to move, to thin, to dissolve, to melt away before his eyes. Soon, none remained on the crest of that

183

headland, save only Aeneas Graham and his charge. Stooping, he folded the pathetic bundle deep inside his coat, and wearily, shakily, turned away and left Rudha nan Altair to the night.

## 22

IN the days that followed, Aeneas Graham fought for that child as hard as he had fought for it on the summit of Rudha nan Altair. It had to live, and it lived. The mildness of the night had helped, of course, and the fire that had borne it company on the table of that grim altar. And its constitution was sound and strong, like that of its mother. For Mairi survived also, and fought gallantly, for the child's sake if not for her own or that of the pale ghost of a man who lurked miserably about the Manse door, daily, to ask for his wife and daughter.

And, her lips unsealed at last, the oath of secrecy that Lachlan Macgillivray had made her swear no longer valid, Mairi talked, in her relief and gratitude. What was there to be silent for, now? In fragments and outbursts and answers to questioning, in formal English and free Gaelic, piece by piece, the story was told.

It was an old story, older than history, older than Columba and Ninian and Christianity, as old as time itself. The bold saints brought Christ to the islands, and established Him there by the fire of their conviction, and by their stout right arms often as not, but it seemed that they did not altogether succeed in dethroning the former deities at the same time. Not on Erismore, at anyrate, a savage storm-girt isle that had worshipped Iolair Mor, the Eagle One, the Storm God of the Seas, who had ruled supreme in the Northern Ocean since the world was born out of the womb of the Mother Tempest. Erismore had accepted Christ as a kindly, humble, harmless divinity, for peace's sake, and largely because of His interest in the fishing and fishermen, and His reputed ability to still the seas. But when storms continued to ravage and assail the islanders, they had restored Iolair Mor alongside the new Christ, for safety. But it made only a difficult partnership, for Iolair Mor's ways were not Christ's ways, and to placate the one often meant offending the other. Uncomfortably duo-theistic, Erismore continued, then, down the centuries.

Thus went the tales and legends and songs of the ceilidh-house. So much, all the West knew, for it had been a situation common enough amongst those islands. But, Mairi imagined, elsewhere such practises and beliefs had faded under the weight of the ages and the constant testimony and progressive control of the Church, faded and died and been forgotten. But not on Erismore—not altogether; faded, yes, hidden away perhaps, and covered up, but not dead, and not forgotten. The remoteness of the place, no doubt, the hostility of its treacherous seas and currents, the inaccessibility of its havenless coasts, accounted for it backsliding—as well as the stresses under which its folk subsisted. But on Erismore, the cult of Iolair Mor, the Storm God, remained something more than just a legend and a story for the sennachies, even when the milder sway and more equivocal doctrines of the Mother Church gave place to the stern yoke of the Kirk of Scotland. Perhaps the later Kirk had been less interested in Erismore than were the early saints. As they would know, there came a time when the minister died and the parish lapsed and the church fell into ruin, and for more than a hundred years Erismore was left to go its own way—until, indeed, Mr. MacBride came to rebuild what had fallen to ruin. The Eagle One had maybe made greater progress than had the Prince of Peace, in those hundred years.

Yet, from all accounts, it was only a half-hearted and cautious sort of worship that Iolair Mor got out of the island, at least in living memory, till Lachlan Mor came back from his travels. Where he had been and what he had been doing in the twenty years that he was away, no one knew. But when he returned he was a very different man from when he went, all agreed. Mairi thought that probably his mind had become affected. But mad or sane, he started up the cult of the Storm God again, not just passively as it had been for centuries, but actively, vigorously, working it up to its full intensity, with himself as High Priest. He did not deny Christ altogether, of course—though she thought that he had little faith in Him, especially where storms were concerned—and got himself appointed Elder and Catechist, as an obvious precaution. It would not be difficult, and him the only man of any learning and experience of the world on the island, as well as its tacksman as his fathers had been before him. So he came to have complete power in Erismore, representing both of the Gods and the laird as well. This was the way of things when Mr. MacBride arrived.

Mairi had been sorry for Mr. MacBride, desperately sorry. He had not had a chance, of course, from the first. She had been young then, a mere girl, but she would have told him, warned him, but for the oath her grandfather had made them all swear. It would have gone ill with anyone who had broken that oath, for Iolair Mor was a jealous god, too, and did not restrict his worst punishments to the next world, like the God of the Kirk. And Lachlan Macgillivray was very zealous in his service. Especially after the great storm in which her father and two other sons of Lachlan's had been drowned. That, she thought, had set the zeal upon his madness—and on his hatred for her mother and herself.

It was the night after she was born, and her mother had refused to do the thing that Iolair Mor demanded, and her husband had supported her. She was a strong woman, was her mother, and not an islander at all, and from the first Lachlan had disapproved of her. But Ian, her father, had loved her deeply, and defied the old man on her account. So she, Mairi, was not offered up to the Storm God—and the next day her father and his brothers, and others as well, were drowned. For that was the price of the Eagle One's goodwill; every first-born female child must be offered up, exposed upon the altar of Rudha nan Altair, for his use and purpose. Few indeed survived. Those who did became Brides of the God, priestesses of the storm, and might not marry mortal men. They were supported by the islanders, and it was their duty to feed the minions of the god, the sea-eagles, with the best of the fish that the fishermen caught, and to lead in the ritual dances and revels of the cult—for Iolair Mor was no sober sanctimonious god. Such were Seana Macvicar, and Kirsty Cameron the midwife. Those who did not survive were taken straight to his Palace of the Winds, and became eagles, to serve their master in a higher sphere. But her mother— her mother disobeyed, and paid for her disobedience; the Eagle One took her, no doubt by the blood-stained hand of Lachlan Mor, her father-in-law.

And since that day, her grandfather had watched her, Mairi, as a cat watches a mouse. She, his grand-daughter, alone upon the island, was a first-born woman child that had not been offered to Iolair Mor on the night of her birth. She, in her person, was responsible for the deaths of her mother and father and uncles. She, one day, would pay the price. Thus he had brought her up, and married her to Ewan that was to be his heir, and prepared her. Only so could the stain be wiped out. She had been in horror when she became pregnant, and terrified lest the child should be a girl. Ewan, though he loved her, was no use to her— he had been quite under the old man's sway. And then Doctor Graham had come, and she had clutched at him as the drowning clutch at a straw. And the straw had held, had saved her, and saved her child. Glory be to God!

All this they learned, and more, marvelling. It was time that it was told.

Lachlan Mor Macgillivray's body was never found. Perhaps the sea-eagles took him to Iolair Mor himself, in his Palace of the Winds in the cold heart of the northern sea, there to play his mad music on the wild harps of the storm. Perhaps his gift for distilling would be much in demand at that riotous court where the tempests were born. Perhaps . . . But no man saw him again, and few spoke of him. If any mourned him, they did not do so openly.

His silent son, Duncan Og, may have been but little affected physically by the blow that Aeneas Graham had dealt him, but in himself the events of that night made a stricken man of him, nevertheless. For days he shut himself within his own house, seeing nobody, and then, one night, he and his patched-up boat disappeared. Where he went, no one ever knew—nor sought to find out.

Ewan Beg worked his hard way to his own salvation. His child's birth-night had added years to his age and something went out of him that would never return. He had not been present at the bacchanal on the headland—indeed, he had been lying deliberately drunk and insensible in his own cowshed throughout that night, a broken reed. His humiliation became a garment for him, and his self-reproach was ever with him. In time, Mairi took him back, for she could not hate him. He was her husband, even if he had failed her; her's was a generous soul, and life for her was starting anew.

As for the people of Erismore, it appeared that the whole affair was to be dismissed and forgotten, by mutual consent. Neither by word nor act nor demeanour was their attitude altered towards the occupants of the Manse—on the face of it, at anyrate, though perhaps a certain wariness of glance and urgency of affability might have been noticed by the noticing. Perhaps, indeed, it was the wisest course. Little was to be gained from a state of hostility and suspicion, on either side. The Gael, whatever his faults and weaknesses, takes ill to churlishness. And Frances and Aeneas, again, were well enough content to let bygones be bygones.

It was perhaps a week after that eventful night, with Mairi and the child fit to be left to their own devices for a while, that the Grahams took a walk round the bay to the headland of Rudha nan Altair. Aeneas had something like a repugnance for the spot, and would gladly have avoided it, but Finlay's musket had never been retrieved, and Frances confessed to a certain fascination, an inclination to look upon the place with enlightened eyes. They found the weapon, without difficulty—indeed, it had been placed, significantly or otherwise, on top of the altar, and lay there rusty a little but undamaged. And that was all that they found. No sign of the ongoings of the previous week remained, whatever traces had been left on the night in question; Lachlan Macgillivray's fiddle and bow were gone, the empty bottles were gone—understandable enough, perhaps, for these were precious—but the ashes of the fires were removed, even the blackened marks of them obliterated, and the splinters of broken glass were gone likewise. Not even a fish scale adhered to that rocky plinth. More than breeze and rain had been busy here. Only the time-worn stones, the weather-polished gravel and grit, the mosses and lichens and thin wiry heather remained. The cycle was complete, the story told, the chapter finished. The man and the woman left that place unspeaking, to the thin sighing of the wind.

At the foot of the hill, they turned and looked back.

"There it is," Frances said. "The source of all the trouble. The answer to the question. Rudha nan Altair—empty, swept and garnished."

"Swept and garnished," the man repeated. "I wonder? You remember the sequel? He went and took seven other devils more wicked than himself—and the last state was worse than the first!"

"No." She shook her head decidedly. "That is over, done, finished with. I know it—I know these people. Lachlan Mor has failed. Their Storm God has failed them—if they ever really believed. They are left ashamed, humiliated. And though they can stand defeat and failure, they cannot abide disgrace. Always that has been the way. And it is you that has done it, Aeneas. You have confounded the Devil. You have finished Finlay's work for him. Finlay can rest in peace, now."

They turned their backs on it all, and stared out over the wimpling limitless sea, calm now under the pale spring sunlight, but heaving gently, inexorably, with its ceaseless swell. And the man's arm slipped as gently round the girl, and he drew him to her as inexorably.

"You are a very . . . adequate sort of man, aren't you, Aeneas," she murmured.

"Am I?"

She glanced at him, and at his look a flush mounted slowly from her throat. "Yes," she whispered, her eyes shining. "And I should know . . . shouldn't I!"

## EPILOGUE

THE factor's hail came up to them as they sat by the roadside, at the first group of outcrops above the township. Always it had been a favourite haunt of the girl's today it was more than that. Aeneas Graham rose, his hand on his wife's shoulder. But still she stared, urgently, her gaze lingering on every feature and vista and landmark, of croft and bay and cliff and sea, as though she could not see enough of them, familiar as they all must be to her. And yet, perhaps, there was something strange about it all, some aspect of the view that was not so familiar. For though the rocks and heather and waves could not change, the works of men's hands, so much less enduring, could—and had done. It was amazing indeed, how they had changed, all of them— eloquent testimony to Ezra Mitchell's thoroughness. And though such represented only an inconsiderable proportion of that wide panorama, it was remarkable how they drew and held the eye. Well might she stare.

From that viewpoint, thirty houses, perhaps, were visible— the Manse, two that could be termed farmhouses, and the rest crofts and black-houses. And of them all, only two, the Manse and Ruaigmore, now supported a roof, and of the rest few indeed were more than a heap of stones and turf. About the tiny irregular fields, scratched wherever the grudging soil allowed a foot of depth, the dry-stone dykes were levelled and scattered. No small shaggy cattle nor long-maned garrons grazed on the rough pasture. No figures worked at the hay—though it was mid-July, and the bog-hay ripe for cutting—nor at the peat- digging, nor about the byres and steadings. There were no byres and steadings any more, save at Ruaigmore, and there only the factor's men were busy—and not at farmwork. Indeed, except for them, there was not any sign of life on all the island, nor any movement save the sparkle of the burns in the sun, and the cloud-shadows at their quiet drifting, and the single plume of smoke that rose up from the curing-shed near the pier—not from its usually so busy chimney, now, but from the last charred embers of its fallen roof. The other buildings and crofts could have shown a plume like that, too, of course—but not today; that was all done with, finished. And beyond the skerries, far out in the Sound, two boats sailed, small and lonely-seeming on the empty glittering plain of the sea, westwards towards the faint blur that was Barra of the Outer Hebrides, the last of the fishing-boats of Erismore, bearing Ewan Macgillivray and his wife and daughter and such of their worldly goods as they could carry, seeking fresh fishing-grounds and pastures new—but scarcely seeking hopefully.

But the factor's hail had been peremptory, and it was not to be supposed that he would look kindly on any delay to his sailing, on account of a woman's mere sentimental mooning. And, unfortunately, he was in a position to show his preferences, with no uncertain voice; he held a sheriff's warrant in his pocket for the clearance of the whole island, for the eviction of all tenants, for the distraint and impounding of all goods, chattels, effects, stock, and unmovable property, in lieu of unpaid rents. All this he had, and more; full powers to exert his master's will on Lord Dunalastair's property of Erismore, now ripe for improvement—with a sheriff-officer and half-a-dozen of the laird's minions to help him do it. He was in no state to be trifled with, was Ezra Mitchell; in the last week they had been left in no doubt about that. Even Aeneas Graham had to admit it, grimly. It was a couple of days, at least, since he had ceased protesting, in anything more active than his general attitude.

Even the factor, of course, had not been able legally to dispossess the occupants of the Manse before the next Martinmas term, the doctor having paid the stipulated rent in full when the creature had come surveying the island's possibilities previously. At first Aeneas was for staying on, to thwart him—for the estate wanted the Manse as residence for the sheep-run manager, that was going to make pounds out of Erismore's upheaved acres where the crofters' rents had made only shillings—but Frances had convinced him otherwise; there could be neither sense nor satisfaction in remaining once the islanders were gone, with only a disgruntled manager and two Lowland shepherds and some thousands of baa-ing sheep for company, even to spite Dunalastair and his factor. Better to go now, with the others, than to wait on, in barren discomfort. She had been right, of course, and he had agreed; but it had gone against the grain.

They walked down the track together, in silence. There was nothing to say; all that could be said had been said, in reproach and pleading, in anger and sorrow. What little they could do, they had done—what tragically little—to mitigate the blow, with sympathy and a kind word, with helping hands and a little organizing ability. Perhaps their presence had restrained the factor's men from the worst excesses; there had been no bloodshed, at anyrate, and a minimum of blows—though that, it may be, was accounted for more by the people's stunned acceptance of their fate rather than by mediating influence. They knew that their cause was hopeless, of course; this clearance and eviction was an old story, wind of which had come to them from the mainland for many years, where whole provinces had been depopulated and handed over to the nibbling sheep. And the war was over now, and their menfolk no longer needed to fill the Highland regiments. What use to kick against the pricks? Advice, Aeneas and Frances had given; but how inadequate, when the only choice lay between going to one of the already over-populated islands of the Outer Hebrides—for the mainland was barred to them—or sailing in one of the dreaded immigrant ships for the Canadas, provided by thoughtful authority anxious to fill the vacuum of a tenuous empire. Some small help they may have given in the matter of bargaining with the factor over goods and plenishings, but of what avail was that when there was so pitifully little space allowed in the boats for household goods to be transported—and Mitchell paid no gold for property left behind. Only the man's doctoring skill had been of real service—to prolong the agony of the ailing and the aged. That was the way it had been, that past unholy week.

They did not pause at the Manse. All their things that they

were taking were already down at the pier, stowed in the factor's ketch. Mitchell, by his way of it, had been very generous, offering them passage to Tobermory, and infinitely more storage-space for their belongings than had been the lot of the islanders. It would have been crazy to refuse it, yet the acceptance stuck in Aeneas Graham's throat; but he owed it to Frances—they were her things, after all—and that much he could do for her, the last bitter dose.

On the vessel, they were awaited impatiently. Everyone else was aboard, and anxious to be gone from this barbarous place. Only two of the factor's men were left, as caretakers of the island till the manager and the shepherds and the sheep arrived, housed in Ruaigmore and well-armed, to see that none of the islanders came skulking back; not that there was anything to come back for—Mitchell had seen to that. But one never could tell, with obstinate ignorant peasantry, absurdly bound to their barren bits of rock and heather. Without more ado these two unfortunates now cast off the ropes, with bawled laments as to their ill-luck, and the factor's thoughtlessness in not even leaving them one or two of the island's women to beguile their solitary waiting. That was goodbye to Erismore.

Frances and Aeneas stood in the stern and watched the island recede, as one of the Eorsa fishermen, specially brought for the purpose, piloted the ketch through the gap in the skerries— perhaps Mitchell had been wise not to rely on one of the Erismore men for this last service. The girl's eyes were clouded, swimming, as she watched, and her husband's frown was black as it had ever been.

"That is it, then—that is the end," Frances said brokenly. "We thought that the chapter was finished, that day on Rudha nan Altair, didn't we! We did not know . . ."

The man's grip on her arm hurt. "Swept and garnished—you remember?" he said harshly. "Seven other devils—we little thought they would be baa-ing ones!" He laughed, a single mirthless bark. "We had a pagan, offering new-born babes for the sake of all the island. Now, we have Christian men," and he jerked his head backward, to indicate their fellow-passengers, "who sacrifice a whole people for yellow gold—a golden image with horns and trotters!"

She bit her lip. "This is judgment, do you think—the price to pay for what they did . . . ?"

"Maybe."

"And yet Lachlan Mor did not live to see it."

"Nor Finlay, either."

"No. Almost I thank God for that. It would have broken his heart. But it is a heavy price to pay."

The man did not answer, for a moment. "Yes," he said, at length. "A heavy price. But nothing to the price of these others' sin. All Scotland will pay that price, before the count is closed."

And that was the truth, too.